COURTING BECCA

"My parents are hosting a party this Saturday at their home," Matt said. "Will you come with me?"

"Your mamm didn't approve of me the first time we met in your office. It was obvious by the frown on her face. I'm nervous about meeting her again."

Matt moved the candle to the side and leaned forward. "My father will be a gentleman. As far as my mother goes, I told her I expected her to treat you with respect."

"I fear I'm not sophisticated enough for your mamm. I may embarrass her by coming in my plain clothes."

"You are a beautiful woman, and I will be proud to have you on my arm in any dress you choose to wear."

"I can see how important it is to you, so yes, I'll go with you."

"We will have a good time. It will be fun for me to show you the house where I spent my childhood." He rose and offered her his hand. "Miss Yost, may I have this dance?"

She giggled and rose. "I don't know how to dance, and we don't have any music."

"I will teach you and hum a tune."

He showed her where to put her hands and counted each step. As he hummed, she followed his lead and caught on

"I get lost in the s

"I like having you

"I am blessed to ha

BOOK YOUR PLACE ON OUR WEBSITE AND MAKE THE READING CONNECTION!

We've created a customized website just for our very special readers, where you can get the inside scoop on everything that's going on with Zebra, Pinnacle and Kensington books.

When you come online, you'll have the exciting opportunity to:

- View covers of upcoming books
- Read sample chapters
- Learn about our future publishing schedule (listed by publication month *and author*)
- Find out when your favorite authors will be visiting a city near you
- Search for and order backlist books from our online catalog
- Check out author bios and background information
- Send e-mail to your favorite authors
- Meet the Kensington staff online
- Join us in weekly chats with authors, readers and other guests
- Get writing guidelines
- AND MUCH MORE!

**Visit our website at
http://www.kensingtonbooks.com**

Change of Heart

MOLLY JEBBER

ZEBRA BOOKS
KENSINGTON PUBLISHING CORP.
http://www.kensingtonbooks.com

ZEBRA BOOKS are published by

Kensington Publishing Corp.
119 West 40th Street
New York, NY 10018

All Kensington titles, imprints, and distributed lines are available at special quantity discounts for bulk purchases for sales promotion, premiums, fund-raising, educational, or institutional use.

Special book excerpts or customized printings can also be created to fit specific needs. For details, write or phone the office of the Kensington Sales Manager: Attn.: Sales Department. Kensington Publishing Corp., 119 West 40th Street, New York, NY 10018. Phone: 1-800-221-2647.

Zebra and the Z logo Reg. U.S. Pat. & TM Off.

First Printing: July 2015
ISBN-13: 978-1-4201-3761-3
ISBN-10: 1-4201-3761-1

First Electronic Edition: July 2015
eISBN-13: 978-1-4201-3762-0
eISBN-10: 1-4201-3762-X

10 9 8 7 6 5 4 3 2 1

Printed in the United States of America

To my soul mate and husband,
Ed,
for his loving support.
I couldn't do this without you.

Chapter One

Massillon, Ohio, 1899

Becca Yost sighed, as David Garber's face flooded her mind. She pictured herself standing in front of their friends and family as he told her he couldn't marry her three weeks ago on her wedding day. A memory she would like to forget. Time away from home was a good idea. Besides, a visit to her sister was long overdue.

Her neighbors had made the long ride from home to Massillon, Ohio, an enjoyable one. *What a relief.* The Eblings hadn't mentioned David.

The buggy stopped, and Becca bid the couple farewell. The hot sun warmed her cheeks, and the sky was cloudless. Hoisting her bag over her shoulder, she headed downtown. The Ohio-Erie Canal sparkled in the sunlight. Passengers stepped into a boat at the dock. Maybe she would take a boat ride while she was here. On the corner, a peddler and an older man with a weathered face bartered over a handcrafted wooden cane. She smoothed her plain dress and righted her black kapp as she eyed three pretty women who wore colorful dresses with lace trim. What would it be like to wear a printed dress? She mustn't let her mind go there.

A newspaper boy stepped in front of her. "Do you want to buy a paper, miss?"

She shook her head. Maybe she should buy one. No, her parents wouldn't like it and neither would the bishop.

She reached First Street and peeked in the window of Ned's Milliner's Shop. Hats decorated with colorful ribbons and bows lined the shelves. She pressed her nose to the glass of a dress shop. White petticoats hung on a rack. Calico dresses caught her eye. Did Ruth wear these types of dresses? As she passed Myrtle's Bakery, she breathed in the aroma of fresh bread drifting in the air. No wonder Ruth loved living here. The colors, smells, and sounds were all so exciting, compared to her life in Berlin, Ohio, where men and women wore plain clothes and refused to have anything to do with world news or modern conveniences.

Becca held the old letter Ruth had sent months ago with her handwritten map on it. She grinned. Memories flooded her mind. She had missed their late-night talks. What a great idea she and her sister had had to sew a pocket on a quilt and tuck a meaningful letter inside before giving it to a loved one. Ruth wrote she'd had trouble retaining keepsake pocket quilts in stock. How many heartfelt letters had been tucked inside pocket quilts and given to loved ones? No matter. It was a blessing that family, friends, and now strangers who bought them would pass keepsake pocket quilts on to their loved ones for years to come.

The huckster bartered with a patron over a walking stick and raised his voice. She winced and crossed the street. She read her map. Should she have let Ruth know she was coming? *No.* Surprising her sister was more fun. As she passed the post office, she found North Street. According to Ruth's map, she should turn here.

In the street, a boy cracked a whip with a loud snap. She jerked and tripped on a big stick and fell. "Ouch!" Her mind went blank for a few moments. She blinked a few times and recovered. A slender, tall man stood before her.

"Dr. Matt Carrington. Are you hurt?" He offered his hand.

She blushed and gripped his fingers, as she struggled to stand. "I'm Becca Yost." She patted the dust off her dress. "I'm not hurt, but I'm quite embarrassed."

He snapped his fingers, and his deep green eyes widened. "You are Ruth Smith's sister. Her late husband, Caleb, and I were friends. They told me about you. I am stunned at how much you look like Ruth. Are you sure you are all right?"

"Yes. I'm fine." He was kind and polite. They did look alike, but Ruth didn't have an ugly red birthmark the size of a small apple on top of her right hand like Becca did.

"Wait here a moment, and I will be right back."

Dr. Carrington walked over to the boy and jerked the whip out of his hand. "This is no place for you to play with a whip." He pointed at Becca. "Come with me. You are going to apologize to Miss Yost for your bad behavior."

Dr. Carrington and the boy reached her. "This is Roy Wallace. He has something he would like to say to you." He nudged the boy's arm.

Roy removed his hat. "I am sorry for scaring you."

Seeing how cute he was, with his curly black hair and big brown eyes, she choked back a desperate laugh and gently tapped his nose. "You frightened me with your whip, but I accept your apology."

Roy gripped his suspenders and shuffled his feet. "May I go, Dr. Carrington?"

"Yes, but you behave yourself. I do not want to hear this whip crack again, do you understand me?"

"Yes, sir."

He handed the whip back to Roy and pointed to the general store. "Your father is loading his buck wagon, and I suggest you join him."

The boy scampered across the street. "Roy is nine, and he is always into mischief. He and his parents are patients of mine. Are you here to visit Ruth?"

"Yes. My visit's a surprise."

"She will be delighted." He wrinkled his forehead and pointed to her sleeve. "You're bleeding."

She touched her arm. Wet, she pushed her sleeve up and gasped. A cut oozed with blood.

He lifted a stick stained red. "You must have landed on this." He dropped the stick to the ground, pulled out a clean handkerchief from his shirt pocket, and handed the crisp cloth to her. "Press this on the cut to slow the bleeding. Come with me to my office next door. Let me bandage

your arm. Then I will show you where Ruth lives."
He lifted her bag from the ground and slung it over
his shoulder.

Becca followed him. Yes, she remembered Dr.
Carrington. Ruth had written to her in one of her
letters about him. She'd described him as nice,
caring, and smart. She'd left out the word *handsome*.

He opened the door. "The exam room is on the
right."

She glimpsed inside a room on her way down the
narrow hall. A handcrafted oak desk caught her eye.
Neat piles of paper were stacked on top. *Nice office*.
In a separate room, she scooted onto an exam table.
No patients sat in the waiting room, and a nurse
hadn't joined them. "Do you have a nurse who
works with you?"

He dropped her bag onto a chair. "No. I wish I
did. I put the word out, but no one has responded."

She cleared her throat. She was alone with a man.
But he was a doctor and a friend of Ruth's. Should
she leave?

"Ruth is a nice lady. Caleb and I met for coffee
every Friday morning in my office. I sat with them
on Sunday mornings in church. Caleb and I fished
at least once a week. I have not dipped a pole in the
water since his death. It is not the same without him.
He was a good friend."

Becca stared at her lap. Had Caleb explained to
Dr. Carrington why she and her parents had not
visited Ruth? Would he ask her why she chose to visit
her today? *Please don't*.

He pulled saline, ointment, and bandages from a
cabinet, and then he tended to her wound. "Much

to your relief, I am sure, you do not need stitches. Are you in any pain?"

She shook her head. Dr. Carrington had been a perfect gentleman. "I'm a little sore, but I'm fine otherwise. I'll find Ruth's house. I don't want to take you away from your work."

"This is my day off. I came in to clear my desk and order supplies. It is no bother to take you to Ruth's house, and I have done enough work for today. Are you allergic to any medications or foods?"

"I'm not aware of any."

Dr. Carrington removed a small bottle from a cabinet, shook out two pills, and handed them to Becca. "This medicine should help relieve your soreness." He poured her a glass of water and passed it to her.

She noticed his hands. Callous free, and his nails didn't have one speck of dirt underneath. She swallowed the pills, passed the glass back to him, and scooted off the table. "Is there somewhere I can change my clothes? My dress is ripped, dust covered, and stained with blood."

"You can change in this room. There is a wash-basin, a pitcher of water, and clean towels on the table in the corner." He walked out and shut the door.

She washed her face and hands and then pulled a clean dress out of her bag. After she had finished changing her clothes, she went to his office.

He carried her bag and ushered her outside. "Ruth's house is not far."

She winced as two men lifted a sheet of metal from a spring wagon and struggled not to drop it.

She and Dr. Carrington waited to let them pass. "How did Massillon grow to this size?"

Dr. Carrington walked alongside her. "The railroad and canal played a part in helping the town grow. Massillon has thrived because of the wheat, steel, glass, and metal industries. In 1845, the Russell brothers built a threshing machine. Their invention won them first prize at the Ohio State Fair. The two men we passed are sons of the two inventors. They opened their metal company a month ago. My father is friends with the Russells." He chuckled and rubbed his chin. "This tidbit of information is one of my father's favorite stories to share."

She could've listened to him talk about Massillon all day. His enthusiasm for the city was infectious. Ruth sent letters about the latest fashions, but not about new inventions, history, or world news. These things were interesting. The next time a paperboy offered her a newspaper, she'd buy one.

He stopped and pointed. "This is Ruth's house. Have I bored you? I get carried away talking about the history of this place."

"No. I enjoyed our conversation. Would you like to come in and say hello to Ruth?"

He shook his head. "You and Ruth have a lot to talk about. I would be in the way. Are you staying long?"

Her stomach clenched. She accepted her bag from him. She didn't want to ever leave Ruth again. No one laughed at her jokes, lifted her spirits, or understood her like Ruth. She would have to return to her life in Berlin in a few weeks. Her sister's empty bed beside hers came to mind. Her heart stung. She would make this decision later. "I'm not sure yet." She blocked her eyes from the sun. "You've been kind, and I appreciate all your help today."

"I enjoyed your company. Visit my office in a few days, and I will check your arm. I want to make sure your wound does not get infected. Please give my best wishes to Ruth."

She had never been alone with a man, except for her daed. Dr. Carrington had soon put her at ease with his calm voice, kind words, and polite manners. She could understand why Caleb and Ruth had such nice things to say about him. "I'll do both."

He walked away.

She liked his crisp white shirt, creased black pants, and shiny boots. His neat appearance matched the way he kept his office.

After he left, she turned to Ruth's white house. A high-backed rocking chair sat on the porch. Red and yellow tulips and deep blue hyacinths planted in a pot scented the air. Her heart raced as she ran up the steps and knocked on the door.

Ruth appeared and yelped. "What a wonderful surprise to find you on my doorstep!"

Becca embraced her. "I've missed you so much." Her eyes swept Ruth from head to toe. Two years older, her sister hadn't changed a bit in the three years they had been apart. Aside from her birthmark, she and Ruth were mirror images of each other with their narrow waists, light blond hair, and blue eyes. "What a sight you are. Your printed blue dress is beautiful, and I like your hair in ringlets tied back. I'm used to my hair being in a bun."

"You are as sweet as ever. I made the dress, and I like wearing my hair in ringlets the best. I have missed you. Come in." She ushered her into the kitchen. "Have a seat." She poured Becca a glass of water and sat across from her. "I have not received a letter from you since before your wedding. Where is your husband?"

She heaved a big sigh. "Three weeks ago, on our wedding day, and in front of our parents and friends, David Garber told me he couldn't marry me. First, I was stunned, then angry, then sad. My emotions ran together all at once. We hardly knew each other, but I had agreed to go along with Amish tradition and have Daed choose my husband. I was relieved and disappointed at the same time not knowing if David and I would be happy together or not."

Ruth brought her hand to her mouth. "Did he explain why he would not marry you?"

"He had visited his uncle in Lancaster, Pennsylvania, for two months before the wedding. While he stayed there, he met a woman who cared for his uncle's sick wife. She cooked and joined them for dinner every day. During those times, he grew fond of her."

"Why did he wait until your wedding day to tell you about this woman?"

Becca removed her shoes. "Because he had arranged with Daed to marry me, and he didn't want to dishonor me or our parents by going back on his word. When the time came for him to say his vows, he knew he couldn't go through with the marriage. This other woman meant too much to him."

A picture of David formed in her mind. She considered him attractive with his medium height, slightly overweight frame, brown hair, and green eyes. She had looked forward to learning more about him after their wedding day. *No longer.* Now distrustful and thoughtless came to mind. At least David had been honest with her though.

She sighed. "In the end, he did me a favor."

Ruth crinkled her nose. "What a terrible spot he put you in. Did he leave right away? What did you do?"

"He left in a hurry. I cried, and our parents and Grace comforted me. She is truly a best friend. She stood by my side most of the day. Friends had cooked chicken, potatoes, green beans, and pies for the after-wedding meal. I appreciated all their hard work, but I wasn't hungry. Not wanting to hurt their feelings, I nibbled on the food. I left early, and I walked to my favorite maple tree by the neighbors' pond to pray and ponder what to do with my life. I'm twenty and an old maid."

"You are not an old maid. I have faith you will either meet someone or Father will find the right man for you to marry when the time is right. In the meantime, I am thrilled you chose to come to me for comfort."

Becca hugged herself. It was as if she and Ruth hadn't spent time apart. Ruth had changed her life, but not her heart. "I'm ready to put the unfortunate day behind me. Grace understood this, but our parents and my other friends didn't. They wouldn't stop offering sympathy. I needed time out of town for a while, and visiting you came to mind." Becca touched a dishtowel. No doubt, the rose on the fabric was her sister's handiwork. Ruth had taught her a similar pattern when they were younger. In the corner, a handcrafted maple cabinet stood tall. She ran her hand along the arm of the chair. The etched detailing matched the table where she and Ruth sat. Her sister's house was cozy.

"You may stay as long as you like." Ruth rose and placed two large pots of water on the hot stove.

Becca lifted a picture of Ruth and Caleb from a shelf. The smiling couple sat close. "When you left your Amish life behind to marry Caleb, we mourned the loss of you for a long time."

"You did not mention this in any of your letters."

"I didn't want to upset you. When I told Mamm and Daed Caleb had a heart attack and died, they asked me if you were coming home. When I told them you weren't, they cried. I explained you had built a life in Massillon and had your mending shop to manage. They asked me not to speak about you because hearing about you hurt them too much."

She had missed Ruth's stories at mealtime and playing games with her on family night. She and her parents rarely played games anymore. The absence of her sister's laughter and excitement ruined the fun. "I'm grateful our parents allowed me to write to you. They didn't want me to come to your house, but they understood how painful it's been for me not to visit you. Mamm and Daed were ready to let me do anything to lighten my dark mood. Shunning our friends who choose to leave our community isn't a rule I agree with."

"I do not either, but Amish law is not going to change according to my circumstances. I miss our parents, and I pray for them every day. I will always be grateful for my Amish upbringing, but I have no desire to go back to Berlin. I have grown roots here, and I cannot imagine living anywhere else."

Life without Caleb for the last year mustn't have been easy for her sister, but Ruth had never once complained. "Do you struggle to make a living here?"

"No. The mending shop provides a comfortable living. I am anxious to show it to you. I love working there." Ruth stood. "Are you tired? You must have gotten up early this morning to come here. I have warmed water for your bath so you can soak in the tub and relax. Are you hungry?" She lifted the heavy pot of water from the stove.

Becca followed Ruth to the washroom with the other pot. *She's taking care of me just like she used to. Visiting here was a great idea.* "I'm wide awake. I would like to wash this dirt off me. I'll help you make dinner when I'm done with my bath. I don't want to trouble you."

Ruth kissed her cheek. "I have missed taking care of you. You enjoy your bath, and I will warm some leftover vegetable soup I have in the icebox." Taking Becca's bucket, Ruth glanced over her shoulder. "Everything you need is in the washroom and bedroom. My old Amish clothes are in the clothes press. You are welcome to wear them."

"I may take you up on your offer. I may not have

brought enough of mine." She kissed Ruth's cheek before shutting the door.

Becca slid the fabric off her body and placed the garment on a chair. She stepped in the tub, eased herself into the water, and draped her bandaged arm over the side. She breathed in the scent of honeysuckle drifting through the open window. Spending time with Ruth was even better than she had imagined. Her mind flooded with memories. She had loved sharing a bedroom with Ruth. They would sneak to the kitchen for late-night snacks and eat them in bed, giggle about the silliest things, and make up stories.

The water cooled, and she stepped out of the tub. She toweled off, got dressed, and headed to the kitchen.

Savory vegetable soup aroma caught her senses. Steam rose from the mixture sitting in a bowl. "I've missed your cooking, and this smells delicious."

Ruth served them. "I like cooking for two again. Is there a reason you are speaking more English than Pennsylvania Dutch?"

Becca inhaled the wonderful fragrance of Ruth's soup and sipped some from her spoon. "I suspect my spending time with Hester is the main reason I don't use our language much since she isn't Amish. I speak Pennsylvania Dutch when I refer to Mamm or Daed or kapp or boppli. I'm not used to you speaking properly."

"After living here, I have gotten used to speaking like my friends. I like Hester. It is a shame she never married. She must get lonely. It was generous of her to teach you and Grace midwifery."

"She never got over being jilted by the love of her life at seventeen. She's thirty and not interested in getting married. She works hard and likes living alone without anyone telling her what to do. I'll always be grateful to her for sharing her books with us and allowing us to help her until we were confident enough to birth boppli by ourselves. I made her a keepsake pocket quilt like the one you made me. I wrote her a letter, put it in the pocket, and stitched string on it to tie it closed. She wept when I handed it to her."

"I am touched you are carrying on our keepsake tradition. I keep the one I made for Caleb on the back of this chair. After we married, he wrote me a letter and slipped it in the pocket of the quilt with the one I wrote to him. I read the letters now and then." She lifted the quilt and pulled it close. "The quilt reminds me of the wonderful memories we made together."

"I want to make Grace another pocket quilt while I'm here. She baked my favorite cookies, made me a new dress and kapp, and worked hard to take my mind off David's rejection. She fears her birthmark covering her left cheek is why men refuse to arrange with her daed to marry her. At twenty, she fears there will not be many available Amish left in Berlin. I hope she's wrong. Her big green eyes and brown hair are pretty. She's tall and thin. She's sweet, smart, and loving. The name Grace describes her well. She possesses all the qualities a man would want. It saddens me neither of us are married."

Ruth covered Becca's hand. "Don't fret about you or Grace getting married. God has a plan for each of you. I believe He will find you both husbands when the time is right."

Becca pushed up her sleeve and scratched the skin around her bandage. "I hope you're right."

Ruth's eyes widened. "When did you hurt yourself?"

Becca recounted her story of how she met Dr. Carrington. "Did Caleb explain to him why I haven't visited you?"

"Yes, Caleb and I explained how you are to shun me, since I left. I told him our parents did allow us to write letters. He must have been surprised when you told him you were coming to visit me. Did he ask you any questions?"

"No. He was a gentleman."

"He is a fine man. I am glad he was there to help you." She sighed and pushed a stray hair from her cheek. "I worry about him. He works such long hours. He really needs a nurse, but he cannot find anyone who is interested in the job." She straightened in her chair and leaned forward. "Becca, you should consider working for him. You will need something to do if you stay in town for a while, and you would be easy for him to train since you have worked as a midwife for the last several years. I am not suggesting you ask him about the nursing job right away, but I know you. You will be bored in a few days and want something to do, and this job would be perfect."

Becca sucked in her bottom lip. She had always wanted to work as a nurse in a doctor's office, but she hadn't imagined it possible. "What about when we didn't have patients to tend to? We would be alone."

Ruth raised her hand in a dismissive wave. "Dorothy Watts works for him, and she is a friend of mine. She is sixty-three and moves around faster than I do. She is a kind woman who takes care of his office duties, and she will be there most of the time. Matt is an honorable and trustworthy man. If he agrees, work for him a few days. Then decide if you want to continue."

"I'm not sure how long I'll stay in Massillon. He needs someone he can depend on."

"Explain it to him. I suspect he will be appreciative for whatever help you offer."

She would miss birthing boppli with Hester. As a nurse, she'd learn how to tend to a variety of patient needs. "I'll ponder the idea."

Ruth patted her hand. "You do what makes you feel comfortable."

"If I'm going to consider working for Dr. Carrington, I need to know more about him. You talk about him as if he's perfect. Is there anything you don't like about him?"

"I like him, but I do not appreciate how his mother treats others. Matt does not agree with Eloise Carrington's prejudiced opinion about people who she doesn't believe live up to her high standards. When Caleb and I first met her, she studied us from head to toe. Her pinched face made her disapproval of us obvious. He is twenty-six and unmarried. I suspect it is because she is too overbearing for the women he has courted in the past. I pity the woman Matt does marry. I have not met his father."

She pictured his mamm in her mind as an elegant and pleasant woman. "Did Caleb mention how rude she was to the two of you to Dr. Carrington?"

"No. Caleb already knew Matt had spoken with her about her behavior toward his friends a number of times. She ignores him. He claims she can be nice, but I have my doubts." Ruth wiped her hands. "Enough talk for tonight, little sister. Go to bed, and I will take care of the dishes." She shooed her out of the kitchen.

In the spare bedroom, Becca peeled back covers layered on the bed and climbed in. She pulled the thin top quilt onto her legs and reached for the King James Bible on the nightstand but left it unopened. She tugged her sleeve over her bandage. Dr. Matt Carrington's face flooded her mind. His structured jawline, kind eyes, and interesting personality were unlike any other man she'd ever met. She suspected he would be an excellent teacher. *Yes,* she would talk to him soon about working for him.

Chapter Two

Matt walked into his practice and was pleased that it was Becca who stood talking to Dorothy. It had been one week since he had escorted her to Ruth's house. Thoughts of her had filled his mind often since then. He had hoped their paths would cross before now. Her innocent blue eyes matched a brilliant sky on a clear day, and her plain Amish dress did nothing to diminish her attractive figure. "Miss Yost, it is nice to see you."

"Please, call me Becca. Are you busy? I can make an appointment or come back later."

He shook his head. The shyness she displayed added to her charm. "You do not need an appointment. You are welcome in this office anytime. And please, call me Matt."

Dorothy circled her arm around Becca's waist and glanced at him. "Becca told me about her fall and how you helped her. She and I have been getting acquainted, and I have learned she is a midwife. Ruth suggested she talk to you about your need for a nurse. With her experience birthing babies, she would be easy to train. You two should chat about working together."

Matt winked at Becca. "I agree, and we will discuss it right after I check her arm."

Becca's cheeks pinked. "I don't want to put you on the spot."

Matt waved a dismissive hand. "You are not putting me on the spot at all. You are doing me a favor. I could use the help." How impressive. Midwives worked long hours and had to handle mothers in pain and nervous fathers while birthing babies at the same time. He had had a few of those experiences. He gestured for her to follow him to the exam room. Once inside, he pulled two chairs across from each other. "Have a seat. Please pull up your sleeve for me."

Becca did. "I removed the bandage after a few days."

Matt examined the cut. "It has healed nicely." He leaned back. "How is Ruth? Are you enjoying your time with her?"

"She's doing fine, and I love spending time with her. She has such a nice mending shop, and I've enjoyed meeting her friends, but I'm not used to having spare time. When I'm at home in Berlin, I'm busy delivering boppli."

"Tell me about your experience as a midwife."

"Hester Harris is a nurse, midwife, and a close friend who trained me. She let me borrow her medical books and tested me to make sure I understood the material. We work together when we can. Most of the time, I work alone. I've been a midwife for two years."

"I do deliver babies, but the majority of my patients are either ill or injured. I need a nurse in the worst way. If you will accept the job, I will teach you about medications, how to assist me, and my way of writing down patient notes."

"I would like to try it, but I'm not sure how long I'm staying in Massillon."

"No problem. I would appreciate having your help for as long as you are here."

She tilted her head and grinned. "I accept."

"All right, we will work together for a week and then talk. If you and I are content with our arrangement, you can stay as long as you like. Do you have any questions for me?"

He had missed dinner and worked long hours many days tending to patients. The paperwork mounted, and a nurse would make things easier for him. Besides, he found her innocent personality refreshing.

"When would you like me to start?"

"Eight o'clock tomorrow morning? I can pay you seven dollars a week."

"I'll see you in the morning."

He escorted her to Dorothy's desk. "Becca has agreed to join us starting tomorrow."

Dorothy lifted her spectacles and patted her gray-haired bun. "I am thrilled. Do not bring your dinner. I cook for us on the potbellied stove in the back room every workday. Is there any kind of food you do not like?"

"I love everything."

"Your words are music to my ears."

She waved and shut the door behind her.

Dorothy tapped her pencil on the desk. "Your mouth could not stretch any wider. I believe you are excited about her working here."

"Yes, I am."

The next morning, Matt paced the floor. He could not remember the last time he had been this anxious. Becca was like a breath of fresh air. Beautiful and she shared his passion for medicine.

"Are your feet on fire?" Dorothy poured coffee in a mug. "You are as nervous as a father waiting for his baby's birth."

Becca opened the door and swept in. "The rain's hitting the ground hard." She put her dripping umbrella in the corner.

"Good morning. Have some coffee." Dorothy passed her a mug.

"This is yummy, but I don't expect you to wait on me."

Dorothy patted her hand. "I spoil Matt, and I am going to spoil you. I enjoy it."

"You won't get any argument from me." Becca's soft sweet voice echoed in his mind.

"Are you ready for your first day?"

"Yes. I'm anxious to get started."

Matt gestured toward the exam room, showed her his routine and how he would like her to pencil his notes.

Dorothy pushed the door open and peeked in. "I

am sorry to interrupt, but Clyde Peterson is here for his appointment."

Clyde Peterson passed Dorothy and sauntered in wearing muddy boots and a sweat-stained hat. Thick suspenders secured sagging pants over his round stomach. A worn gray shirt clung to his over-weight frame. He threw his hat on a chair. His black hair was matted to his head. He frowned at Becca and climbed onto the table. "Who's this?"

Oh no. Matt washed and dried his hands. Clyde would not hesitate to speak his mind, and the scowl on his face meant trouble. He could be a grump. "Say hello to Miss Yost, my nurse."

"No Amish girl's going to touch me. They're strange, dress alike, and think they're better than us."

Matt fought to hold his temper. Any other patient besides Clyde Peterson would have been better to start their day. He inhaled and exhaled. "She is here to stay, and you will treat her with respect."

Becca chimed in. "Mr. Peterson, please call me Becca. Why don't you let me help you today, and if at any time you are uncomfortable, I'll step out of the room."

Clyde grumbled and let her help him out of his shirt.

After Matt removed the man's shoulder bandage, thick green fluid oozed from the wound. Matt glanced at Becca. "Last week a rugged board with nail ends sticking out of it fell from a shelf in Clyde's workshop and landed on his shoulder. As you can see, it has become infected. Please hand me a syringe, gauze, tape, and a bottle of saline from the top shelf in the cabinet closest to the wall."

She hurried to the cabinet and gathered his requests. Her gentle hand touched his each time she passed an item to him. She had soft skin and delicate fingers.

"Clyde, this is going to hurt."

"Doc, how much longer you gonna be?"

"I am finished with your shoulder, but I have to give you a shot in your backside. I need you to lower your pants."

Becca turned her back.

He slid off the table, undid his pants, and pulled them low enough for Matt to administer the shot.

"All finished."

Clyde buttoned his pants, pulled up his suspenders, and allowed Becca to help him into his shirt. He bowed his head to her. "Sorry about earlier."

She shrugged. "I don't know what you're talking about."

"I have some tomatoes in my wagon. Would ya like a few?"

"I love tomatoes, and I'll look forward to biting into one for supper."

"You can call me Clyde."

"Please, call me Becca."

Becca had gained Clyde's confidence in her in minutes. She continued to amaze him. He walked Clyde out, while she readied the room for the next patient.

He treated a variety of patients with fevers, cuts, coughs, and sprains. She worked all day with only minutes between patients to grab a bite of Dorothy's rabbit stew without complaining. "Dorothy leaves and locks the door around five. It is fifteen after five." Matt rotated his neck and shoulders. "Are you ready to run away?"

"No. I enjoyed it, and the day flew by."

He liked her unpretentious way, and her natural beauty captivated him. "You were a big help to me today. I apologize for Clyde's behavior. A patient expressing prejudice against you did not occur to me."

"I'm glad he relaxed."

He opened the door for her. "You have worked one day with me, and I am spoiled already."

"Good. I like nursing and working here." She lifted her bag from a drawer. "Have a nice evening. I'll see you in the morning."

Matt shut the door. She had swept into his life like a pretty spring day.

Four weeks later on a Saturday, Becca milked Ruth's cow then carried the half-full pail inside and poured it in a pitcher. "It's a beautiful day outside."

Ruth grabbed a basket. "Come and talk to me while I gather eggs."

In the backyard, a protesting hen pecked at Becca's heels. She shook her head as Ruth petted their heads while she collected eggs and placed them in her basket. "You're the only person I know who can pet chickens without getting pecked at. They pester me."

"I do not want to chat about these chickens. I want to talk about you and Matt." Ruth pushed open the kitchen door and stepped inside.

Becca remembered her first day in Massillon. Time had passed quickly since she had begun to work for Matt. His patience, hearty laugh, kind eyes, and attention when she spoke were all things she liked about him. Work had been busy, and she loved it. She pulled plates from the cupboard. "I find nursing exciting. Matt's an excellent teacher, and he's patient. He doesn't even flinch when I drop things half a dozen times a day."

Ruth laughed and rolled her eyes. "You drop things because you are always in such a hurry to do everything." Ruth cracked an egg on the side of the skillet. "Matt visited me at the shop yesterday. He is thrilled to have you as his nurse, and I believe he is smitten with you. It is the lilt in his voice when he talks about you." She tapped Becca's nose. "You are giddy when you speak about him. Do you like him more than you would a friend? Am I right? Are you fond of him?"

Becca giggled and held her stomach. "I can't hide anything from you. I never could. Yes. I can't help it. He hangs the moon. What am I going to do? I love it here. I don't want to leave you or Matt, but I miss our parents and my friends. I like birthing boppli, but I love nursing more. Mamm and Daed wouldn't be happy with my working for an Englischer. Nor would they like me learning about the world and getting excited about it at the same time. After reading one newspaper, I can't wait to read the next."

"I am sorry you are in such turmoil, but I love having you here. Of course, you are welcome to live with me if you choose to stay in Massillon. It is a difficult decision. Pray and ask God for guidance."

Becca's stomach flipped. Could she leave her Amish life behind? Her parents and friends would shun her. She suspected Grace wouldn't. She hoped her best friend would agree to write letters to stay in touch. The thought of leaving those she loved sickened her, but no more than the thought of leaving Ruth and Matt. She no longer believed God turned away from those who left Amish life if those same people remained faithful to Him. Ruth had taught her this by her example. She leaned more toward choosing Massillon as her home because of this. "I hadn't intended on moving here. I must come to a decision soon, because our parents and Grace deserve to know what I'm doing. They must wonder why I haven't written and told them when I'm coming home." She rubbed her temples. "I don't want to ponder what to do about where I want to live, but I must."

"Put it out of your mind for today. After breakfast, we will walk to my shop. I want to introduce you to Margaret Tuttle, my seamstress. She is sixty-five and beautiful. She has been in Columbus, Ohio, visiting friends ever since you got here. She came home yesterday, and we caught up on our news. She often works when we are closed to catch up on her mending. It would be a perfect time for you to meet her. Our visit with her will brighten your day and hers."

Becca and Ruth finished breakfast and then strolled downtown. The sun heated their cheeks, and puffy white clouds decorated the sky. A ball hit Becca's leg. She threw it to the boy who stood a few feet away with his arms held out. He ran and joined his friends. Two women were working in their gardens. What beautiful roses they were planting. She waved to townsfolk who were patients of Matt's or friends of Ruth's. Her sister and her late husband, Caleb, had chosen the right neighborhood to build their home. Close enough to walk to town but far enough away from the hustle and bustle.

The bell clanged when Ruth opened the door to the shop. A petite older woman with a sparkle in her eyes and dimples in her rosy cheeks greeted them.

Margaret clasped Becca's hand. "You must be Becca. The two of you could pass for twins."

Ruth put her arm around Margaret's waist. "This elegant woman is like a mother to me. I love her dearly. Last year, when I got sick with a fever, she came to my house and nursed me back to health." She pulled her friend close. "I would be lost without you, Margaret."

The older woman blushed. "I feel the same way." She patted Ruth's cheek and leaned in to her.

The bell clanged over the door again, and a woman entered. "Ruth, I am sorry to bother you on your day off, but may I show you the rip in my dress? I found it when I left the general store."

"Please come in." She glanced over her shoulder. "Becca, you and Margaret visit while I take care of Mrs. Sanderson."

Becca liked the older woman on sight. She had her gray hair wound in a bun and spectacles perched on her nose. She represented the perfect picture of a grandmother. "It's a pleasure to meet you. I appreciate all you have done for my sister."

"I am a widow and alone. My husband died last year. We did not have any children. Ruth is like a daughter to me." She lowered her voice to a whisper. "From what I have heard your sister has blossomed since you have been staying with her. She misses Caleb, and it broke her heart to lose him. She has never gotten over it. She confides in me about this often. She is excited and happy you are here. You are like a bright ray of sunshine in her life."

Ruth finished with Mrs. Sanderson and joined Becca and Margaret. "Come and sit with me at the drawing table. I will show you a dress in *Godey's Lady's Book* similar to the one I am designing. Margaret, I found a dress in the catalog I would like to make for you. I will point it out to you." She flipped through the pages of the book.

Margaret's eyes brightened. "I like the green one you picked out for me. I would love it if you would make it for me."

"I will draw a pattern for it tomorrow." She patted Becca's hand. "Is there anything you would like me to make for you?"

Becca shook her head. "No thank you. Not yet." She glanced at the pages with Margaret and Ruth. She liked a lot of the dresses offered in *Godey's Lady's Book,* but she wanted to wait a little longer before trying on one of Ruth's dresses or having her make her one. She was comfortable in her plain clothes. It was a part of her past she wasn't ready to let go of yet.

An hour later, Margaret yawned and stretched her arms. "I would love to talk more, but I must finish my mending. If I do not, I will be behind in my work for the rest of the week."

Ruth closed the book. "It is getting late in the afternoon. We better head home." Ruth and Becca hugged her friend and left.

Walking past the many shops and restaurants on

Main Street, Becca pondered what Margaret had told her about Ruth since Caleb's death. Her sister hadn't indicated her sadness in the letters she sent. Since Becca had been here, they had laughed, stayed up late and chatted, worshipped in Ruth's church, and enjoyed picnics, shopping, and dining together. She had enjoyed herself. She had no doubt Ruth had too. She couldn't imagine leaving her sister to go home.

What did the future hold for her and Matt? She must find out. She had grown roots in Massillon. She couldn't go back to her old life and be happy. Yes, she would tell her parents and Grace she had chosen to make a life in Massillon soon. Ruth's voice jerked her out of her thoughts.

"Matt is sitting by the window at Lizzie's. No one is with him. I am hungry. We should join him." Ruth hurried to the restaurant.

Good idea. Becca followed her sister. She pushed returning to Berlin to talk to her parents out of her mind.

As soon as they walked through the door, Matt stood and beckoned to them. "Come and sit with me."

Dishes clanged and patrons' conversations buzzed. Becca and Ruth squeezed through the narrow pathway between chairs to Matt's table.

Always the gentleman, Matt seated them before he sat.

Lizzie removed a pencil from behind her ear. She blew a strawberry blond hair from her ruddy face. "Becca, you've ordered chicken and dumplings every time you've come in. Are you ordering it today?" Hands on her hips, she cocked her head.

"Yes. Did you bake any cobbler this morning?"

"I baked a fresh cherry cobbler an hour ago. I'll set a piece aside for you."

Ruth ordered the same meal as Becca. Matt told them he had ordered the venison stew earlier.

The door chimed when Lizzie left to pass their orders on to the cook. Becca glanced up. David. Her heart thudded against her chest. She had hoped to never run into him again. What could he want? *Nothing I would care to discuss.*

He approached her, holding his hat. "Will you step outside with me for a few minutes? I need to talk to you."

Her face heated. *No,* but she would. She wanted him out of here before he said anything to embarrass her further. She took a deep breath and gestured to Ruth and Matt. "David, this is Dr. Matt Carrington, and this is my sister, Ruth Smith."

Matt stood and shook David's hand.

"Hello, Mrs. Smith." He fidgeted with his hat.

Ruth stayed seated and gave him a curt nod.

David eyed Becca. "What I have to say won't take long."

No, it won't. She couldn't stand the sight of him. He had approached her in front of a roomful of people just like on their wedding day. Why hadn't he waited until she left the restaurant and approached her then? "I'll be right back." She followed him out the door. "How did you find me?"

"When I returned from Lancaster, my parents told me you left to visit your schweschder in Massillon. When I arrived here, I asked the owner of the general store if he knew Ruth Smith, and he told me where she lived. On the way to her haus, I recognized you through the restaurant window."

Hand on hip, she squinted. "Why are you here?"

"Is there somewhere quiet where we can talk?"

She pointed across the street. The least amount of time she spent with him the better. A walk too far would add to this awkwardness. She would remain as close to Lizzie's as possible. "The post office is closed. We can sit on the bench by the front door. No one will bother us."

Her heart thudded against her ribs, as he followed her. She had nothing to say to him, and she could care less about anything he had to say to her. She hoped he would make this meeting a short one.

In front of the post office, she waited for him to speak.

He passed his hat from one hand to the other. "I'm sorry for leaving you the way I did. I would like to make it up to you by asking you to marry me."

She narrowed her eyes. He must be out of his mind. "No, I am not interested in marrying you. Why aren't you marrying the woman in Lancaster?"

He bowed his head and spoke in a whisper. "She refused to wed me. I told her I had arranged with your daed to marry you but changed my mind at the last minute. It didn't sit well with her. I would've kumme to you earlier, but I stayed in Lancaster for a while to help my uncle build an addition to his haus. I've given this a lot of thought. You and I should get married. I need to follow through with the commitment I made to your daed to wed you. Besides, we are both twenty and should be married by now."

She clenched her jaw. She would never marry a man who wanted to be wed to another woman. Besides, she cared about someone else. Someone she could trust. "As I stated, I won't marry you."

"You're getting older, and there aren't many available men in our community left. You should reconsider." David stared at the birthmark on her hand.

She hid her hand under her apron and squinted. "Like I said, I'm not interested." The more he prattled on, the more stern and coldhearted his tone became. If she had married him, she pictured her life as a miserable one.

He stood and mashed his hat on his head. "You'll be sorry. I could've provided a good living for you. I intend to find a fraa, and I won't be available when you return to Berlin." He stuffed his hands in his pockets. "I'm staying at Daisy's Boarding House tonight and leaving in the morning. If you change your mind, you can find me there." He stomped off.

She heaved a sigh. She had no intention of changing her mind about not marrying him. Too bad he couldn't leave tonight. She hoped he found someone else to marry soon. Then he wouldn't bother her anymore. She waited until he turned the corner before heading to the restaurant. As she pushed the door open, they waved her over. Her chicken and dumplings sat on the table.

Matt seated her. "Are you all right?"

She sipped lemonade to gather her thoughts. David was an arrogant man. How dare he come here and assume she'd marry him after what he did to her. She thought her head would explode. He had glanced at her birthmark, as if to remind her she was flawed. He had traits she knew she didn't want in a husband. "Yes, I'm fine."

Ruth patted her hand. "I told Matt about your unfortunate wedding day. What did David want?"

She recounted her conversation with David. She opened her mouth to speak about what a dishonest and heartless man he appeared to be but shut it. Bad mouthing David wouldn't make her feel any better, and it would cast a bad light on her character. She swallowed hard. "I'm glad it's over, and he's gone."

Matt pushed his back against the chair. "I am glad you refused to take him up on his offer and sent him on his way, because I would be lost without you."

Her heart soared. He couldn't have said anything more perfect. Each day she liked Matt more, and it warmed her heart to learn he valued her. She didn't want to, but she would need to leave him for a little while. She had to deliver her news about leaving Berlin for good to her parents and Grace in person, rather than letting them know in a letter. It wouldn't be an easy conversation to have with them. She would wait for a week or two.

Chapter Three

Monday morning, Matt greeted Dorothy then joined Becca in the exam room, where she stocked supplies. The sun shone bright through the window and showcased her flawless skin.

She dropped thermometers in a container of alcohol. "I'm sorry David interrupted our dinner yesterday."

"Do not apologize. You did the right thing sending him on his way. He does not deserve you."

She blushed and dropped a box of cotton.

He bent to pick it up, and their hands touched. He met her gaze and held it. *Those eyes, how beautiful.* The door burst open and interrupted them. Micah, a little boy with tousled brown hair and freckles across his nose, hurried toward him. "Dr. Matt, I falled and am bleedin'." He held his arm up.

Matt grabbed a clean towel and held it on the wound. "Miss Yost and I will fix you right up."

Dorothy entered the room. "I apologize. He ran right past me before I could catch him."

Matt waved a dismissive hand. "Micah can be a handful. I understand. Will his mother join us?"

Dorothy rolled her eyes. "No, she prefers to stay with me."

Mrs. Shepler had not joined her son on any of their visits. She had not touched her son or spoken a kind word to him. Why? He shrugged his shoulders. "No problem."

After Dorothy shut the door, Becca held the cloth in place. "Let me help you climb onto the exam table, Micah. How old are you?"

He held up four fingers and his thumb.

"Five?"

"Yep, I am. Is the red spot on your hand a birf-mark?"

"Yes, it is."

He lifted his pant leg and showed a birthmark the size of a coin. "I like yours better than mine. Last time I came here, Dr. Matt told me God gives special people birfmarks. He calls them angel kisses."

She often hid her hand in the folds of her skirt when she didn't need to use it. She was beautiful to him with or without the birthmark. Micah had delivered his message to her in the right way.

"Dr. Matt's a wise man." She winked at Matt then patted Micah's back. "Your birthmark's a beauty, and you're definitely special."

Matt grinned at her then leaned toward the child. "Becca is going to wash your hands and arm. When she is finished, I will have a look at your cut."

Becca gently removed Micah's shirt. She readied

soap and water then washed Micah's hands and injured arm.

Matt strolled to the medicine cabinet and removed two syringes. He filled one with numbing medicine and the other one with an antibiotic. He hid them behind his back, walked across the room, and leaned close to Becca's ear. "I suspect his cut will need stitches."

The small boy whirled around and flung himself into Becca's arms. "No, no. Not stitches!"

"Dr. Matt will give you medicine to make it not hurt."

"If it hurts, let me know. I will stop and administer more numbing medicine."

Micah clutched Becca's arm with his good hand. "Please, don't let go."

"I'm not going anywhere, and it'll all be over before you know it."

Matt removed the cloth and administered the shot.

Micah closed his eyes tight and whimpered.

He waited a few minutes and then stitched Micah's arm. All the while stifling his chuckle as the child talked nonstop to Becca about his wooden train set. "All right, brave boy. I am finished. You may join Dorothy and your mother in the other room."

Following them to Dorothy's desk, he liked how Becca had handled Micah. She had gained the little boy's trust. Her patience and way with the child had made treating him much easier.

Dorothy handed Micah a piece of candy. "How is your arm?"

"Dr. Matt and Becca made it all better."

The child's mother, Leah Shepler, squinted at Becca and did not bother to address her. Matt crossed his arms against his chest. "Do you have any questions, Mrs. Shepler?"

Her reticule slid off her wrist. She caught it, removed a silver coin from inside, and pressed it in Dorothy's palm. She stood straight and tall, her dark, black ringlets bouncing, as she jutted her chin. "No, I do not, and Micah and I must be on our way."

The child hugged Becca before skipping to his mother. Mrs. Shepler did not glance back as she shut the door.

Matt waited for Becca to comment about Mrs. Shepler's rude behavior, but she did not. She had not spoken a negative word about anyone since she began working for him. "Micah does not take easily to everyone, but he warmed to you right away."

Her cheeks flushed pink. "He's a dear little boy, and I love children."

Matt smoothed back his hair. "He wore me out. Maybe we will have a few minutes to catch our breath before the next patient comes in."

The door swung open. Mr. Waxman limped in with a gaping leg wound.

Matt whispered in Becca's ear. "I could have used a *few* more minutes before our next patient."

Becca chuckled and joined him in supporting Mr. Waxman to the exam room. Blood flowed from Mr. Waxman's open cut on his lower leg.

"How did you hurt yourself?" Matt held his breath

a moment to avoid gagging. He supported the man to the exam table. Mr. Waxman reeked of alcohol and body odor. He must have started drinking early in the day and neglected bathing for quite some time.

"I fell off my horse."

Matt assessed the wound and told Becca what he needed to treat the injury.

Becca did not flinch or grimace. She stayed right by his side and comforted Mr. Waxman when he cried out in pain.

She squeezed Mr. Waxman's shoulder. "Hold on. It won't take much longer."

Matt finished suturing Mr. Waxman's leg and applied a bandage to the wound. He passed the man pills to take to ward off infection. He escorted Mr. Waxman to the door and another patient came in. He and Becca skipped dinner.

The clock struck five. Matt sighed and turned his window sign to CLOSED, then removed his stethoscope and hung it on a peg.

Becca yawned and removed her reticule from a drawer. She moved to the door. "We had a long day. Go home and get some rest."

He bid her farewell and shut the door. Then he gathered his belongings and headed for the livery.

On his ride home, he noticed a wagon in front of Ruth's house with an older Amish couple and young woman inside. He steered his horse a little closer and squinted. Becca and Ruth walked toward them. His heart sank. The couple must be her parents. Who was the woman with them? Would she go home with them? He was fond of Becca. He should have told her this. Would he ever have another opportunity to talk to her?

Becca held Ruth's hand tight as they walked outside to greet their parents and Grace. Not going home before today had been the right decision. It had forced her parents to face Ruth after three long years, but would this make things better between them or worse?

Joseph and Elizabeth Yost stepped out of the buggy.

Her mamm appeared older than her daed, even though they were both forty. She liked Mamm's plump soft body and smooth, flawless skin. She had full rosy cheeks and big blue eyes. Wrinkles had deepened on Mamm's forehead and chin. Was it from the worry she had caused her mamm? She hoped not.

Ruth ran to hug them. Becca's eyes filled with tears as she hugged Grace and watched her parents and sister hold each other and cry. She had prayed often for her parents to reunite with her sister. She hoped they would be delighted Ruth's devotion to God hadn't wavered and realize she was the same sweet daughter they raised.

Grace whispered in her ear. "I've missed you, dear friend."

"I'm glad you came. I have something important to tell you and my parents."

Ruth stepped back and kissed Grace's cheek. She

motioned to her parents and Grace. "Please, come inside."

Becca hugged her daed. She loved wrapping her arms around his thin frame and having his long arms around her. She inhaled the scent of tobacco in his shirt then peered into his dark brown eyes. "What a nice surprise to find you and Mamm outside Ruth's door."

She stepped to Mamm and circled her arms around her overweight soft body. She separated from her and pushed a stray golden hair back in her mamm's kapp. "I'm happy you're here." She searched her mamm's sad blue eyes and shut her mouth.

Mamm and Daed stepped inside the house and sat in chairs. They hadn't spoken to either her or Ruth. Were they angry, sad, or overwhelmed with emotion? Why wouldn't her parents say something?

Daed removed his hat. "Becca, David's parents told us he plans to visit and ask you to marry him again. We came to warn you and to ask you to kumme home with us."

"David already came to ask me to marry him, and I told him no." She recounted her awkward and disappointing conversation with David.

Daed raised his eyebrows. "Would you like me to tell him to leave you alone?"

She shook her head. "No, it isn't necessary. He got my message loud and clear."

Mamm put her hand on Becca's shoulder. "You've been in Massillon long enough. It's time for you to kumme home. Our friends and relatives have put the unpleasant marriage ceremony behind them."

Grace bobbed her head up and down. She straightened her kapp over her brown hair wound in a bun.

Becca gripped her apron. "David isn't keeping me from coming home." She cleared her throat. "I've been working as a nurse for Dr. Carrington. His office is in town, close to Ruth's Mending Shop. I've learned about medications and how to help him treat patients with a variety of illnesses and injuries. I enjoy nursing more than I did being a midwife." She paused to give herself time to gather the courage to continue. "I've worshipped in Ruth's church, and she and I have enjoyed being together. I can't imagine not spending time with her. I'm happy here. I'm going to stay in Massillon and live with Ruth." She had talked too fast. She shouldn't have blurted her news out all at once. This was a lot of information for her parents and Grace to take in.

Mamm brought her hand to her chest. "No, Becca. Please don't do this to us."

Daed bowed his head and clasped his hands. He shook his head. "You will be shunned by your friends in Berlin. It's a sin for you to leave your Amish life behind."

Grace wiped a tear from her heart-shaped face and clasped her friend's hand.

Mamm studied Ruth. "You can open a mending shop for the Amish community in Berlin. I'll help you. Please, kumme home. We miss you. Our lives haven't been the same since you left. Becca can continue to work for Hester. We can be a family again."

Ruth gently squeezed Mamm's fingers. "Please try and understand. I have my home, church, and friends here. It took time to make my business a success. I have customers who visit my shop on a regular basis. They like my work and trust me. I appreciate my Amish upbringing, but to live by Amish rules is not for me." She reached for her Bible. "I have not abandoned my faith in God. I pray and read my Bible every day. In that respect, I am the same daughter you have always known."

Becca chimed in. "In spite of wanting to live in Massillon, my faith and devotion to God hasn't wavered and won't in the future either."

Daed straightened. "I don't believe you can be devoted to God, living in the outside world." He held up his hands. "I understand you don't agree with me. Let's not argue about it." He pursed his lips. "On another note, Becca, I don't like you working for an Englischer."

"Matt Carrington's a fine doctor, and he has taught me a lot about nursing. He's faithful to God and a gentleman. You would like him."

Mamm scooted her chair closer to Becca. "You called him Matt. Do you have feelings for this mann? Is he another reason you wish to stay in Massillon?"

Becca swallowed around the lump in her throat. What if Matt asked to court her? She would say yes. She had to tell them she cared for him. Matt was a popular doctor in town. She wouldn't want anyone else to tell them, and their friends and neighbors from Berlin visited Massillon on occasion to buy special supplies. She and Matt had attended church, he had come to Ruth's for dinner, and they had been to restaurants together. Even though Ruth was with them on these occasions, Mamm and Daed wouldn't approve. She must tell them the truth. "Yes. He and I are friends at this point. He hasn't asked to court me. I would like him to." She paused and waited for one of them to respond to her news.

Mamm squinted at Ruth. "Did you have anything to do with Becca meeting Dr. Carrington? Have you influenced her to remain here?"

Before Ruth could answer, Becca raised her hand. "I met Dr. Carrington on my first day here. I suffered a minor injury on my way to Ruth's house. He bandaged it for me and led me here. Later, she suggested I work for him, but she's not to blame for my being fond of him. I am. Ruth trusts him. Matt and Caleb were good friends. He has an excellent reputation in town."

Daed leaned forward. "If he doesn't ask to court you soon, will you kumme home?"

Becca left her chair and knelt before him. She covered his hands with hers. "No, I want to make a life for myself here with or without Matt. I love you and Mamm with all my heart, but I can't live my life for you."

Ruth knelt beside Becca. "I will take excellent care of her, and all of you are always welcome in our house. We would love it if you would visit regularly."

Mamm stood. "We're disappointed you both have chosen to leave the Amish order. Your daed and I are bound by Amish law to shun you, but I don't want to separate myself from my dochders anymore." Her lip quivered as she addressed Daed. "I've been miserable not being able to visit Ruth. I can't stand the thought of not visiting our dochders again. They can't kumme home again, but may we write to them? Maybe visit them once in a while? They're determined to live here. Nothing we say will change their minds. We must accept they're not kumming home."

Daed paused for a moment with his hand on his chin.

Becca struggled to keep silent. Would he agree with Mamm? It would be an answer to her prayer if he did.

His eyes looked from Mamm to Ruth and to Becca. "I agree with your mamm. We'll write and visit you once in a while." He bit his upper lip. "Ruth, I'm sorry we didn't come and support you during your time of sorrow. We should have been here to comfort you when Caleb died. We hoped you would return to Berlin."

Ruth met his gaze. "I understand."

Becca stood and held open her arms.

The Yost family circled in a hug.

Grace joined them.

Becca hugged herself. Her life was moving forward and falling into place. Her parents had agreed to visit, and they showed how much they loved them by making this decision to bend Amish law for them. She could move on with her life with peace in her heart. She no longer had to fret about not seeing them again. She stepped back. "You've been traveling all day. Are you hungry? We have a pot of vegetable soup in the icebox. I'll warm it for you."

Her parents and Grace followed her into the kitchen. Ruth made a fresh pan of biscuits and Becca heated the soup. She wiped a tear from her eye, as she listened to Daed's prayer of thanks. What a great day.

Mamm and Grace answered Becca's and Ruth's questions about their friends and what was going on at home. Mamm shared that she'd been doing her usual chores, cooking for community suppers and sewing dresses for her friends.

Grace chatted about the boppli she had helped come into the world with Hester.

Ruth shared with Mamm and Daed more details about her mending shop. She paused and rested her hand on Becca's arm. "Talk about what you've learned while working with Matt."

Becca curved her lips in a wide smile. "I've learned how to treat serious open wounds, apply stitches, fill syringes with medicine, and administer shots. I could go on and on explaining what I've learned, but it would take all day. I love nursing. One patient, Clyde Peterson, didn't want an Amish nurse in the room with him. I asked him to let me stay and help Matt treat him. When he left, he apologized for his behavior and offered me tomatoes." She chuckled.

Her parents threw her a wry grin. Their comments were few. Her new life went against their beliefs. Maybe she and Ruth shouldn't have been so forthcoming. *No,* if they were going to visit, she and her sister needed to be open and honest about their life here. Would they agree to visit Ruth's Mending Shop and meet Matt before they went home?

Becca readied the third bedroom for them. She spread sheets and a blanket on the sofa for Grace and then joined her family and Grace in the kitchen. "Your beds are ready." She folded her hands in front of her. "Would you like to visit Ruth's shop and meet Matt in the morning before you go?"

She held her breath. Her sister stiffened and kept silent. She might have gone too far. Maybe she shouldn't have suggested it. She couldn't read either one of her parents' faces.

Mamm looked at Daed with pleading eyes.

Daed raked a hand through his hair. "Yes, but it must be quick. I want to get home before dark."

Grace pulled Becca aside. "My parents won't be happy about you leaving our Amish community, but I'm sure they will let me write to you. Maybe they will let me kumme to town with your parents again when they visit you. I'll miss you, but I'm happy for you. I'm excited about meeting Dr. Carrington."

Becca valued her best friend. Grace had always loved her unconditionally. "I was hoping we could write letters to each other. I would love it if you could come with my parents when they come to Massillon. Follow me to my room. I have something for you."

Grace followed her.

She opened a drawer, pulled out a quilt, and passed it to Grace. "I made you another pocket quilt." She patted the pocket on the quilt tied closed with string. "Wait to read the letter tucked inside until you arrive home and are alone."

Grace hugged the quilt to her chest. "I'll treasure this always. It will remind me of the memories we've created together, like the first one you made me."

She carried another quilt to the kitchen and handed it to her mamm. "I wrote you a letter and put it in this pocket."

Mamm accepted the quilt. "I'll read it to your daed when we get home. It will comfort me until we meet again."

Her parents' dedication to the church and Amish order had been apparent to her since she was a child. They had compromised their values by not following the Amish rules for the sake of their daughters. Grace had agreed to do the same for the sake of their friendship. She loved them. She would never forget this day.

In the morning, Ruth and Becca got up early and cooked eggs and warmed homemade bread for their guests.

Becca's heart raced when her parents commended Ruth on how well she had decorated her home. Her sister's face beamed.

They walked to Ruth's shop together, and Mamm and Grace accepted Ruth's gifts of plain dark blue, gray, black, and white fabrics and thread. Her sister introduced them to Margaret, and they had a pleasant conversation.

After leaving Ruth's shop, Becca ushered them inside the medical office. She introduced them to Dorothy. Becca stifled her chuckle when Dorothy circled them each in a hug. Mamm was at a loss for words then recovered quickly and returned the gesture. Becca grinned. Grace seemed to like

Dorothy. It showed in the way she talked to her. Her friend and Dorothy chattered on and on as they got acquainted. Becca hadn't met a person yet who didn't like Dorothy.

She searched for Matt and found him in his office. "My parents and a friend are in town for a visit. They're in the other room talking to Dorothy. Matt, I told them I will not be returning home. I'm going to remain in Massillon. They've agreed to bend the Amish rules and write and visit Ruth and me now and then."

Matt eyes widened. "Becca, I'm happy for you and for me."

She laughed. "I found it difficult to share my decision with them, but they accepted it much better than I anticipated. We better not keep them waiting. Will you come and meet them?"

"Yes, of course." He walked out and offered his hand to her daed. "I am Dr. Matt Carrington, Mr. Yost. Call me Matt. It is nice to meet you. It is a pleasure to work with your daughter and my patients adore her."

Becca left them alone. She glanced over her shoulder and listened to Matt speak to her daed. He treated her daed with respect. She had trusted him enough to bring her daed to meet him. She wasn't disappointed.

Joseph Yost shook Matt's hand. "Becca's always been a hard worker. She has a gut heart. The outside world and working for you is exciting for her. My dochder isn't used to cruel or unkind people. She's bound to run into a few. Please take gut care of her."

"I am fond of your daughter, sir, and I assure you I have honorable intentions toward her. I will take good care of her and Ruth."

"My dochders claim you are a fine mann. After meeting you, I agree with them. I'm sure we'll meet again. We're planning to visit now and then."

"Your dochders must be delighted. They make it no secret how much they care about you and Mrs. Yost."

"It was nice meeting you."

Her mamm joined her daed and Matt.

"I'm pleased to meet you, Mrs. Yost. I was telling your husband how much I appreciate Becca and the hard work she does for me in the office. I am also rather fond of her."

Becca wanted to shout with glee. Matt and her parents had a great first meeting. They liked him. She read their faces. She never imagined them meeting Matt, let alone accepting him. Her pulse raced. He'd told Daed and Mamm he was fond of her.

Grace nudged her arm. "May I meet Dr. Carrington?"

Becca grasped her friend's hand. "Of course. Come with me." She approached Matt. "Matt, I would like you to meet Grace Blauch."

"You must be Becca's best friend. She told me what a valuable friend you are to her. It's nice to meet you."

Grace's cheeks pinked. "Her friendship means a lot to me, too. I hope you will take gut care of her."

"Rest assured. I will. I hope you will visit us again soon."

"I hope to kumme with Mr. and Mrs. Yost when they visit. I'll write to Becca and keep in touch."

They bid Matt and Dorothy farewell and walked home.

Grace hooked her arm through Becca's. "He is handsome and kind. I can tell he loves you. It's the way he looks at you."

"There is no doubt in my mind. I love him. I can't help it." Daed had arranged for her to wed David. She didn't know him. Would she have liked him? Would she have fallen in love with him? Those questions had flashed in her mind often before David left her alone on their wedding day. David had done her a favor. She and Matt had gotten to know each other. She liked and loved Matt. "He listens to me and offers good advice. He's good-looking, smart, kind, and he has a good sense of humor. I respect and admire him as a person and as a doctor."

Grace smiled. "I'm happy for you."

They arrived at Ruth's. Her parents and Grace gathered their belongings, and Becca and Ruth followed them outside.

Mamm tied her bag. "Becca, do you need anything from home?"

"I don't. Grace can go through my room and take what she wants."

Grace's brown eyes danced. "I would be delighted to have your things. I will think of you when I wear your clothes and kapps."

"You can drop whatever of mine you don't want in the charity box."

"I will share your dresses with two other women who are our size." She put her hand on Becca's shoulder. "Do you want me to share your news with Hester, or will you write to her and tell her yourself? She'll be excited to learn about Dr. Carrington."

"I'll write her a letter and explain everything."

Grace put her hands on Becca's shoulders. "I was hoping you would. She would be hurt if she didn't hear your news from you."

"I understand." Becca squeezed Grace's hand and then left to help Daed ready his buggy and horse. Then they joined Mamm and Ruth standing outside. Becca and Ruth bid their loved ones farewell and waited until they were out of sight before heading inside the house.

"I'm surprised they came, Ruth. They accepted my leaving much better than I anticipated they would."

"They did not flinch when you told them your news. I suspect they had already guessed you might stay, since you had not written and told them when you planned to come home. The fact we love God with all our hearts must also make this a little easier for them. At least I can tell it did for Mamm. I am relieved they have agreed to visit. It is truly a miracle."

Becca removed her kapp and smoothed her hair. "I never thought our parents would bend the Amish rules. What a relief. I suspected Grace would support my decision. I'm glad she came with them. Writing letters back and forth with Grace and our parents makes my decision to live here much easier."

The next morning, Becca awoke to the sweet aroma of fresh baked cinnamon rolls and coffee. She washed her face and hands and dressed. She joined Ruth for breakfast. "I'm going to get fat if you keep making these delicious cinnamon rolls."

"We need to celebrate this morning. I have my family back. Something I had not imagined possible. It is a great day." She waved her hands.

Becca moaned and bit into a soft gooey roll. She drank milk. "Yes it is." Her sister had reason to celebrate. They both did. The fear of never seeing their parents again had been erased.

Ruth glimpsed at the clock. "It is late, and I have got to get to work. I have a load of fabric being delivered today."

"I'm running late too. I'll see you tonight." Becca headed for the office. As she got closer, she squinted when a woman held her protruding stomach and groaned. A man opened the door to Matt's office. She hurried to help them.

Inside, Dorothy rushed to the couple. She stepped back when she saw Becca.

The woman cried out. "Please, help me. My baby is coming."

Becca and the man supported the woman as they escorted her to the exam room and helped her lie down. The stench of vomit, sweat, and blood from the woman's clothes filled the air. The pregnant woman's gown clung to her body. Damp hair matted to her head framed her sickly white face.

Dorothy fretted in the doorway. "Please meet Mr. and Mrs. Piper. What do you want me to do?"

She liked them at first sight. Both were short, medium build, and could have been mistaken for brother and sister with their small frames, dark hair, and round, pale faces. "I'm Becca Yost. Please call me Becca." She glanced over her shoulder. "Dorothy, where's Dr. Carrington?"

"He is not here yet. He had some errands to run this morning." Dorothy twisted her fingers. "Do you want me to find him?"

"No. I'll be fine taking care of Mrs. Piper. Would you mind making us some fresh coffee?" She didn't want Dorothy to worry and, at the same time, wanted her to feel useful.

The man wiped beads of sweat from his forehead. "My wife, Gretchen, has been in pain all night. I fear something is wrong with the baby."

"I'm an experienced midwife. Dorothy makes great coffee. Go relax and have a cup with her while I examine your wife."

Color returned to his face. He kissed his wife's forehead before he hurried to leave.

When he shut the door behind him, she stifled a chuckle. He was obviously relieved to escape. Dorothy would keep him occupied until his bundle of joy made his or her appearance. His absence would allow her to fully concentrate on Gretchen. She missed helping mamms birth their boppli. How exciting. She pulled clean sheets from a drawer. "How long have you been having severe pain?"

The woman winced and gripped her stomach. "The pains have gotten worse the last few hours."

Becca washed her hands then lifted the woman's skirts and draped her with clean sheets. The boppli was in position. She rushed to pull two pillows out of a cabinet. "I'm going to stuff these behind your back and help you into a sitting position. Get ready to push." She then positioned herself to help the boppli enter the world.

"Gretchen, push on the count of three. One, two, three, push."

The patient screamed. Sweat dripped from her forehead as she pushed.

"The boppli is crowning. Push again for me."

The young mamm screamed and pushed again.

Becca helped ease the boppli out the rest of the way. She placed the squalling boppli on Gretchen's chest, cut the umbilical cord, and clamped it with a clothespin. "You have a son." She lifted the infant from the mamm's chest. "Your boppli needs a little attention. You relax and get ready to hold him in a few minutes."

She cleared his mouth and nostrils then checked him to make sure he was healthy and washed him. After swaddling him in a boppli blanket, she placed him on the mamm's chest. "The blanket is a gift to you from Dr. Carrington. Your son's a handsome little fellow."

Becca removed the afterbirth from Mrs. Piper and discarded the bloody mess in the trash bin. Relieved Gretchen didn't require suturing, she dipped a rag in clean water and washed the woman's sweaty, beaming face. She then slid a clean sheet under Gretchen. "Would you like a clean dress? We keep a few here for new mamms. They are plain, dark blue, and are not formfitting. It would be suitable for you to wear home. You may return it if you wish."

"Yes. Thank you. You can throw my soiled dress

away. We own a farm, and I ripped the hem of the dress yesterday helping my husband feed the animals."

Becca helped her change, while Gretchen balanced the newborn in her arms. She covered her with a thin blanket.

Matt poked his head in. "Are you doing all right in here?"

Becca waved him in. "Yes. We're doing great. Would you ask Mr. Piper to come in?"

Matt opened the door wide, and Mr. Piper walked in and smoothed his wife's hair. "He is tiny." He shook Matt's hand. "Thank you both for your help."

Gretchen touched Becca's arm. "You did a great job taking care of me and my baby. I am going to tell my friends about you."

"You're too kind. I'm glad you and your son are healthy. Enjoy him."

Becca and Matt left the couple alone for an hour to relax. Mr. Piper and Matt supported the new mamm and walked her to the buggy. Becca carried the boppli and followed them.

She, Matt, and Dorothy waved good-bye.

Dorothy chuckled. "The poor man did not have a chance to take his buggy to the livery. It is a good thing the baby did not take long coming into this world, or their horse would not be fit to take them home." She linked her arm through Matt's. "Becca did a great job. She helped bring the infant into this world with ease. She calmed Mr. Piper and comforted his wife, all at the same time."

"I keep feed in the shed outside. I fed and watered

their horse earlier." He rubbed Becca's shoulder. "I am blessed to have her here."

Becca thought her heart would burst at hearing his words.

"I will leave you two alone to catch your breath before another patient shows up. Besides, I have some work to do." Dorothy squeezed Becca's hand before returning to her desk.

Becca and Matt headed for the exam room.

Matt leaned back in a chair. "You did a great job with Mr. and Mrs. Piper. I should have been here to help you."

"I enjoyed birthing the couple's boppli. It allowed me to practice being a midwife again." She flattened her palms on her lap and leaned forward. "All right. Enough talk about Mr. and Mrs. Piper. The anticipation of what you think of my parents is keeping me on the edge of my seat. How did you like meeting them?"

"It stunned me they came to visit you and Ruth, because of their strong belief to shun her for leaving the Amish community. I enjoyed meeting them."

"They surprised us. We are thrilled they've agreed to write and visit us. Ruth and I consider it a miracle from God."

"I am relieved you have decided to stay here. I cannot imagine what I would do without you." He moved closer to her and clasped her hand. "Becca, you are more than a friend to me. I have grown fond of you. Will you please allow me to court you?"

Her heart raced. "Yes! Yes! I hoped you would ask."

He stood and gently pulled her to her feet. He pulled her close and lowered his head to kiss her.

Her heart raced. She closed her eyes and lifted her chin in anticipation of their first kiss. His lips touched hers. Nothing could have prepared her for the overwhelming joy and burst of excitement she felt. She and David hadn't courted, hadn't shared past life experiences or had meaningful conversations. An arranged marriage seemed strange to her now that she had met and gotten to know Matt. She wanted to meet his parents, spend more time with him, and find out if they were right for each other. When would she meet his parents? Ruth didn't have anything pleasant to say about Mrs. Carrington. Her sister's words echoed in her mind.

Chapter Four

A week later, the bell clanged in the waiting room. With the tone of a squeaky wooden door hinge, his mother spoke to Dorothy. He groaned and rubbed his temples. Why was she here? A meeting with his mother was not the way he wanted to start his day. Her heels pounded the floor as if she were headed into battle. He had avoided talking to Becca about his parents. He slapped a hand to his head. *Big mistake.* No telling what his mother would say to her, and there was no time to warn her.

Eloise Carrington swung open the door. "Do not stare at me. Say something. Why have you not bothered to visit your father or me?" She darted her eyes from Becca to him. "Is this the woman I have been hearing about?"

Matt rose. His mother's entrance and dramatic performance as she pulled off her thin white gloves sent needles up his spine. His mother had not paused between questions to allow him to answer her. Of course, this was nothing new. She had not been in his office five minutes, and she had insulted Becca already.

He put his hand on Becca's shoulder. "If you are referring to the nurse I have hired, then yes, this is Becca Yost." He gestured to his mother. "Becca, this is my mother, Eloise Carrington."

Matt raked a hand through his hair. He did not want to risk his mother insulting Becca further. He would rather she be in a pleasant mood when she and Becca had a chance to get to know each other. "Becca, would you mind going over the supplies we need to order with Dorothy?"

Becca bowed her head. "I would be glad to. Mrs. Carrington, it was nice to meet you."

Mrs. Carrington gave her a curt nod, as if to dismiss her.

Becca left and shut the door behind her.

Matt gritted his teeth to keep from saying something he would regret.

His mother crossed her arms against her chest. "Are you out of your mind? An Amish girl is not a suitable nurse for you."

He did not want to discuss Becca with his mother. Her prejudice had always troubled him.

She pointed at his chest. "You must consider your reputation. It is unusual for an Amish girl to work with a man outside her community. Gossip is you are rather comfortable around each other. I do not understand why you would want to work and associate with a girl who has lived such a backward life. Her dowdy Amish clothes are disgusting."

He removed her finger from his chest. "The Amish are plain, hardworking people who make

God a priority in their lives. Fancy clothes and material possessions do not matter to them. For your information, she has left her Amish life. She will remain in Massillon and live with her sister, Ruth. She is a sweet woman, who I admire for many reasons, and we are officially courting." He stood straight and refused to turn his eyes from hers.

Eloise jutted her chin. "You are out of your mind. She has been raised in a sheltered community and could not begin to fit into our society." She broke their gaze. "You need a refined woman. I will find you one."

Matt stepped back. "I resent your insults about Becca. She has all the qualities I am looking for in a woman. I expect you to treat her with kindness. If you refuse to honor my request, then we have nothing more to say to each other. You ruined my courtship with Mary Stetson. Do not try and do the same thing with Becca." The minute the words flew out of his mouth, he regretted them. He did not want to talk about Mary Stetson with his mother ever again.

Eloise Carrington narrowed her eyes. "She wanted your money. I saved you from her. She came from a poor family and did not know the first thing about etiquette or how to fit into our world."

He matched her glare and stood firm. "I did not care. I loved her."

"She did not love you, or she would not have taken the generous bank note I handed to her on the condition she leave town."

"You lied to her. You pushed her away with your rude behavior. You convinced her she did not fit into our social circle and never would because she came from a poor family. You caught her alone several times and continued to humiliate her."

She scoffed. "I did you a favor running Mary off."

"She left because she could not imagine having you for a mother-in-law. She accepted your money because her father was dying and needed expensive treatment."

"How do you know?"

"I received a letter from her weeks later. Her father died, and she did not want me to think she had taken the money for herself. I would have gone to her, but she told me in the letter she had met someone." The agony of the letter came rushing back to him.

"I believe she lied about her father. Furthermore, she would not have fallen in love with someone else so soon if you were important to her."

"I am not convinced she did meet someone. I believe she knew I would try to persuade her to come back but had made up her mind she could not put up with you, Mother."

Her nostrils flared. "Nonetheless, she must not have meant too much to you, or you would have gone to her and found out if she had met someone."

"Communication is important to me in a relationship. She should have trusted me enough to tell me about your disgusting offer. I would have refused to have anything to do with you and given her the money myself. Nonetheless, it is over and done with, and I will not discuss this with you any longer." It had taken time, but he had forgiven his mother for causing his and Mary's separation two years ago.

It did not do either of them any good to argue about Mary.

"I agree. There has been enough said about Mary Stetson." She patted his arm. "Besides, I have some exciting news to tell you."

Matt read the determination in her face. He dreaded her announcement. He abhorred her arrogance but admired her spunk, drive, and elegant taste. She had always doted on him and, even though she was opinionated, he had forgiven her shortcomings.

Moving to the mirror on his wall, his mother pinched her cheeks and righted her hat. "Beatrice Bloomingdale will arrive on the afternoon stagecoach to dine with us at the Massillon Restaurant. She is a beautiful girl from a fine family. Her father is a surgeon at Columbus Hospital. She helps her mother plan the most successful and wonderful parties." She brushed a thread from his shoulder. "Her parents are friends with many prominent physicians in Boston, New York, and Chicago. I expect you to join us for supper."

She knew he was courting Becca. Why was she matching him with Beatrice Bloomingdale? He gritted his teeth. He would bring Becca. "I will be happy to come and meet Miss Bloomingdale if Becca is invited."

"Fine. Bring her." Eloise fluttered her fingers at him. "I will meet Beatrice at the stagecoach. We will meet you and Becca at the Massillon Restaurant around six-thirty. Beatrice is staying with your father and me. She leaves on the morning train to go back to Canton."

Matt followed his mother to the door and waved good-bye. Well, what a surprise. She had not argued about Becca coming to supper. What did she have up her sleeve? He shrugged. Whatever plan she had in mind, he would not stand for her being rude to Becca. He would take her with him, and if his mother misbehaved, they would leave.

He moved next to Dorothy. She sat at her desk. "Where did Becca go?"

Dorothy focused on her paperwork. "She went to the general store for coffee. I asked her to fetch it for me. I did not want her here when your mother left. Mrs. Carrington was rude from the minute she came in. I am used to your mother's arrogant attitude, but Becca is not."

"I understand, and I told Mother she is to treat Becca with respect. If she does not, I will distance myself from her. I also told her my news."

She cocked her head. "Have you told me this news?"

He shook his head. "Becca and I are officially courting."

Dorothy rose and danced a little jig. "I hoped you would ask her to court you. I am thrilled. Her parents must be sad she will not be returning home to live with them. It is selfish of me, but I am glad she has decided to stay here. I would miss her if she left us."

"Yes, her parents are upset she is going to live with Ruth, but they agreed to bend the Amish rules and visit their daughters now and then. They are humble and kind people."

"Your mother is not going to show Becca the

same kindness her parents showed you anytime soon. It was evident in her behavior today. Your father is a gentleman. He may treat Becca with kindness."

"I am hoping my father will be welcoming to Becca when he meets her. He is not near as judgmental as Mother."

"I hope you are right."

"When they get to know her, they will love her."

The door swung open. Becca came into the office and handed Dorothy the coffee. "Here you go, Dorothy." She dropped her reticule in a drawer. "Matt, did your mamm leave?"

"Yes, she did. She invited us to supper tonight. She has a friend from out of town joining her. I would like you to go with me."

Becca paled. Uncertainty filled her blue eyes. "Maybe you should go alone."

"I would appreciate it if you would join me. It will give Mother a chance to get to know you." Should he go alone? No, he would take her with him. Becca had to interact with his mother sometime. She was the woman he had chosen to be with. His mother needed to understand this.

She sighed. "What time should I be ready?"

"I will pick you up at six."

Matt and Becca treated patients all day. Five came, and Matt shrugged out of his doctor's jacket. He hung it on a hook. "You must be exhausted. I hope you are not too tired to join me for supper this evening."

She opened the door. "No. I'll change clothes,

splash water on my face, and be ready at six." She waved to Dorothy and him before leaving.

He shut the door behind her. She did not want to go to supper with his mother. He could sense her apprehension in her voice. He did not blame her after the way his mother dismissed her today. Becca put others before herself. Another trait he admired about her. Yes, he loved Becca more each day.

Becca hurried home. She didn't have much time to get ready before Matt would arrive. Ruth must still be at work. A knock at the door startled her. She answered it. An older man slightly bent over with gray hair and a wrinkled face stood on the porch.

"My name is Jared White. My neighbors told me you are a midwife and a nurse who works for Dr. Carrington. They told me where you live. My granddaughter, Naomi White, is pregnant. She is in terrible pain and has been vomiting all night. She needs you. Will you help her?"

"Of course. Let me grab my bag." She lifted her medical bag she had put together a few weeks ago for just such an occasion. She wrote a note to Matt and taped it to the front door. He would arrive soon to take her to supper. He would have to go without her. She had hoped to win Mrs. Carrington over tonight. She shook her head. It was more important to help Naomi White this evening. She would have other opportunities to meet with Mrs. Carrington. "Let's go."

They climbed in Mr. White's buggy, and he guided

the horses to his house. He didn't speak on the way there. His hands trembled as he held the reins.

Her heart raced. He loved his granddaughter. His concern and expression told her so. She hoped his granddaughter and her boppli would be fine when this was all over.

He stopped in front of a house. "You go on in. I will take care of the horses."

Becca stepped out of the buggy. Naomi White's last name was the same as her grandfather's. The young woman must not be married. Where was the boppli's daed? She hoped Miss White wouldn't have to raise her boppli alone.

A shrill scream rang out. She opened the door. Miss White lay in a small bedroom drenched in sweat. Blood spread over the white bed sheets beneath her swollen stomach and thin arms and legs.

Pale and in obvious pain, the distressed woman reached for Becca. "Something is wrong with my baby. I know it. The pain is unbearable."

"Miss White, my name is Becca Yost. Please call me Becca. I'll do everything I can for you and your boppli." She pulled out a small blanket, antiseptic, thread, and sterile needles from her supplies.

Mr. White rushed in. "I will take care of the horse and buggy later. What can I do?"

Becca liked the woman's grandfather. Maybe giving him a task would calm him. "Mr. White, will you please fetch me two pots of clean water and several towels?"

He left the room.

Miss White winced and held her stomach. "Please, call me Naomi. Becca, I am scared. Please help me."

Becca threw one blood-soaked towel after another to the floor. Naomi had lost a lot of blood. Mamm and boppli were in trouble. She must get this boppli out as fast as possible. "I will do my best." She didn't like the amount of blood coming from the woman.

Mr. White hurried into the room and put Becca's requests on the floor beside her.

Her heart raced. She opened her mouth to offer comforting words but closed it. *Oh no.* The infant's head appeared too big.

"Naomi, push as hard as you can."

"I cannot. It hurts."

She positioned herself at the end of the bed. "Please try."

The woman cried out in pain and pushed.

Becca yelped when the boppli and blood gushed onto the bed. She cut and tied off the umbilical cord. The newborn's body lay limp and blue. The boppli girl's arms and legs twisted in the wrong direction and her toes were absent.

Naomi lifted her head and asked in a weak voice, "Is my baby all right? She is not crying."

Becca patted the woman's leg. "You rest and relax." She turned her back and wiped the infant's face and blew small puffs of air into the boppli's tiny mouth. No sound came from the newborn. The cold, tiny, lifeless body didn't respond to any of her efforts to revive it. She closed her eyes for a moment. Stillborn infants were the most difficult births to witness. Next, it was the mamm's obvious anguish and pain. She hoped not to experience either. She listened. A familiar voice sounded outside the door. Matt. She heaved a big sigh. He had come at the right time.

He opened the door and rushed to her. In seconds, he assessed the situation. "Let me try reviving the infant."

She passed him the newborn. "I've tried everything." She checked Naomi. The bleeding had stopped. She applied sutures.

Matt worked with the boppli, but she didn't respond to his ministrations.

Naomi sobbed. "Dr. Carrington, please do not let my baby die."

Matt's face turned somber as he cradled the motionless boppli. "I am sorry. Becca and I have done everything we can to save her, but your daughter did not make it. There is nothing more we can do. Would you like to hold her?"

Naomi wept and held out her arms.

Becca accepted the dead boppli from him, wrapped her little body in a soft blanket, and then tenderly placed the infant in Naomi's arms as her own tears dripped onto her cheeks. She smoothed Naomi's damp matted hair while the bereft young mamm held her dead boppli girl. Her heart broke, witnessing the woman's pain.

Matt moved next to Naomi. "I am sorry for your loss. If you need me, please send your grandfather to my office. I will come to you. I will step out now so Becca can help you change."

Naomi caressed her boppli's cheek as tears streamed down her own cheeks.

Matt left and closed the door behind him.

Becca cleaned and helped her change into a

fresh gown as the new mamm moved the boppli from one arm to the other. Becca offered to hold the boppli while Naomi changed, but she wouldn't let go of her daughter. Becca couldn't blame her. What a shock to find out her boppli had died. She couldn't imagine experiencing Naomi's pain. "Is there anything else we can do for you?"

Naomi grabbed Becca's hand. "Please visit me tomorrow. I don't have another woman to talk to about my problems. Would you mind coming back here tomorrow evening?"

Becca smoothed the sorrowful woman's matted dark brown hair. "I will be here at six." Becca cleaned up her mess and discarded the bloody rags in a flour sack. She stepped out of the room then handed it to Mr. White to throw away. She gathered her other things and stood by Matt's side.

Matt shook his hand. "Please let me know if you need anything."

"I appreciate you both coming here today and helping us. Thank you both."

Becca left with Matt and climbed in his buggy. "Thank you for coming. My heart goes out to Naomi. Do you know her well?"

"Naomi White is sixteen. When she was fourteen, her parents died in a house fire in Canton, Ohio. She came here to live with her grandparents right after her parents' deaths." He clucked at the horse and drew a breath. "A year ago, Naomi's grandfather hired a carpenter, Samuel Keller, to help him build an addition to his house. Naomi fell in love with the young workman and got pregnant. When she told Samuel about the baby, he left town."

Becca's mouth opened. "My heart aches for her. She is mourning the loss of the man she loves and her boppli."

"At least she has her grandfather. He is sixty-two and in good health. He is a fine man."

She raised her eyebrows. "What happened to the grandmother?"

"She died of a heart attack six months ago. She was a kind woman. I am sure Mr. White and Naomi miss her."

"I'll include them in my prayers tonight before bed." She glanced at Matt. He had come to her rescue again. She found comfort having him by her side in such a sad situation. He had shown compassion and had not passed judgment on the unwed mamm. She admired him for that.

They approached the Massillon Restaurant.

She yawned and stretched her arms. "I hope you told your mamm and her friend why we weren't able to join them for dinner."

Matt stopped in front of the livery. "When I found your note, I did stop by the Massillon Restaurant and told Mother why we would not be joining them. She understood. My father is a surgeon. She is used to patients' needs taking priority over dinners and parties." He steered his horse toward the livery. "Mother and her friend would have headed home by now. I am going to take you to dine there anyway before I take you home."

"I'm starving. It sounds good to me."

He stopped and handed the reins to the liveryman, and they walked to the restaurant.

"You haven't told me much about your parents. Tell me more about them."

The waitress delivered their food and a basket of warm bread.

Matt lathered butter on a slice of bread. "My father and I are close. In spite of being a busy surgeon, he found time to take me fishing and target shooting. I asked a lot of questions concerning his work as I grew older, and he answered each one in a way I could understand. His patience in explaining why he had to do different types of surgeries for his patients generated an interest in me to become a doctor."

"Are you close to your mamm?"

Matt wiped his mouth with his napkin. "I love my mother. She bought me the finest clothes, read me stories before bed, and took me to dinner in town at least twice a week. She taught me proper manners from the time I was a child. She is too caught up in what she considers appropriate dress and behavior, though. Acceptance in high society is of primary importance to her. She is prejudiced against people who do not live up to her social standards. We have argued about this subject many times."

Ruth had also told her Mrs. Carrington looked down on people not up to her social standards. When she met her, Mrs. Carrington lived up to what she had heard about her. It explained her cold attitude toward her. Ruth was right. Mrs. Carrington might be a problem. She certainly didn't fit into Mrs. Carrington's social circle. "She didn't appear to approve of me as your nurse."

He sighed. "I have not visited my parents for a few weeks. It is unusual for me not to do so. She was upset with me and in a bad mood. Do not take it personally." He covered her hand with his. "I told her you were more than my nurse. I told her we are courting."

Becca stopped chewing. She stared at Matt for a moment then swallowed. "What did she say?"

Matt shrugged and glanced away. "She was stunned. She does not understand Amish culture. She will be fine once she gets to know you. I will arrange a time for you and me to have dinner with my parents sometime soon."

Umm. She doubted Mrs. Carrington had anything nice to say regarding her after the way she treated her when they first met. She hoped the woman would like her when they had a chance to finally sit and chat. With what she had been told about Mrs. Carrington so far, she doubted it.

She pushed Mrs. Carrington out of her mind and listened to Matt talk about the patients they had treated in the last two days. They finished their meal, and he delivered her to Ruth's house. He kissed her good-bye, and her heart raced. Her life had changed for the better. The decision to leave her Amish life overwhelmed her at first, but after spending time with Ruth and meeting Matt, she had no doubt she had done the right thing. Yes, she looked forward to her future in Massillon.

* * *

Matt went home and guided his horse into the barn. His mother's buggy was inside. What was she doing here?

His mother was in the sitting room, sipping tea. "It is time you came home. Where have you been?"

"I had no idea you would be here. I told you Becca and I went to help a young woman birth her baby. It took longer than I expected. The baby died. We stayed to comfort the family as much as we could. After we were finished, I escorted Becca to the Massillon Restaurant for supper before I dropped her off at Ruth's." He placed his bag on the floor and sat. "Did you enjoy your evening?"

"I am sorry the young woman suffered such a horrible loss." She placed her teacup on the small table beside her. "To answer your question, supper was disappointing since you did not join Beatrice and me, but I understand you were busy. I dropped her off at my house and then came here. I need to get back to her. I stopped by to tell you Beatrice has agreed to stay over another day and night. I expect you to join us for supper tomorrow at six at the Massillon Restaurant."

Matt rubbed his chin. "I am not interested in dining with you and Beatrice alone. Becca has promised to visit the young woman who lost her baby tomorrow night. She won't be able to join us."

Mrs. Carrington's face reddened. "You are being rude. Beatrice and her parents are friends of mine and your father's. I expect you to dine with us. Do not be late."

He opened his mouth to protest. She hurried to leave and shut the door behind her before he could

say anything. He groaned. His mother was the
pushiest woman he had ever met. To keep the peace,
he would go and be nice since the Bloomingdales
were friends of his parents. He wished Becca could
join them, but it would not be fair to ask her to
change her plans for him. Naomi White needed
her. Maybe it was for the best. He did not know
Beatrice. She might be as brash as his mother.

Chapter Five

Becca couldn't sleep. Heavy raindrops pelted the roof and ground outside. Thunder boomed, and then lightning bolts lit up the dark night. She shuddered and tightened her grip on the mug. The candle on the kitchen table flickered and offered little light in the dim room. Matt's words about his mamm flooded her mind. She tossed and turned.

Mrs. Carrington was like no other woman she had ever come across. The woman's stern tone set her teeth on edge. She had to stop fretting about what Mrs. Carrington thought of her and pray for guidance on what to say when they met again.

The next morning, she climbed out of bed and dressed. Becca headed to the kitchen and told Ruth she had met Naomi White. She recounted the story of delivering the young woman's boppli. She explained the infant's daed had left town upon learning Naomi was carrying his child. "I'm going to her house tonight to listen to her woes."

Ruth pressed a palm to her heart. "What a tragic

story. She is young to have suffered such pain in her life already."

Becca and Ruth finished their coffee and left for work. When Becca entered the office, she put her reticule in a drawer and lifted her white nurse's apron Ruth had made for her. She told Dorothy about meeting Naomi White.

Dorothy patted Becca's shoulder. "It is nice of you to spend time with her."

Becca kissed Dorothy on the cheek and picked up a biscuit before following Matt to the exam room.

Matt draped a stethoscope around his neck. "Good morning. I have news. Mother was at my house last night when I got home. Her friend is staying another day, and Mother insists I join them for supper. I wish you could join us too. I dread going without you."

Becca placed a clean sheet on the exam table. Why would Miss Bloomingdale stay over another day to meet Matt? She didn't want to sound jealous, but she wanted to know more about this woman. "If I hadn't promised to meet with Naomi tonight, I would join you. What do you know about your mamm's friend?"

"I will miss you, but Naomi needs you. I am glad you are going to comfort her. Beatrice Bloomingdale is a young woman from Canton, Ohio. Her father is a surgeon, and my parents and hers have become friends. Our fathers met at a surgeons' research meeting in Canton a couple of months ago. If Mother is playing matchmaker, you have nothing to worry about."

Becca's cheeks heated. "I trust you." She checked the drawers to make sure they were filled with the appropriate supplies. Miss Bloomingdale must be the perfect fit for Matt, according to Mrs. Carrington, or why would she introduce her to him? What if Matt found Miss Bloomingdale more interesting than herself? She had to stop her mind from going there.

She worked alongside Matt to treat patients with a range of injuries and illnesses nonstop until the last patient left at five-fifteen.

Matt yawned. "The last thing I want to do is go to supper with my mother and Miss Bloomingdale." He put his hands on Becca's shoulders and kissed her. "I would rather you and I were spending the evening together."

Her heart soared. Again he said all the right things. She believed him. On the other hand, Mrs. Carrington caused her concern.

She bid him farewell and headed home. Ruth was in the kitchen mixing ingredients for butter cookies. A touch of flour coated her hair. "I have one batch made, and I have started on the second. Could you put the first batch in the basket on the table?"

"Yes, I'd be glad too." She recounted her concerns to Ruth about Mrs. Carrington and Miss Bloomingdale.

"Matt is having dinner with his mother and this woman because he is a gentleman. Do not give Miss Bloomingdale another thought."

Becca scooped the cookies from the pan and put them in the basket. "I'm not worried about Matt and Miss Bloomingdale. I'm worried Matt's mamm will continue to play matchmaker for him."

"I suspect Matt will bring your name up more than once this evening. I have no doubt he will make it clear to both of them he is courting you." She winked.

Becca chuckled. She hadn't thought of Matt discussing her at supper. She liked the idea. She felt better already as she bid Ruth good-bye and headed for Naomi's house. She walked and enjoyed the warm night air. She arrived and rapped on the door.

Pale and with dark circles under her eyes, Naomi waved her in. "I am glad you are here. I have had a difficult day. I named my daughter Isabella. My grandfather and I buried her this morning." She wiped a tear. "My body is healing, but I am not sure my heart ever will."

She followed Naomi to the parlor and sat next to her. "I have not experienced the loss of a child. I can't imagine what you must be going through."

Naomi frowned. "I cannot stay in this town another day. Our neighbors stare at me like I am evil because I was pregnant and unwed. They are not the least bit sympathetic about Isabella's death."

Becca pulled her chair close to Naomi. "I'm sorry you're experiencing such cruel behavior from your neighbors. Ruth and I are always willing to listen to you, and you can visit us anytime."

"I appreciate how you and Dr. Carrington helped me when you delivered Isabella. You are the only woman who has offered to spend time with me."

"You can trust me. Please share whatever you like."

Naomi pulled a letter from her sleeve and unfolded it. She handed it to Becca. She recounted the story of how she met Samuel and why he left. "In the letter, Samuel asks me to forgive him for leaving. He wants to marry me and says he is ready to be a father."

She handed the letter back without reading it. "What do you want to do?"

"I am not sure. Can I trust him? He left when I needed him most."

She covered Naomi's hand. "I don't know Samuel, so I'm not sure what advice I can offer. Perhaps he needed time to get used to the idea of being a daed. When you told him, he must've been overwhelmed."

Naomi put the letter in her sleeve. "He is seventeen, and we had planned to court for a longer period. He most likely was overwhelmed when I told him I was pregnant. I believe he is truly sorry. He told his boss about me and the baby, and the farmer offered Samuel a house on his property to live in as part of his wages. The house has a small second bedroom, and it would have been perfect for our daughter."

"The house sounds nice." She rubbed Naomi's arm. "Do you love Samuel?"

"I do love him, and I forgive him. We all make mistakes. My grandfather liked Samuel and was disappointed in him when he left. He will support me in whatever I decide. He always has."

"You're fortunate to have such a loving grand-father. You do what will make you happy."

Naomi's eyes widened and the sadness softened. "Discussing my love for Samuel with you has made me realize how much I miss him. I will not be content until I am with him again." She clasped her hands. "I am going to leave the day after tomorrow and tell him I will marry him."

Becca put her hand to Naomi's cheek. "You need to wait a week and rest before you go."

"I will be fine. My body is doing better than my dark mood, and reuniting with Samuel will lift my spirits. He is excited about the baby. I dread telling him she died. At least we will be able to mourn her passing together."

She chatted with Naomi for an hour and left. Matt's face came to mind as she walked home. Would Matt mention her name while dining with his mamm and Beatrice Bloomingdale? How would his mamm respond?

Matt slapped cologne on his face and neck. He reconsidered, grabbed a towel, and wiped it off. The forced supper with Beatrice and his mother exasperated him. His mother put him in situations he loathed, and he planned to put a stop to it.

Mother should show her softer side more often. He was sure she did with his father, or how could the man stand to put up with her day in and day out. No wonder his father traveled so often. His parents' marriage was not like the one he wanted. He wanted a wife he would enjoy spending time with, namely Becca.

He went to the barn to ready his horse and left. After he delivered his horse to the livery, he strolled to the Massillon Restaurant. He paused in the doorway. His mother and the woman she was with sat a few feet away from where he stood and whispered something. A moment later, they laughed. He shook his head and headed for their table.

His mother glanced at him. "Son, you are late." She sighed and touched Beatrice's arm. "Well, never mind. Sit."

He ignored his mother's subtle rebuke and held out his hand to her guest. "I am sorry to have kept you waiting. It is a pleasure to meet you again. I apologize for having to rush off after meeting you last evening."

"I am delighted to see you again. Your mother has told me about your practice and what a charming man you are. I am looking forward to getting to know you while we dine."

He sat. Spending a lot of time with her was not something he intended to do. He would not engage her in much conversation while they dined, nor would he linger after supper. Her expensive dress flattered her small frame, and her brown hair in ringlet curls outlined her delicate heart-shaped face. *Attractive yes,* but her mannerisms reminded him too much of his mother. It was the way she moved and tilted her head to one side when she talked. He struggled not to wince when she prattled on in her high-pitched voice.

She put her hand on his upper arm. "Your mother is quite proud of you. She has sung your praises every time we have run into each other in the last few months. I had to come and see for myself if you were as handsome and interesting as she claims you are." She eyed him from head to toe. "I must agree with her. You are every bit as handsome as she claims."

He wanted to shrug her arm off but did not. Her facetious words sickened him.

A waitress served them water and then penciled their orders. Miss Bloomingdale spread her napkin on her lap. "Your mother told me you hired an Amish woman to help you in your office. I see the Amish as plain and simple people. You are kind to take pity on her and offer her a job."

He fisted his hands in his lap. Why did his mother share her concerns about Becca with Miss Bloomingdale? She must have thought the woman would help plead her case against Becca. His mother was wrong. Nonetheless, Miss Bloomingdale did not mince words. She got right to the point.

He would too. "On the contrary, Miss Bloomingdale, I did not hire her out of pity. Miss Yost is intelligent and an excellent nurse. Furthermore, she is someone I have taken a personal interest in."

His mother frowned. "Beatrice, he will not listen to me. Talk some sense into him."

"I do have to agree with your mother. You have built a practice where your patients trust you, and having an Amish woman for a nurse cannot be comfortable for them. Nor would she be a suitable woman for you to court, considering your social standing."

The waitress delivered their food.

He dipped his spoon in his potato soup. "My patients are fond of Becca, and my social standing is none of your concern."

Miss Bloomingdale's cheeks flamed.

His mother raised her voice. "Mind your manners. Beatrice is only offering her advice."

Beatrice cleared her throat. "Please forgive me. We can talk about something else."

His mother put her hand on Beatrice's arm. "We should talk about you, dear." She sat back. "Beatrice is a great hostess. She has been hired by most of our friends to plan and organize many parties to help raise money for school books. It has been a pleasure working with her. She is quite the world traveler, too."

Beatrice waved a dismissive hand. "You flatter me."

Matt closed his eyes for a moment. Miss Bloomingdale's insincere apology sickened him. She had made it clear by her aggressive actions and words she thought she was the woman for him. She was in for quite a disappointment, because he had no intention of spending any more time with her after they dined. This woman was forward and tiresome.

His mother lifted her chin. "Go on, Beatrice. Tell Matt about your trip to Washington, DC, and meeting the President and First Lady, Ida Saxton McKinley."

Miss Bloomingdale bragged about the money her father donated to Washington to help build schools there. Then she gave a detailed description of her tour of the White House as she presented a picture of President William McKinley and the First Lady.

Matt did not ask any questions as she prattled on. A little over half an hour had passed, when the woman yawned. He suggested they leave and bid the two women farewell. After retrieving his horse from the livery, he headed home. His polite but distant behavior toward Miss Bloomingdale was meant to discourage his mother from any further attempts to play matchmaker. His mother had found her younger twin in Beatrice Bloomingdale. Would his mother honor his request to stop trying to set him up? He doubted it.

The next morning, Matt sat in the reception area across from Dorothy and bit into a piece of rhubarb pie and sipped hot tea. "This hits the spot. I got up late and skipped breakfast."

Dorothy refreshed his cup. "I am glad to see you chipper. After meeting your mother and her friend last night, I suspected you would be in a bad mood today."

"She is stubborn. Even after I told her Becca had agreed to court me, she tried to match Miss Bloomingdale and me. I made it clear to both of them I am not interested in courting anyone but Becca."

Becca entered and joined them. "The sky is gray, and the rain is steady." She placed her dripping parasol in the corner of the room and hung her damp shawl on a coat hook.

Dorothy passed her hot coffee and a plate of

warm blueberry bread. "Matt is telling me about his dining experience with his mother last night."

She raised her eyebrows. "Start at the beginning."

Matt chuckled. "There is not much to tell. Miss Bloomingdale is a brash woman. Her laugh, mannerisms, and opinions about life in general are the opposite of mine. No matter, they understand I am not available. Next, Miss Bloomingdale chattered on and on about meeting President McKinley and the First Lady. I might have found this part of the conversation interesting, if anyone else but Miss Bloomingdale had been talking about it."

Dorothy laughed and almost dropped her coffee cup. "You must have been miserable having to spend the evening with such an arrogant woman."

"Yes, miserable would describe the evening quite well."

The door opened and startled the three of them.

A bodacious woman in a low-cut dress and tangled red hair hanging halfway down her back barged in. She held a blood-soaked towel to her cheek. Her two front teeth were missing. "I'm Gertrude Evans. I work over at the Horseshoe Saloon. A fight broke out between two men. One of the men threw a glass at the other man. It hit me instead. Will you look at it for me, Doc?"

"Yes. I am Dr. Carrington. This is Dorothy Watts, and this is Becca Yost, my nurse."

The woman picked up Dorothy's trash can and spit a disgusting wad of tobacco in it.

Dorothy winced.

Matt stifled his chuckle and followed Becca and

Miss Evans into the exam room. "If you will have a seat on the table, I will take a look at your cheek."

Matt removed the towel from her wound. The bleeding had slowed. "Becca, will you please gather what I need to suture Miss Evans's wound. I will clean it."

Becca gathered what he needed and brought them to him.

"Cute little nurse you got there, Doc. Are you and she courtin'?"

"I do not discuss my personal life with my patients."

"Whew, Doc, you're a little grumpy. You might want to come visit me. I'll lighten your mood. Why, I'll only charge you half as much as I charge other men."

Becca blushed.

"Miss Evans, please remain still while I suture your cut. If you cooperate, I will do my best to leave you with the smallest scar possible for this type of wound." He paused. "You owe Miss Yost an apology for your rude remark." He waited for her reply.

"Sorry. I shouldn't have been so mouthy. I'll behave."

"I accept your apology. You can call me Becca."

"Call me Gertrude. I don't like bein' called Miss Evans. I'm only twenty-three. It makes me feel like an old woman."

Matt could not believe it. Becca did not judge Gertrude and treated her with respect, even after the woman had been offensive. She amazed him once again.

After the patient left, Dorothy pushed through the door. "Gertrude Evans has to be the most brazen woman we have ever had in this office. I had to fight the urge to gag when she spit tobacco in my trash can."

Matt and Becca held their stomachs and laughed. Matt caught his breath. "She is different."

"She obviously leads a hard life. I don't understand what goes on in a saloon, and I don't want to. I've had men stagger into me when I walk by there. They smell like alcohol and struggle to stand. I don't understand why she would want to work in a saloon."

The sheriff burst in and interrupted Becca. He breathed heavy and bent over to rest a minute. His hat fell off his bald head, and a button popped off his tight-fitting shirt covering his round stomach. His ruddy face was streaked with dirt.

Matt put his hand on the sheriff's shoulder. "Something is wrong. What is it?"

"Micah fell again. I told his mother I would find you. She said the boy is asking for Becca. I've got my wagon outside. We can all ride together."

Becca's face drained of color. "How bad is he hurt?"

"His mother told me Micah worked all afternoon building a mound of dirt. He jumped off the back porch, aiming for the pile. Instead, he landed on a pile of wood. She managed to walk him in the house and to bed but said he complained of a headache."

Matt grabbed his bag. "Dorothy, if anyone comes in, explain to them Becca and I had to tend to a patient and will be back as soon as we can."

Becca and Matt climbed in the sheriff's wagon.

The wheels bounced on the uneven ground and rocked Matt into her.

Becca straightened the hem of her dress. "He might have broken a bone. I hope his injuries aren't serious."

The sheriff spit tobacco on the ground. "I didn't see him. She came running outside when I stopped by her house. I check on all the widows who live outside of town at least once a week." He shook his head. "There's a sad story. Leah Shepler doesn't give her child much attention. Micah resembles his father. She's bitter and angry her husband left her for another woman a few years ago. She is twenty-eight and hasn't remarried. She delivers her baked goods to the bakery to sell and washes clothes for her neighbors to make a living. The boy fends for himself most of the time."

Tying the rope to the hitching rail, the sheriff gestured toward the house. "Go and help Micah. I'll be in the house in a few minutes."

Matt escorted Becca inside. They greeted Mrs. Shepler, and she hustled them to Micah's room.

"He is in pain but brave. I am worried he has hurt himself real bad this time."

Micah grunted and moved to sit up. "I falled again. My back and head hurts."

"You're not warm, but let me check your temperature." Becca removed a thermometer from Matt's bag and put it under Micah's tongue. She chatted with him until it was time to remove it.

Her tenderness with Micah reminded Matt of all her positive qualities. He moved next to her and bent to Micah. "I will be gentle." He eased the pressure of his hand each time the child groaned. He examined the large lump on his head and bandaged a bloody scrape on his back.

"You were a brave boy. My hands pressing on your body with these bruises must have hurt."

The child grimaced when he shifted in the bed, searching for a comfortable position.

Matt returned the stethoscope to his bag, pulled out a bottle of medicine, and handed it to Mrs. Shepler. "A teaspoon every four hours for the next two days will help relieve his pain. Nothing is broken. His aches should get better and his bruises should fade in the next few days."

Mrs. Shepler whispered in Matt's ear. "I apologize for my behavior toward Becca the last time I brought Micah to you. I resented her because I have been a terrible mother to my little boy. She shows him unconditional love, which is something I have not been doing. I was jealous. He talks nonstop about how nice and kind she was to him in your office. Two things I need to do."

"I understand. None of us are perfect. I'm glad you have had a change of heart toward Micah. Thank you for sharing this news with me."

They bid Micah and his mother good-bye and climbed in the wagon. On the way back to the office, Matt recounted Micah's physical condition to the sheriff. He shared with both of them Micah's mother's confession about her treatment of Micah and jealousy toward Becca.

"I'm glad the boy's all right." The sheriff spat tobacco juice on the ground.

Becca grimaced every time he spit. "I'm glad

Mrs. Shepler has had a change of heart toward Micah. They will enjoy a much better relationship because of it." She reached over Matt and tapped the sheriff's arm. "I worry about you. You should give up that nasty habit."

Matt stifled his chuckle at her discomfort with the sheriff's tobacco habit.

"You are forty-two. You may not make it to forty-three if you keep chewing tobacco."

"Aw, I'll be all right. I love the stuff."

The wagon stopped in front of Matt's office. The sheriff lifted his hat. "By the way, I hear congratulations are in order."

Matt eyed him. "Congratulations for what?"

"Dorothy told me you two are courting. Best news I've heard in a long time." He chuckled, flicked the reins, and left them standing there.

Becca's face reddened.

Matt shook his head. The sheriff gossiped more than anyone else. He followed Becca inside the office. "I'm glad Dorothy told the biggest gossip in town about us courting." He laughed and held her hand. "I want the whole world to find out."

Becca's cheeks pinked. "I'm tickled about it too."

Dorothy had left a note stating she finished her work and had gone home. An hour later, patients trickled in with various complaints.

Matt treated the last patient. After the patient left, he circled his arms around her. "Becca Yost, I must say it. I love you." Before she could say anything, he pressed his lips against hers. She stirred him like no other woman. He loved everything about her.

"I love you, too."

His heart raced. He had found the perfect woman. Working alongside his potential wife had not entered his mind. He looked forward to tending to patients with her help each workday. She understood when he talked about medications, research, and treatments. Her smile lit up a room, and her eyes sparkled like blue diamonds. He enjoyed the sound of her sweet voice and infectious laugh. Kind and caring, she had a gentle heart. Their conversations about any subject matter had been interesting. She was strong and able to handle the most difficult situations with ease and wisdom. She possessed all the qualities he wanted in a wife. He was ready to share his life and home with her. When should he ask her to marry him? She'd had to adjust to life outside the Amish community. Should he give her more time?

Chapter Six

Becca awoke to the aroma of hot coffee. She stared at the ceiling and hugged herself. Last night Matt said he loved her.

Ruth would be delighted to hear her news. She scrambled out of bed and dressed. In the kitchen, she joined Ruth. "Yum. I love the smell of hot coffee."

Ruth whipped eggs in a bowl. "You look chipper this morning."

"I have news."

The eggs sizzled as Ruth poured them into the hot iron skillet. "Do not keep me waiting. What is it?"

"Matt told me he loves me. I told him I love him, too." She bounced on her toes. "Ruth, I'm about to burst. I'm so excited."

She clapped her hands. "What wonderful news. I love watching your life flourish with all these good things happening to you. Soon we'll be planning your wedding." She checked the eggs and scooped the food onto their plates.

"Matt's mamm is my concern."

Ruth sat across the table from her. "He has let her know you are the one for him. This is not her decision to make. Do not let her spoil your happiness."

Becca poured two glasses of milk from the pitcher and handed one to Ruth. "You're right. Matt's everything I could ever want in a husband. I shouldn't fret about Mrs. Carrington's opinion of me. We haven't had much time to get acquainted."

"Maybe your next meeting with Matt's mother will be a pleasant one." She glanced at the clock, rose, and rinsed her plate. "I'll see you tonight."

Becca swallowed the last of her coffee and hurried to work.

Dorothy hurried to embrace her. "The sheriff stopped by and told me Micah is all right."

"Yes, he has a few nasty cuts and bruises on his back, but he'll be fine. He scares me. He's not afraid of heights. I worry about him."

"You are good with children. They love you. You are going to make a great mother someday."

Matt walked in. "I agree with Dorothy. You will make a good mother someday."

Becca's cheeks warmed.

Matt motioned for her to follow him into his office. He gathered her into his arms. "I could not wait to see you this morning. Let me take you to Lizzie's tomorrow night for supper. I wish we could go tonight, but my father needs my notes on some important influenza research. I promised to mail the material to him tomorrow. Do you mind?"

Becca's heart thumped at the sight of him. The sound of his voice calmed her. He was the one for her. He loved her, and she loved him. It had changed

everything for the better between them. "No, I
don't mind at all."

Patients trailed in for treatment one right after
another. She loved the flirty glances Matt threw her
way and the times he managed to sneak a squeeze
of her hand between patients. The last patient de-
parted at five-thirty Becca readied the exam room
for the next morning.

Matt gently tugged on her arm and pulled her
close. His lips pressed against hers. Her eyes closed
as she held her lips on his. She didn't want their kiss
to end.

Matt stepped back and kept his hands on her
waist. "Our first kiss was special, but all of them will
be memorable."

As she strolled home, Becca's lips tingled from
his kiss. She loved and admired the man. He treated
her with respect and continued to teach her about
medications and patient treatments. She spent time
with him in and outside of work. Could her life get
any better?

The next evening, as Matt and Becca enjoyed
dining at Lizzie's. The sheriff rushed in the door
and bolted to Matt and Becca's table. His face was
stricken. "I need your help. My best friend Jim
Abington is hurt bad."

Matt rose and lifted his bag. The sheriff normally
handled the most difficult situations with case, but
not this one. "Take me to him."

Becca lifted her reticule. "I'm coming too."

Matt held her hand and clasped his bag in his

other hand. He and Becca followed the sheriff outside and climbed into his buggy.

"What happened, Sheriff?"

"Jim was cutting wood for a fence and sliced his leg. His injury looks like fresh meat, Doc."

Every morning, Jim and the sheriff sat on the bench outside the livery drinking coffee and gossiping before heading off to work.

Matt patted the sheriff on the back. "Try not to worry. We will do everything we can for him."

The sheriff spit tobacco over the side of the buggy.

Jim's house came into view. The sheriff prodded his horse to go faster. Jim Abington's wife, Clara, and the neighbors were gathered around Mr. Abington's body stretched out on the ground. Color had drained from his face. Matt knelt and placed his hand over Clara's. The woman's small body trembled. Her stray brown hairs from her bun clung to her neck from sweat. She pressed a large blood-soaked towel firmly on the wound. He removed the towel. Blood gushed over Jim's leg.

Clara gasped. "Doc, please don't let Jim die. You gotta do something."

Becca grabbed a clean towel from his bag and applied pressure. "The blood's not clotting."

Matt motioned for the neighbors to move. "Please step away and let us have some room."

Becca sat on the ground next to where Matt knelt over the patient and handed him everything he asked for from his bag.

Matt examined the injury again. The sheriff

had been right. The man's leg wound resembled butchered meat. It continued to bleed. The man's arms were muscular. His legs were long.

He glanced at Becca and kept his voice low. "This is one of the worst injuries we have treated. How are you holding up?"

"Don't worry about me. I'm fine. I can handle whatever I need to. Tell me how I can help you."

"Hand me a tourniquet from my bag." He applied it to Jim's upper thigh and the blood slowed. "Men, help me move him inside."

The men gently lifted their friend and carried him to a bedroom where they lowered him on a bed.

"Thanks, men. Becca and I will take it from here. Please clear the room."

Matt irrigated the wound with Becca's help. "Becca, pull the anesthetic bottle from my bag and draw a syringe of medicine. I don't want Mr. Abington to wake up while I do the necessary suturing."

She worked as fast as she could.

He finished, washed over his handiwork, and applied a large pressure bandage. He met Becca's eyes. "This was a difficult situation. You were calm and handled Jim's wound with ease. I admire you for it."

Becca blushed and poured water in the bowl. "It provided me with another opportunity to learn more from you on how to assist with these types of injuries. I like working by your side, no matter how difficult the circumstances are." She dipped a towel in the water and then held it out to him. "Let me wash your hands."

Matt obliged, and Becca wiped the blood from them.

Jim groaned and moved his hand to touch his leg.

Matt grabbed his hand and leaned close to the man's ear. "Jim, Dr. Carrington. Do you recognize me? I am here to help you. You have a nasty wound, and I need you to stay as still as possible. You have lost a lot of blood, and I just finished stitching you up. If you move too much, the bleeding may start up again."

Their patient groaned again.

Becca dumped the bloody water outside. She returned to the bedroom and knelt next to Matt.

"He needs a shot for the pain to help him relax and keep still."

She moved to his black bag, drew the pain medicine in a syringe, and administered it in the man's arm.

Matt patted the man's cheeks. "Jim, open your eyes."

The man's eyes fluttered until he focused. He spoke in a whisper. "Will I lose my leg? It hurts, Doc. You gotta save my leg."

"I have given you something for the pain. I will come and check on you tomorrow. Stay off your feet and relax for a few days, until we see how it is healing. We do not want any type of infection. I have taken all the precautions we can. I will leave you some pain pills."

Clara Abington stepped in the room and faced Matt and Becca. "You saved my husband's life."

"We are happy to help. Do not let him rise for a few days." Matt held her hand in his. "I will apply a clean dressing tomorrow. If you need me in the meantime, send one of your neighbors to my home or office. I will come right away."

The woman thanked them.

The sheriff entered and went to his friend. "Jim, old buddy, you scared me. Either do what Matt says, or you'll have to answer to me. I'll visit you tomorrow. We'll have our coffee at your house in the morning."

Matt motioned to Becca. They went outside and climbed in the buggy.

The sheriff headed toward them and heaved a big sigh. "Jim and I go way back. We've loaned each other money and caught more fish and gutted more deer than I can count over the past twenty years. Thank you both for what you did this evening. I'm in your debt."

"You do not owe either of us anything. We are happy to help. Jim is going to be fine. Your friend will be as good as new before you know it."

The sheriff reined in his horse in front of Ruth's. They jumped out and bid him farewell.

The light shone on the porch steps through the window. Becca swiped a bug from Matt's shirt. "Do you want to come in?"

He wanted to spend more time with her, but he struggled to stay awake. Sweat pasted his blood-stained shirt to his body. "Look at us. We are a mess."

"You're right. I can't wait to get out of these clothes. I got my share of blood splatter too."

He yawned and covered his mouth. "I better go home, bathe, and put on fresh bedclothes. In spite of Jim Abington's accident, I enjoyed our inter-rupted night out together." He kissed her.

"I always enjoy time with you, no matter where we are." She caressed his cheek before bidding him good night.

Matt walked with heavy feet to the livery. His large muscular brown horse shook his head and neighed. Matt steered him toward home. He breathed in the fresh air and glanced at the full moon. He looked forward to sharing a lifetime of beautiful nights like this one with Becca.

Soon, he would have to arrange a meeting for his parents to get to know Becca better. His mother was rude to people outside of her social circle. He didn't understand how several of the staff she em-ployed could work for her as long as they had. She barked orders and didn't speak one kind word to them in his presence. He doubted Becca would ever meet her high standards for a daughter-in-law. If his mother was unkind, it might be their last meeting with his parents. He loved his parents, but he wouldn't stand for his mother's distasteful behavior toward Becca. He wasn't sure about his father. Not as judgmental, but he could be high-minded as well. He shook his head. He'd hope for the best.

The next morning, Matt sat at his desk and tapped his lip with a pencil. He listened to the sound of Becca's voice greeting Dorothy in the next room.

The two women escorted a little boy to his office.

"This little one needs attention. He fell and hurt his arm."

Matt guessed the dirty-faced boy at about six. His shabby clothes were too big and had holes in them.

The child squinted and held out his arm. "I fell."

Dorothy left the room.

Becca stooped to look into the child's eyes. "What's your name?"

"Benjamin Evans."

"My name's Becca." She pointed. "This is Dr. Matt. We're going to make your arm better." She guided him to the next room with Matt by her side. "Can you climb up on this table for me?" She offered him her hand.

Benjamin didn't hesitate to wrap his small fingers around hers.

Gertrude Evans charged in. "Benjamin, are ya in here? There you are."

Benjamin cowered and his lips trembled.

Her hand behind his back, Becca helped him climb on a stool to sit on the exam table.

The child gripped her arm and hid his face against it.

Matt bit his tongue and approached Miss Evans. She wore the same garish dress she'd had on the day he treated the cut to her head a few weeks ago. He noticed the small boy's face paled when his mother barged in the room. Why was Benjamin afraid of his mother? Why were his clothes torn and his hair matted? The child looked as if he had not had a decent bath or meal for a while. He was skin and bones. "Hello, Miss Evans. We met when you were here for treatment the last time. You have a nice little boy. We'll take good care of him."

"Yep, I remember meetin' ya." She squinted at her son. "I didn't want no kids. He was a mistake I made six years ago. Gotta watch after and feed him, and I don't have time to take care of him. He's a pain in my side." The woman shifted her bodacious body to one side and put her hands on her hips. "He went and hurt himself, and I had to take time out of my day and bring him here. I told him to stay out of trouble."

Matt crossed one arm on his chest and his other hand fisted under his chin. Her obvious disgust concerning the boy sent chills up his spine. He glanced at Benjamin. The child hung his head and would not acknowledge his mother. She smelled of alcohol. Was she slurring her words or did she always talk this way? It was ten in the morning. Way too early in the day for anyone to be drinking. Those things did not matter. What did matter to him was how she treated this little boy. He stood feet apart and arms crossed. "Do you know how he fell?"

"I have no idea." Benjamin's mother lifted the trash can and spit tobacco in it. "He'll tell ya what happened."

"Are you going to stay here with Benjamin?"

"I don't have time to wait while you check him out. I've got work to do. Send him to the saloon when you're done patchin' him up."

Her exaggerated hip-swaying walk turned Matt's stomach as she left the room. What had Benjamin been exposed to in the saloon?

Becca had washed Benjamin's hands and face.

"After Dr. Matt is finished taking care of your arm, we'll find a cookie for you. We keep a fresh supply in the office."

Benjamin tugged at Becca's sleeve. "Will ya stay with me?"

She caressed his cheek. "Yes."

The child's stomach growled.

Matt tousled the boy's hair. "Are you hungry?"

Benjamin held his tummy. "Yep."

Becca glanced at Matt and frowned. She patted Benjamin's head. "Dorothy brought vegetable soup and homemade bread for dinner today. She would love to share it with you when Dr. Matt is finished treating your wound. Then you can have a cookie. Hold your arm out for Dr. Matt."

"It hurts."

Matt examined his lower arm. "I will be careful." He pressed around Benjamin's swollen skin. "No broken bones. Try to move your arm again for me."

Benjamin leaned into Becca and shook his head. She kept her arm around his waist. "Raise it a little at a time. You can do it."

He raised it until it was almost straight then pulled it back.

"You are going to be all right." Matt gestured to Becca. "His arm is swollen and bruised, but it should heal fine in a week or so."

She helped him off the table. "It's time to find you something to eat."

The small boy grabbed Becca's hand.

Matt followed them. He and Benjamin sat while Becca and Dorothy served vegetable soup, retrieved milk from the icebox, and then joined them. "The poor boy is starving. He is devouring everything on his plate."

Dorothy finished her food in a hurry. "I am going across the street for a few minutes. I will be back."

Matt suspected she would buy clothes or toys for Benjamin. She had been quiet through dinner, and it was not like her. It was difficult not to stare at Benjamin's skinny frame and his insatiable hunger. The small boy chewed and swallowed the food like it was his last meal. He stayed close to make sure the child did not choke. "Slow down there, little fella. I do not want you to get a stomachache."

The little boy lowered his head and slowed his eating.

Becca cleared the table. She leaned close to Matt's ear. "We need to talk away from him." She pushed a plate and bowl toward the child. "Here's more vegetable soup and bread. Take your time and eat what you like. We'll be right back."

Matt followed Becca to his office.

"I'm worried about Benjamin. What kind of place is a saloon for a little boy? He's too young to fend for himself."

"His mother smelled of alcohol. I suspect she entertains men for money and serves drinks."

She flattened her hand against her forehead. "Where's he while she's *entertaining?*"

He put his finger to his lips and pointed to Benjamin. "I do not want him to overhear us." He sighed. "I do not know where he sleeps or spends his time during the day. He stated he fell jumping off a box outside the saloon. The bruises on his back looked suspiciously like handprints to me." Matt shook his head. "He cannot be more than six."

She wrung her hands and paced. "We have to do something. He can't go back there, Matt."

He circled his arms around her to calm her. "Mrs. Evans may not like our interfering."

She stepped away and paced. "I must help this child. I'll go and talk to her."

"You will do no such thing. You cannot go inside the saloon. There are some unsavory and dangerous men who hang out there."

She opened the door and glanced over her shoulder. "Keep Benjamin here a little longer."

Chapter Seven

Becca ran out the door on her way to the saloon. She glanced over her shoulder. A patient holding her ear and groaning had stopped Matt. *Good.* She would have time to find Gertrude before Matt could come and insist she leave. Her heart slammed against her chest as she pushed through the saloon's wooden doors. The stench of alcohol and tobacco nauseated her. Her eyes darted around the room. Men with dusty clothes, long hair, cowboy boots, and heavy eyes sat half out of their chairs. Card players wearing Stetsons, coattails, and ascots concentrated on their cards and threw money to the center of the table. Women dressed in tight and low-cut dresses carried bottles of liquor and glasses on trays. Others sat on men's laps.

The music stopped. A hot blush rose from her neck to her forehead. She wanted to scream for the men and women to stop staring. Matt had been right when he told her this was a bad idea. She didn't care. Someone had to help Benjamin, and it might as well be her.

She approached Gertrude Evans. "I need to talk to you about Benjamin."

"I'm kinda busy, sugar. I don't have time to chat. Besides, I doubt you and I would find much to talk about." Gertrude used her fingernail to remove a piece of tobacco from between her teeth. "If you're done with Benjamin, you tell him to come back to the saloon. You better run along before one of these men wraps their arms around your tiny waist."

"I would like to help you with Benjamin, if you don't mind."

Gertrude stepped back. "What do ya mean? Are you gonna take him off my hands?"

Becca fought to control her temper. What a terrible thing for a mamm to say about her child. "My sister, Ruth, owns the mending shop not far from here. Margaret is a seamstress who works for her. Between the three of us, we could watch him during the day while you work."

Gertrude scowled and jutted her chin. "I live and work here. I don't have time to take him to your sister's mendin' shop every day."

Blocking out everyone else in the room, she concentrated on Gertrude. If she didn't, her knees would buckle. "What if he lived with Ruth and me? We live down the street. You could visit him anytime you want."

Gertrude leaned close to Becca. "I would like to get rid of him. Sometimes he spoils the mood when I'm with a man." She winked. "You know what I mean? You'd be helpin' me out. You're not goin' to charge me money for takin' care of him, are ya? 'Cause I'm not payin' you to do this."

She shut her mouth. *No,* she didn't know what Gertrude meant. Nor did she want to. She was here to help Benjamin. "No, his care will not cost you a cent. We would like to care for him as long as you let us."

A man's hand grabbed Becca's arm, and she jerked away from him.

The bearded man sneered and chuckled. "This one needs new clothes, Gertrude. She needs to show some skin." He sat and patted his lap. "Come sit with me, sweetie." He grabbed her arm.

Gertrude slapped his arm away from Becca. "You leave her alone."

Her skin crawled. How did Gertrude stand this place? She didn't understand women like her, women who talked tough, revealed too much of their bodies, and allowed men to do who knew what to them. "If you don't mind, I'll take Benjamin home with me." She grabbed a pencil and paper on the bar and wrote Ruth's address on it. She passed the note to Gertrude.

Gertrude stuffed the paper in her pocket. "I'll go upstairs and put his clothes in a bag." She lifted a dirty glass and swigged a small amount of liquor. "You better come with me. These men are ready to pounce on you. They like the young ones best."

She shivered and followed Gertrude. Upon entering the small room, her eyes swept from the lace undergarments hung on hooks in the small washroom to the bed covered with soiled, rumpled sheets. On the floor in the small closet, a dirt-stained toy dog lay on a pillow and blankets. Her stomach tightened. Benjamin slept in the closet.

What did he hear? How much time did he spend in this dark, cramped space? She eyed the slide lock on the door. Did she lock him in the closet? He must've been afraid she wouldn't let him out. Angry words flooded her mind. She fought the urge to tell Gertrude what she thought of her but shut her mouth for the child's sake.

"I don't know anyone willin' to take on someone else's kid." Gertrude handed her a bag with a tattered shirt. "Appreciate it."

Becca walked over, grabbed the dog, and stuffed it in the bag. She raced downstairs and outside. She paused and caught her breath. It would take a long time to erase what she had seen and heard in the last few minutes.

Matt's long legs strode toward her. She expected smoke to roll out of his ears to match his stern grimace. Instead, he held her elbow and guided her to the office through the back door.

Eyes narrowed, he let go of her arm. "I told you not to go in the saloon. You could have been harmed. You put me in a terrible position in not being able to go after you when Mrs. Bell came in to have me examine a boil on her ear. I would have gone to talk to Gertrude myself after our last patient."

Hands on her hips, she leaned forward. "I couldn't stand to take him back to her even for a minute. A saloon's no place for a child. You should've seen her room. There are sinful outfits lining her washroom, and Benjamin's bed is nothing more than a bunch of blankets on a dirty floor in her closet. How can a mamm have such a cold attitude toward her child. Where is he?"

"Dorothy is with him. She bought him new clothes, a small wooden train, and a picture book." He removed a thread from her collar. "You should have seen his eyes when she delivered them. His grin stretched from ear to ear."

"Matt, Gertrude said Benjamin got in the way of her entertaining. She has no problem with him living with Ruth and me. She couldn't wait to get rid of him. How can a mamm hand over her child to a stranger?"

"A mother giving up her child is appalling, but Gertrude is not like the women you are used to. Benjamin is blessed to have you and Ruth."

"I'll check on him before I leave to tell Ruth what happened today. She'll be thrilled to have a child in the house."

Dorothy was reading to the boy.

Glancing up, he skipped to her and lifted the small train. "Dorothy bought me this." He picked up the small red shirt and blue pants. "She bought me bedclothes, too." He held them with pride and pressed the clothes to his face. "I haven't ever had bedclothes before."

Becca patted his shoulder. "What is your book about?"

"Animals. I want to hear it again."

She patted his head. "Dorothy has been kind to you. Did you thank her?"

"Yep, I did."

"I need to speak to Dorothy. You enjoy your book, and I'll be back in a minute."

The child sat on the floor and flipped through the pages.

Becca gestured for Dorothy to join her away from him. She recounted her experience with Gertrude and described Benjamin's living conditions in the saloon. "I'm going to take him to live with Ruth and me today. I need to talk to her. Are you all right with Benjamin staying here a little longer?"

"Take your time." Dorothy removed her spectacles. "I am enjoying this little one. He has captured my heart. It is wonderful what you and Ruth are doing for him."

She hurried to the mending shop and stepped inside. Ruth looked up from the material she held. "What brings you here at this time of day?"

Pulling her aside and out of earshot from customers, she told her what had happened.

Ruth shook her head in disapproval. "First, you should have let Matt go to the saloon. You were out of your mind going to such a sinful place alone."

"I couldn't wait. Benjamin needed help. It doesn't matter. The ordeal is over, and I'm fine."

Shaking her finger, Ruth scolded her. "Do not ever go there again."

She would do it again for the little boy, but she would refrain from making this statement to Ruth to avoid an argument. "I won't."

Ruth's face softened. "Of course he can live with us." She put her hand on Becca's shoulder. "I cannot believe this is happening. I have always wanted a child. Margaret and I can both care for him here. She does not have any family, and she loves children."

"Wait until you meet him. Your heart will melt. He's pitiful and needs us. He's with Dorothy at the office. I'll bring him here and introduce the two of you."

"God has given us a wonderful gift today."

"After meeting his mamm, I'm sure he has not been cuddled, kissed, or treasured as a child deserves."

She kissed Ruth's cheek and walked to the medical office. She stepped inside and approached Benjamin. "I would like to take you to meet my sister, Ruth. Will you come with me?"

"Where is your sister?"

"She's not far." Becca glanced over her shoulder and eyed Dorothy. "Please let Matt know Benjamin and I are going to the shop to meet Ruth before heading home in case he needs me for something. Otherwise, I'll see you both in the morning."

Dorothy hugged them good-bye.

Benjamin stepped outside with Becca. The little boy's eyebrows lifted. "I don't want to leave. I want to stay here. Please don't make me go back home to my ma."

She squeezed his hand. He didn't know her or Ruth. She envisioned him being upset when she suggested he live with them. However, he might take the news better than she had anticipated. "Benjamin, I talked to your mamm. She told me you can come live with my sister and me for a while. What do you think?"

He paused then spoke in a low tone. "Do you have any men who live at your house?"

"No. Why do you ask?"

He raised solemn eyes to her. "Dr. Matt's okay, but men at the saloon push me and yell at me. I'm scared of 'em. Bad men hurt my ma. I hear her scream when I'm in the closet."

Becca swallowed around the knot in her throat. The child confirmed her fears. Gertrude had not cared what Benjamin heard. She lifted his chin with her finger. "You don't need to worry. No men live with us. You will be safe with Ruth and me." She pointed to Ruth's house down the street. "We live right over there."

"All right, then I'll go to your house."

Becca bit her upper lip. This child had endured more heartache than any child ever should. She would give him all the love she could muster. She knew Ruth would too. "You will like my sister. She loves children, and I told her all about you. She's eager to meet you."

Ruth stood outside and met them halfway. She offered her hand. "Hello, Benjamin. I am Ruth, Becca's sister. It is nice to meet you."

Benjamin scuffed the toe of his shabby boot in the dirt.

Her sister pulled a piece of candy rolled in a handkerchief from her pocket. "Would you like this?"

He lifted it from her fingers.

Benjamin held both their hands, as they walked to their house. Inside, he ran from room to room. "Your house is big." He smoothed his hands along the pillows decorating the sofa, quilts on racks and beds, tabletops, and furniture. He opened the closet door. "This closet is much bigger than the one I sleep in."

Ruth shot Becca a sad look. "He thinks he is sleeping in the closet."

Becca circled her arm around his shoulders. "We'll fill your closet with clothes. You'll sleep here on the bed." She patted the bed.

He stared with wide eyes. "This is my room and bed?"

Becca pointed. "Go look at the rest of the house." They were strangers, but Gertrude didn't ask one question. Benjamin came with them without hesitation. It seemed unnatural for a mamm and her son. How sad his life must have been to be unloved and unwanted.

She and Ruth plopped on the sofa. Becca patted her lap, and he sat. "Ruth will take you to her shop in the morning where you will meet Margaret. She's a kind woman who likes to play games. You will enjoy spending time with her. Then, in a few weeks, one of us will take you to school."

"I don't know how to play games."

Becca bit her lip. The neglected child had lived a sheltered life. They would introduce him to games, puzzles, books, and a variety of toys. "Margaret will teach you how to play games, work puzzles, read books, and draw pictures."

Benjamin clapped. "She sounds nice like Dorothy." He sat quiet for a moment. "Does Ma know where I am?"

Becca doubted the woman would visit her son, and she hoped not. Nonetheless, she and Ruth didn't have any legal right to the child. She would have to let Gertrude visit if she showed up. "Yes."

His mouth quivered. "Please don't let Ma come.

She hits me and hollers at me. Ma locks me in the closet, and I'm always afraid she'll forget and not let me out. She's mean."

Becca held him tight. His distress broke her heart. She understood his fear. Her jaw clenched. She hoped Benjamin never had to face his mamm again, but she couldn't make promises she might not be able to keep.

Ruth sat next to her and rubbed Benjamin's back.

"Ouch." He drew away from her.

Ruth raised his shirt, and covered her mouth. "Becca, look." His bony back was covered with black-and-blue bruises.

Becca whispered in Ruth's ear. "Matt found the bruises when he examined him. We didn't question him about them. He has been through enough. Since he is with us, there is no reason to broach the subject with him. No matter. We will have to do our best to protect him from harm. If she comes here, one of us will need to fetch Matt to come and stay with us until she is gone. If he is here, she will be less likely to raise a hand to Benjamin."

Ruth's lips trembled. "I agree. We are no match for a woman like Gertrude if she became violent."

Becca glanced at the bruises on his back and then put her hands on the child's cheeks. "We're happy to have you here with us. Tomorrow, we'll go shopping and buy clothes, books, and toys to decorate your shelves. If you could have anything you wanted, what would it be?"

He tapped his lip with his finger. "A new fluffy toy dog."

"I'm sure we can find one."

What had happened in this boy's life to cause him to trust two people he barely knew? He had accepted her and Ruth without hesitation.

She wanted him to relax and find comfort here. Maybe if he put his belongings in drawers it would give him a sense of permanence. "Let's go to your room and put the clothes Dorothy bought you in your drawers." She handed him the new clothes first. She opened the bag Gertrude had given her and lifted the dirty tattered shirt. How pitiful. She wadded the bag with the shirt inside and set it aside. Later, she would throw it away.

He tucked the clothes in the drawer and shut it. He eyed his dirty stuffed dog on the bed, where Becca had put it earlier. He left it there.

What were his thoughts? He had asked for a new toy dog. Did his old one remind him of his life in the saloon? "We need to feed you and then you need a bath."

Ruth tousled his hair. "How would you like an egg sandwich and fried potatoes?"

Benjamin rubbed his stomach. "It sounds good to me. Do you have any cookies?"

"We'll make cookies before we feed you and give you a bath. Would you like to join us?"

Benjamin tugged at her apron. "I don't know how to make cookies."

"Ruth and I will show you. You will love it." Becca laughed as he followed her sister's instructions as to what and where to get the ingredients. She waited until her sister and Benjamin began stirring the mixture, then she dipped her hand in the flour bin and threw the white powder on Ruth. Handing him the flour bin, she winked.

He plunged his hand in the white mixture, grabbed a handful, and tossed it on her as he squealed with pleasure.

Becca plopped in a chair. Flour coated her kapp, Ruth and Benjamin's hair, and their clothes.

Benjamin giggled until tears stained his powdered face.

Ruth sat and pulled him on her lap. "You are adorable."

"I want to make a mess with flour again sometime."

Becca glanced at Ruth and stood. "We will do it again on another day, but this dirty kitchen reminds me why we don't want to do it too often."

She and Benjamin cleaned the kitchen while Ruth fried eggs for sandwiches. Before sitting at the table, she pumped water in two large pots and warmed them on the hot stove.

When supper was ready, Becca and Ruth joined Benjamin at the table. She loved his laughter ringing in her ears and the sparkle in his eyes. He seemed like he didn't have a care in the world as he babbled on about what fun it was to make the cookies. She finished her meal. "It's time for your bath, young man."

Becca carried the pots to the tub and poured the warm water in. She passed Benjamin soap and a rag. The bruises were many on his back. What kind of problems would she and her sister experience with this child? She hoped they were able to deal with whatever came their way. She helped him wash, dried him off, and handed him his new bedclothes. She kissed his cheek. "You smell much better."

He dressed and hugged her. "May I please have a cookie?"

"Yes, you may."

He hopped on one leg out of the room to join Ruth in the kitchen.

Becca entered. Ruth handed Benjamin two cookies.

She giggled, as he waited a moment after each bite. "Someone is putting off going to bed."

He laughed then plopped the last bite of his cookie in his mouth. He swallowed it and stood. He held out his palms. "Oh no, my cookies are all gone."

"No more cookies for you, young man. It's time to get you to bed." She tickled him and found his giggle infectious.

Ruth laughed at them and removed his empty plate. "You find your book, and I will read it to you before I tuck you in."

Becca cleaned the dishes and made hot tea, while Ruth read to Benjamin in his room. She set a cup on the table for Ruth. The little boy had already added joy to their lives, and he had only been with them a few hours.

Ruth returned. "He fell asleep when I finished reading the third page of his animal book."

"Life brings such surprises. Yesterday we had no idea he would be in our lives today."

"I am thrilled he is, but you had no business going to the saloon alone. Matt must have been furious with you."

"Yes, he was, but he calmed when he saw I was all right. He had planned on talking to Gertrude after our last patient of the day, but I couldn't stand the thought of Benjamin going back there. Living in a community where mamms love their children has sheltered me from women like Gertrude."

Benjamin cried out and startled them. "Please, don't hit me. Stop it. Mama, stop. It hurts. I promise I'll be good."

The two sisters ran to his room.

Becca sat on the edge of his bed and held him. She turned up the lantern. "Wake up, Benjamin. You're having a bad dream."

He opened his eyes and blinked a few times. He blinked and focused on Becca and Ruth then glanced around his room. He wrapped his arms around Becca. "I dreamed about Mama. She wouldn't stop hitting me. I'm scared. Will you stay with me until I fall asleep?"

She held him and rocked him. "Yes, of course. You're safe. She's not here. Go back to sleep."

Ruth rubbed his arm. "Relax."

He drifted off to sleep, and Becca lowered him on the bed and turned down the lantern. She and Ruth tiptoed out the door.

Ruth followed Becca to the next room. "What if Gertrude wants him back one day? How will we protect him?"

Becca quaked. The saloon was too close for comfort. Gertrude could walk to their house. She didn't want to ever come across Gertrude Evans again. "I have no idea." She reached for Ruth's hand. "We'll pray for guidance and take one day at a time."

* * *

Six weeks later, Becca strolled to Ruth's shop after work. What would she and Ruth do without Margaret? She was a jewel to offer to take Benjamin to school today and watch him at the shop afterward. Maybe they did the wrong thing letting Benjamin stay out of school for five weeks. It broke her heart to know he cried every day this week at school. How much longer would the teacher tolerate Benjamin not participating in class?

What were they going to do? He had to go to school. She hoped Margaret was able to get him to stop crying when she escorted him this morning. The child listened to and obeyed her.

Becca pushed the door open and the bell clanged. Margaret and Benjamin were playing tiddledywinks and waved to her.

Ruth pulled her aside. "Margaret walked with him to school, sat with him at dinner, and introduced him to other boys during playtime. He told her she could go home an hour later. For his reward for being a good boy, she is giving him a pocket quilt for his bed. She promised to write and read him a letter from her that he could tuck in the pocket and it would be their secret. Our keepsake tradition has become popular in this family."

Becca covered her mouth. "What would we do without Margaret? She can get through to him when we can't. I'm touched Margaret wants to pass on our keepsake idea to Benjamin."

"I love her. She is a wise and loving woman. We should have asked her to take him earlier. I hope she is with us for a long time." Ruth yawned and hung her CLOSED sign in the window. "It is time to close the shop."

They walked outside with Margaret and bid her farewell. Becca and Ruth listened to Benjamin chat about his new friends at school as they held his hands on the way home. They stepped inside the house.

Becca put on her apron and pulled leftover chicken noodle soup from the icebox, placed it in a pan, and lit the wood in the stove. She set the table while she waited for the food to heat.

Benjamin wandered into the kitchen and climbed in a chair. "What are you cooking?"

"I'm warming up chicken and noodles. It will be a little while before it's ready. You can play with your train until I call for you."

He jumped like a frog to his room.

Ruth entered and plucked an apple from the fruit bowl. "He would rather spend time in his room than anywhere else, and the simplest things make him happy. By the way, the drawer where he stuffed his tattered toy dog was empty yesterday. I found it in the trash. He hasn't said a word about it, and neither have I."

"He sleeps with his new toy dog every night. I'm not going to say anything about his old dog either. I don't want to remind him of any unpleasant memories of his past life. His nightmares are less frequent. If we say anything about the past, he might start having them more often."

"I worry his mother will show up and ruin his life and ours. I could not stand to lose him. You should ask Matt to visit the saloon and inquire about Gertrude. Maybe she is gone. I would rest a little easier if she was."

Becca bit the inside of her cheek. "I don't want to remind her we have Benjamin. If Matt inquires, she may want to see him."

"Please ask Matt to find out if she is working at the saloon. If she is not, we can all relax."

Chapter Eight

Matt noticed the frown on Becca's face when she came to work. "You look upset."

"I'm worried about Gertrude. I'm afraid she will show up on our porch one day. Would you mind visiting the saloon and finding out if she is in town? I would rest easier if I knew she was no longer in Massillon."

He rubbed his forehead. "I will head over there. If any patients come in, tell them I will be right back."

Matt kissed her check and headed for the popular drinking establishment. He walked across the boardwalk and pushed through the doors. It was early for loud piano music. The men in dusty cowboy hats with tobacco wads in their mouths who sat at the bar did not seem to think so. He stood in the open doorway. Several men played cards. He liked their suits and black bowler hats. He eyed their spit-shined boots. Nice. He surveyed the room. Women in tight, revealing dresses hung on several of the men. There was no sign of Gertrude.

The bartender sat an empty glass on the bar. "What's your poison? Aren't you the doc in town?"

"Yes, I am the doctor in town. No thank you to the drink. I need to speak with Gertrude Evans." Matt spoke in a direct tone to discourage small talk. "Is she here?"

The bartender put the glass on the wooden shelf. "No, she left a few days ago. Left a note sayin' she was leavin' town and gettin' married. If you want company, one of the other ladies would be happy to oblige."

"No. I am here for information. Where did she go?"

"I got no idea, and I don't care." The bartender spit in a spittoon on top of the bar. "Gertrude's got a heart of stone, and I'm better off without her. She didn't get along with the other women, had a temper, and got drunk too often."

Matt raked a hand through his hair. He ignored the come-hither stares and whistles from the women and scowls from the men at the bar. "Thanks for your help." Matt strode out and returned to the office.

Becca stopped stocking supplies. "What did you find out?"

"I have good news. She is no longer working at the saloon and has left town."

Becca clapped. "What a relief. Where did she go?"

"The bartender told me she wrote she was getting married and moving away."

Becca leaned against the table. "What a relief."

Matt pulled Becca into his arms. Benjamin's mother was gone. The boy had adjusted to school, and his nightmares were less frequent. It was time to focus on them. "We have reason to celebrate. Let me cook supper for you tonight. Will you come to my house?"

"I didn't know you could cook. I'm impressed. Of course I'll come."

Six hours later, Matt glimpsed at his watch. The day had passed quickly. With Becca's help, he had treated twice as many patients in a day than his normal load. His shirt was wet with perspiration and his back ached from standing.

Becca latched the door. "I'm exhausted."

Matt laughed and grabbed a towel. "What a day, but I am still going to cook supper for us. You have not changed your mind about joining me, have you?"

"Not a bit. I'm looking forward to it."

He left right after she did to go home and prepare their meal. At six he collected Becca at her home and brought her to his house. "Make yourself comfortable." He eyed her surveying the living room and books lined on shelves. He liked having her in his house.

He lit the fire in the stove then checked the venison and potatoes he had cooked before he left. It should not take too long to heat up. He set the table and lit candles. "Come and have a seat."

She obliged and smoothed her napkin on her lap. "Candles are a nice touch."

"I was afraid you would be insulted when I asked you to come alone to my house."

She blushed. "I shouldn't be here without someone else present, but I trust you and wanted to have time by ourselves."

His spine tingled at the sight of her. "We deserve a nice quiet dinner after the overwhelming number of patients we have treated this week. Besides, I would like to talk to you in private about my parents. I put off taking you to visit them because Benjamin needed our attention and they have been traveling. Since he is settled and they are in town for a while, I would like us to spend time with them."

Becca sprinkled her potatoes with salt. "Do you have a particular date in mind?"

He sensed her hesitation. "I do. My parents are hosting a party this Saturday at their home. Will you come with me?"

"Your mamm didn't approve of me the first time we met in your office. It was obvious by the frown on her face. I'm nervous about meeting her again."

Matt moved the candle to the side and leaned forward. He hoped his mother would be kind to Becca from now on. He had told her if she was not nice to Becca this time, he would not be a part of their lives. He would be surprised if his father was unkind, because he seldom expressed prejudice against anyone. "My father will be a gentleman. As far as my mother goes, I told her I expected her to treat you with respect. I would appreciate it if you would come with me to the party."

She sipped her water. "I fear I'm not sophisticated enough for your mamm. I may embarrass her by coming in my plain clothes."

He needed a few minutes to ponder his thoughts. He rose and served the food then sat.

Leaning in, he met her gaze. "You are a beautiful woman, and I will be proud to have you on my arm in any dress you choose to wear. My mother's idea of what is proper attire for you to wear to this party makes no difference to me."

She toyed with her spoon. "Maybe we should have dinner with them by ourselves, instead of with a lot of other people."

"My friends will be there. I would like to introduce you to them."

"I can see how important it is to you, so yes, I'll go with you."

They chatted through dinner and then pushed their plates aside.

The candlelight caught the glimmer in her eyes. He wanted to hold her. The party would include dancing. Maybe he should teach her a few steps. "We will have a good time. It will be fun for me to show you the house where I spent my childhood." He rose and offered her his hand. "Miss Yost, may I have this dance?"

She giggled and rose. "I don't know how to dance, and we don't have any music."

"I will teach you and hum a tune."

"I'll step all over your feet."

"If you do, I promise not to complain."

He showed her where to put her hands and counted each step. As he hummed, she followed his lead and caught on fast.

"I get lost in the soft hum of your voice."

"I like having you close."

He whirled her around. Faces close, eyes locked, he leaned into her and pressed his lips to hers. Her mouth was soft, moist, and welcoming. Her eyes gleamed.

His heart quickened. "I am blessed to have you in my life."

"I feel the same way."

His heart soared at her words. She had been responsive and sweet. He had the urge to kiss her again but would not push his luck. She had come alone and been comfortable. Now he would break the rest of his news to her. "Come with me to the living room."

She sat quietly beside him on the sofa.

"I showed you a few easy steps, because I wanted to dance with you at the party my parents are hosting. Mother is hiring a piano player and clearing a room for guests to dance. I thought you might enjoy it."

"You were right. I enjoyed it."

"Good." He checked his timepiece. "It is after nine. I better take you home."

He went to the barn and hitched his horse to his buggy and brought it to the front of the house.

Already outside, she climbed in. "The moon's full tonight."

"Like you, it is beautiful."

"It's been a wonderful evening, and one I won't forget."

They chatted along the way about patients. He arrived at Ruth's, secured his horse to the front post, and walked Becca to the door. "I enjoyed tonight too. It was nice having time alone together." He kissed her and left.

Matt reminisced about the time he spent with Becca. Their kisses filled his mind. Her lips were soft and full. Her melodious voice, sunny personality, and the way she trusted him made her the perfect woman for him.

Dark clouds rolled in overhead and covered the brilliant glow of the moon. Her meeting his parents was important. He hoped they would not disappoint him and make her feel uncomfortable. Maybe in a social setting, with other dignitaries present, his mother would at least be cordial to Becca.

Becca closed the door and curled up on the sofa. "Matt wants me to meet his parents Saturday at a party they're hosting. A number of important people will be attending. I suggested we meet his parents when there weren't other people present. I'm not sure how Mrs. Carrington will treat me in front of others. She might embarrass me." Taught not to squabble, she wasn't sure how to handle Mrs. Carrington if she was confronted by her. She shouldn't fret. Matt would intervene if necessary.

"You have to meet them sometime. It may as well be at a party. At least with other people around, she will have to be somewhat nice to you."

"I'm almost certain she'll not approve of my plain clothes and prayer kapp."

"You and I need to root through my closet and choose some of my dresses for you to try on. I have three fancy ones you might like. You would be more comfortable and confident at the party if you were wearing an elegant gown."

Becca followed Ruth to her bedroom and waited while Ruth pulled one dress after another from her closet and set them on the bed. She held one in front of herself and looked in the mirror. It was a soft cream color with a pink sash and covered silk buttons from neck to waist in front.

She had chosen to live in the outside world, but she still wore her Amish clothes. She hugged herself. Her plain clothes provided a sense of security. Once she made the change from plain clothes to English ones, there would be no reason to wear them again. "To step out of my Amish clothes and wear an English dress for the first time and meet Matt's parents might be too much. I don't know what to do."

Becca smoothed her skirt. "I planned to start out simple and someplace familiar, like work." She moaned and held the same cream-colored dress up to the mirror again. "Not a public event where I'll be nervous anyway."

Ruth smacked her lips with obvious disapproval. "I have said all I am going to on the matter. The choice is yours."

Three days later on Saturday at three, Becca answered the door. Matt stood dressed in a handsome black suit and white shirt with a red ascot. She dreaded the party even more. She fretted her plain clothes would embarrass him. "You look handsome."

"Why thank you, miss, and you are as beautiful as ever."

Matt's eyes assured her he meant it. She straightened a loose pin on her plain dark blue Amish dress and tied the strings on her prayer kapp.

He held out his arm and escorted her to the buggy. Becca climbed in. She pressed her hand to her rumbling stomach.

Matt chatted about patients they had treated the past week.

Becca listened and commented when appropriate but couldn't relax. She couldn't push from her mind Mrs. Carrington's disapproving face the day she first met her. She didn't want her nervousness to dampen his happy mood. He was anxious to show her his childhood home and introduce her to his family and friends. She would do her best to win his parents over and enjoy the party.

As Matt steered the horses down a long lane, she viewed the ornate buggies with horses heading for the large, four-pillared house. Several cars were parked in the yard. What would it be like to ride in one?

A porch wrapped around the big white house. Plentiful pots overflowed with hyacinth. Women in elegant long dresses and handsomely garbed men headed for the front door.

Matt pulled in front of the house and handed the reins to the stableman. He climbed out, assisted Becca, and escorted her to the front door.

The butler waved them in. "Master Carrington, it is a pleasure to see you. Come in."

Matt introduced Becca to friends then showed

her each room. "I love this place. I have such fond memories of growing up here."

Becca leaned into him. "Your mamm is an excellent decorator. The carpets, furniture, and paintings are divine."

"I must admit, she does have an eye for decorating." He pointed to a painting of an older couple. "They are my grandparents on my father's side. I admire this picture of them. They were kind to others and loved each other very much."

She stared at them. The man and woman in the picture had rather sour faces and didn't reflect Matt's words. Was there anything positive she could say about this picture? Nothing came to mind. She strolled away from it. "What about your mamm's parents. Were you close to them?"

"No. They died before I was born. They owned a restaurant serving casual fare in Columbus where my mother worked and first met my father. She was an only child. Her answers to my questions about her parents have always been short. I do know her parents lived comfortably, but they were far from wealthy."

Mrs. Carrington worked in a restaurant? She had assumed the woman came from money the way she turned her nose up at those less fortunate than herself.

Matt gestured to a man who resembled him. "My father is standing in the library entryway. Come with me, and I will introduce you." He clasped her hand and moved to Dr. Horace Carrington. "Father, please meet Becca Yost. The woman I have been telling you about."

Matt's daed bowed with tight lips. "Yes, Mrs. Carrington has told me about you. Please help yourself to some refreshments. Dinner will be served in thirty minutes. Matt, we will talk later." He turned his back to them and greeted another guest.

Frowning, Matt pulled her aside. "Becca, I am sorry. My father certainly could have been friendlier."

Becca sucked in her upper lip. The moment was awkward. His daed disapproved of her. She observed Matt's stricken face. It was apparent he was hurt by his daed's abrupt behavior too.

Mrs. Carrington approached them. Her soft cream and subtly elegant pink gown complemented her tall, thin frame. Becca liked her dark hair pinned up in a large bun. A matching hat lined with flowers and a bow sat tilted on her hair. Her necklace and wrist shined bright with diamonds, and gloves matching her gown covered her hands. "There you are, my handsome son." She kissed him on the cheek and ignored Becca.

"Mother, you have met Becca Yost."

"My dear, may I call you Becca?"

Becca's pulse rate increased. Maybe they were off to a good start. "Yes, please do."

Mrs. Carrington scrutinized her from head to toe with her dark brown eyes. "Becca, let me help you. My son neglected to find you a proper dress to wear, and you must change before meeting our guests. I may have something you might fit into. I will have one of the servants see what we can do. Follow me."

Becca's body heated. Her hopeful moment ended. Things were not going well with Mrs. Carrington. Matt's mamm was rude and to come here was a mistake. She didn't move. She had no intention of going anywhere with this woman.

Matt gently squeezed her hand. "Becca is not going to change her clothes. She is dressed fine as she is, and I expect you to treat her with respect."

Pinching her lips, Mrs. Carrington leaned close to Matt. "You and I will need to talk at another time. Bringing her here dressed like this is a mistake. You are hurting your reputation and ours." She walked away in a huff.

He placed his hand on Becca's arm and whisked her into the room where refreshments were displayed on a long table. "I apologize for my mother's behavior. She is wrong about your dress. You are beautiful in your plain clothes."

Becca believed Matt meant what he said, but she couldn't erase Mrs. Carrington's rude words. Women stared and turned away when she opened her mouth to say hello but shut it. "You're kind, but your mamm isn't the only one who disapproves of my dress. The other women frown when they look at me." She wanted to run. His parents and their friends treated her as if she had leprosy.

He poured her a glass of ice water. "They are as rude as my mother. We will avoid them. I will introduce you to my friends, who I know you will enjoy." He put fruit and cheese on a plate and led her to a small table outside.

Matt introduced her to men and women of all ages. She liked the wives of his friends. They were kind and welcoming. She enjoyed talking to them. Several husbands asked their wives to dance. The couples moved across the dance floor.

She sat back. The warm breeze brushed her cheeks. Her eyes followed the couples dancing to the soft piano music drifting through the open doorway.

Matt offered his hand. "Dance with me."

Heart throbbing against her chest, she walked alongside him and stepped inside the room. She liked how the women's skirts swirled, as they glided across the dance floor. She followed Matt's lead and concentrated only on him. It was as if they were alone.

"Why is Eloise Carrington's son with an Amish girl? His mother must be appalled to have her son with one of *those* women."

Becca's eyes darted a glance at the bold, well-dressed woman. Her body tensed, and her magical moment with Matt was shattered.

Matt ushered her to a side room and put his hands on her shoulders. "Do not pay any attention to the brash woman's unkind words. I am the lucki-est man here to have you with me." He caressed her cheek. "I am ready to go home. Are you?"

Becca hooked her arm through his and headed for the front door. Today would forever be burned in her memory.

The butler instructed the stableman to bring Matt's horse and buggy to the front. They climbed in and rode to Ruth's. On the way, Matt insisted his parents' opinions about her did not matter to him.

Becca appreciated his effort to put her at ease, but it didn't work. How would she and Matt have a healthy courtship with his mamm and daed so fervently opposed to her? Before they went to Matt's parents' home, they didn't have a care in the world, but the party had changed everything.

He pulled in front of Ruth's home, got out, and escorted Becca to the door. He caressed her cheek, leaned in, and kissed her lips tenderly. "Please do not ponder on my parents' impoliteness. I will talk to them. If they do not agree to change their attitude, we will not visit them again."

She waited until he was out of sight before going inside. She joined Ruth and plopped in a chair beside her. She recounted what had happened at the party. "His parents want nothing to do with me."

Ruth removed Becca's kapp. "The whole evening was not bad. You enjoyed seeing Matt's home, dancing, and meeting his friends."

"Dr. and Mrs. Carrington are influential and rich. They want him to marry a woman of means. I'm not what they had in mind. A few of his friends tolerated me, and the rest were as discourteous as his mamm with their stares and murmurs. You should've seen the way she frowned at my dress. She despised me and my clothes. I wanted the ground to open up and swallow me whole. I've been living in a dream world. Matt's parents and friends will never accept me."

"If Matt wanted to marry someone from high society, he would have. He chose you."

"Matt is going to talk to his parents and insist they be kind to me. He's already had a conversation with his mamm about her changing her bad behavior toward me the first time we met. She still wasn't nice to me. I suspect she won't listen to him. Even if he refuses to communicate with them, we are bound to run into them. She has no problem showing up unannounced in his office. I don't want continuous confrontations with her. What can I do?"

"You have chosen to live in Massillon, and you want Matt. You need to start wearing English clothes. You should have listened to me and worn an elegant gown. You made yourself stand out by not doing so. I do not understand why you have not started wearing English clothes. Choose a simple Gibson Girl dress from my closet and wear it to work tomorrow."

"Maybe you're right. I'm no longer Amish, and Massillon is definitely my home. It's time for me to put my Amish clothes aside. Let's go pick one out." Becca followed Ruth to her closet where her sister pulled out simple flower-printed dresses. She tried them on and studied herself in the mirror. "This yellow one with the full skirt is my favorite."

"Good choice." Ruth smoothed her hands over the shoulders of the dress and straightened the rounded collar. "It is sweet."

She sashayed at her reflection in the mirror. It was pretty and the color brought out her eyes. "I'll wear this one tomorrow."

Removing pins from Becca's hair, Ruth unwound her bun. Her long blond locks fell to her waist. "Matt is going to love your new look. Let me trim your ends so it is more manageable." Ruth found scissors and shortened Becca's tresses. "Your hair is thicker with some weight taken off. When we have time, I will teach you some different ways to fix it."

"It will take a little time for me to get used to wearing English clothes. They feel strange. Not wearing a kapp will be the easiest thing to get used to. I have never liked them."

"You will be fine. Soon, I suspect you will forget all about your plain clothes." Ruth put her hand on her hip. "You will need some color on your face. We need to enhance your flawless skin and accentuate your high cheekbones. I have some powder for your cheeks and a little light beeswax stain for your lips." Ruth went and got these things and applied them with a delicate touch.

Becca studied herself in the mirror. "I like it."

Ruth stood back. "Good. Now I can tell you about my surprise. The day you told me you were going to remain in Massillon, I started stitching a pink and white dress for you. It is still at the shop. I will bring it home tomorrow." She tapped Becca's nose. "You're going to look beautiful in it. Someday, I hope to stitch you a wedding dress."

"Ruth, I'm truly blessed to have a sister like you. I appreciate all you do for me. And yes, you making my wedding dress someday would be wonderful."

She had considered what marriage to Matt would be like. Something she enjoyed mulling over. It would be different from an Amish wedding where the bride didn't wear a wedding dress or accept a diamond ring on her finger. There were no decorations or flowers. She looked forward to it all one day, but the party had cast a dark cloud over the bright and beautiful future she had pictured with him. His mamm had not only been rude to her but insulted her as well. His daed was definitely not happy about their courtship either. "If Mrs. Carrington has anything to do with it, Matt and I won't ever be married."

Ruth waved her hand. "Do not be silly. Matt is not listening to his mother and neither should you. Your first two meetings with Mrs. Carrington were not positive, but I have high hopes for the next one. English clothes will help her accept you. Matt told you how beautiful you are in your plain clothes. Wait until he sees you in your English dress tomorrow."

She had no doubt Matt would like the change, but she suspected she wouldn't measure up to Mrs. Carrington's standards no matter what she wore.

Chapter Nine

Becca walked to work Monday morning. She touched one of the soft blond ringlets bouncing against her neck. Her hair was pretty. Ruth had insisted on fixing her hair this morning. She ran her hand along the buttons on her arm. Yes, buttons were much better than pins holding her sleeves together. The soft yellow material of the Gibson Girl dress she had chosen swished against her legs. She swallowed hard. Would Matt like her new look? Maybe her hair in ringlets was too fancy.

The sheriff waved. She blushed, waved, and stepped inside the office.

Matt strode over to her. "You look stunning. I love the dress, and your hair is pretty."

Dorothy slapped a hand to her chest and squealed in surprise. "Becca, you are lovely in your Amish clothing, but this yellow Gibson Girl dress flatters your petite frame." She fingered a curl. "It is golden and feels like silk. Ruth must have done your hair. Your sister loves ringlets."

"You both are sweet. And yes, Ruth did help me

with everything. I don't know what I would do without her. She takes excellent care of me."

The sheriff rushed in and startled them. "Matt, a fight broke out at the saloon. A man got hit in the head with a bottle. Will you come with me and take a look at him?"

Becca passed Matt his bag. "Be careful."

Matt and the sheriff rushed out.

A few minutes later, the door slammed and Mrs. Carrington swept in.

Becca stood and stared at her then recovered. "Mrs. Carrington, how are you today? Did Matt know you were coming?"

Becca glanced at Dorothy, who hurried to her desk and didn't say a word. She turned her attention to Mrs. Carrington and waited.

"I am fine, and no, I do not need to make my son aware of when I will visit. I am his mother. I will visit whenever I want to. Where is he?"

Mrs. Carrington didn't make being nice to her easy. "The sheriff stopped by a few minutes ago and asked Matt to join him at the saloon to help an injured man."

"I will wait for him." Matt's mamm studied Becca. "I see you have changed from your plain clothes into a more appropriate dress." She tapped her finger on her chin and circled around Becca. "Although an improvement, this dress is still quite simple and a bit dowdy on you."

Becca gritted her teeth, folded her hands, and refused to respond to the woman's ill-mannered comment. "I'm not sure how long Matt will be gone. Maybe you would like to come back later."

Mrs. Carrington removed her gloves. "Oh dear, I have offended you." She came close. "You and I have gotten off to a bad start. I have an idea. Will you go to Lizzie's for breakfast with me and have a little chat?" She tilted her head, and the feathers on her large hat bobbed. "Will you do it?"

She didn't know what to make of Mrs. Carrington. Matt's mamm bounced from mean to nice all in one conversation. She would go with her to Lizzie's and hope for the best. Maybe this would be a new beginning for them. She glanced at Dorothy and caught the older woman's mouthed *no.* Should she listen to Dorothy and not go? No, she had to take the chance Mrs. Carrington had good intentions. "I can leave the office for an hour." She glanced over her shoulder at Dorothy. "If a patient comes in I can help, come and fetch me. Matt should return soon."

Dorothy pursed her lips with disapproval.

At Lizzie's with Mrs. Carrington, Becca bit into her fried green tomatoes. Not sure what to say, she waited for Matt's mamm to speak.

Mrs. Carrington tapped her index finger on the table. "Did Matt mention Beatrice Bloomingdale?"

"Yes, he did. I'm sorry I wasn't able to join you and your guest for supper. Matt said he explained to you why I wasn't able to attend."

Mrs. Carrington bit into her egg sandwich and dabbed her mouth with the napkin. "Yes, he did. Your absence allowed the two of them to get acquainted. She is a beautiful girl who comes from a prominent family, and she is interested in Matt. He seemed to like her."

Becca pinched off a piece of white bread. Why would Mrs. Carrington bring up Miss Blooming-dale? She must want to make her jealous. Matt and she had discussed Miss Bloomingdale, and she was satisfied Matt had no interest in any other woman but her. Why should she discuss Miss Bloomingdale with anyone, least of all Mrs. Carrington? "I believe you're mistaken. Matt and I are courting. He's not interested in Miss Bloomingdale. I assumed this meeting was so you and I could get to know each other better."

"What more is there to know about you? You are a poor ambitious Amish girl who shed her heritage to encourage a man with money to want to marry you. My son is smart but gullible. I want you out of Matt's life. Name your price. If you agree to leave my son alone, you can start a new life somewhere else and have money to do so."

Shock and anger traveled from head to toe. Did this woman really believe she would take money in exchange for Matt? This had to be the worst insult she had ever received. Mrs. Carrington's words were coldhearted, ruthless, and controlling. "I'm not going anywhere, and no amount of money will keep me away from Matt."

An evil grin spread across Mrs. Carrington's face. "You were at my party. You saw the type of people we mingle with, and you were obviously uncomfortable among them. Admit it. You do not fit into our social circle."

Becca considered leaving but stayed in her seat.

She wouldn't cause a scene or let Matt's mamm think she was weak. Some of Matt's patients sat in the corner. She didn't want to draw their attention. She met Mrs. Carrington's eyes and lowered her voice. "Matt's fine with the way I fit into *his* world."

"My son's friendships extend well beyond this town. Like it or not, he has a lot of friends in high society who will not accept you. It will always be a world you fear because you do not even know how to pretend to blend in."

Becca stiffened. Eloise Carrington's words rang true. The people were polished, smart, and current on all the latest news on politics, inventions, and fashion. Maybe Mrs. Carrington was right. Maybe she would never be comfortable in Matt's world. She glanced at his mamm. The woman's shoulders set back and her mouth tightened in a grim line. No, she would not let Mrs. Carrington ruin what she had with Matt. "I'm going to leave, because this conversation is pointless."

"You will be sorry you did not take me up on my offer. Our family's reputation means everything to me, and I will find other ways to steer Matt away from you until I succeed." She rose and left enough money on the table to cover the bill and tip. Without a word, she flounced out the door and to the stagecoach.

Becca raised a hand to her throat. Mrs. Carrington meant what she threatened. It was apparent in her tone. The breakfast was a disaster. Not at all the truce she hoped for.

The restaurant had emptied, much to her relief. As she left and walked to the office, she thought about what she would tell Matt. She must tell him the truth. Mrs. Carrington told her she would continue to meddle in their lives until he no longer courted her. This would most likely not be the last time they would have to discuss his mamm. She stepped inside and dropped her reticule in the drawer.

Matt and Dorothy were eating oatcakes. He pulled a chair close and motioned for her. "Dorothy would not tell me where you went. What is all the mystery?"

She treasured her wise and loving friend. Dorothy must've had doubts she would want Matt to know about her breakfast with his mamm. Her friend had made it known to her she didn't trust or like Mrs. Carrington. Dorothy had left it their secret. Her friend's actions had always shown she had Becca's best interest at heart.

She kissed Dorothy's cheek and turned to Matt. "Your mamm stopped by minutes after you left and asked me to breakfast."

Matt raised his eyebrows. "How did it go?"

Dorothy winked at Becca. "I am going to visit Ruth. I need buttons for a dress I am making. It will give you time to talk in private."

Becca waited until Dorothy shut the door. She recounted the story of her time spent with his mamm.

Matt's face flushed with anger. "I have had enough of her insults, and to offer you money to stay away from me is inexcusable. I will make it clear to her she is no longer welcome here or in my home until she agrees to be civil to you."

She stared at her hands. "I don't want to come between you and your parents."

"I am going to meet with my father and ask him to reason with her. He is not as judgmental as she is."

"Your daed doesn't approve of me either. His eagerness to get away from me at the party made it apparent. I doubt he'll side with you. She does have a point. I have no idea how to impress people, let alone talk about fashion and politics."

"Those things do not matter to me. You do." He cupped her face in his hands. "You suit me perfectly. I will talk to my father. He and I have always been able to discuss things with an open mind."

She opened her mouth to protest but closed it. She had to at least let him try to reason with his parents.

A week later, Matt rode his horse to his parents' home. He prayed for the right words to use when approaching his father about Becca. She was too important to him to let his mother destroy their happiness. He hoped his father would understand and want to support and help him.

Ah, the pond off to the side with horses grazing in the field made a beautiful picture. He had made good memories here as a child. He rode horses, swam, and fished. As always, the thick green grass and colorful flowers were well cared for by the gardner. He stepped to the front door.

A new butler opened the door. "May I help you, sir?"

Another new butler? He sighed. His mother's demands for perfection were impossible to achieve. He couldn't blame the house staff for not wanting to put up with her. She had few butlers or housemaids who could please her. "I am Matt Carrington. Are my parents here?"

His father met him in the entryway. "It is nice to see you, son. Come in. Your mother is at the neighbor's house planning another party."

He sighed with relief. His timing could not have been better. Mother would have complicated things had she been present. "Good. I would like to talk to you alone before she returns."

Frowning, Dr. Horace Carrington gestured Matt to go to the dining room. "I asked the cook to prepare dinner. Your mother told me to go ahead and eat when I got hungry. We can discuss whatever you like while we dine. Smells like chicken and dumplings. Is it still your favorite?"

Matt followed him to the dining room. "Yes, and I have been craving it." The table was massive for two people. Matt chose a chair close to his father.

Dr. Horace Carrington sat at the head of the table. The quiet cook arranged a large white and pink flowered bowl of steamy hot chicken and dumplings in front of the two men. She dipped servings onto their plates and left.

"What is on your mind?"

"Did Mother tell you anything about her visit to my office the other day? Are you aware she offered Becca Yost money to stay away from me?"

"Yes, she told me about her visit and no, I did not know about the money nor do I agree with her using it to bribe Miss Yost. She does tend to go too far, but her intention is to protect you. Your mother and I want you to choose a suitable wife, and we do not believe a simple Amish woman is a good choice." He mashed a dumpling before taking a bite.

Matt stared at his food. His father's words were unexpected and direct. "A wife who treats others with kindness and is more interested in caring for me than impressing politicians or anyone else is my choice."

Horace moved his fork back and forth without taking a bite. "She wants you to choose the right woman for a wife. Whether you like it or not, you belong to a social circle where a woman like Miss Yost does not fit in. Her level of education and sheltered life are two reasons."

"Your prejudice blinds you from seeing Becca for who she is. If you would have a conversation with her, you would learn she is an interesting woman. I am embarrassed by your and Mother's behavior toward her."

"I do not understand your attraction to this Amish woman. You have nothing in common."

All hope he had of convincing his father to talk to his mother on his behalf dwindled. Maybe he could reason with him. "We have a lot in common. We both enjoy medicine, horses, picnics, and worship, to name a few. Regardless, I am courting Becca Yost, and I do not need your permission."

Horace hissed and lifted the bread basket. "You cannot sway me on this one. I still disapprove of her. What is wrong with Beatrice Bloomingdale?"

Matt stared at his father. "Miss Bloomingdale is Mother."

"Why do you find this to be a problem? Your mother is attractive, clever, and a wonderful wife. In addition, she is a perfect hostess and planner. She fosters influential relationships. You need a wife who can offer you these same things. You should consider Miss Bloomingdale."

Matt scooted his chair. "Miss Bloomingdale is out of the question, whether I was courting Becca or not. You and I have always been able to talk freely. I thought for certain Mother poisoned you on this matter, but I believe you are as narrow-minded as she is."

"You need to listen to us. We have your best interest at heart. The right wife can make or break you in life."

"If you want to maintain a relationship with me, you will need to accept Miss Yost and treat her with respect."

"You are being foolish."

"No, I am not, and until you and Mother can accept Becca, neither of you are welcome to visit my office or my home."

Early the next morning, Matt stared at the pages of a medical book while seated in his favorite chair at home. He pondered his conversation with his father about Becca. He had always been able to communicate with him more than with his mother. His father had made it clear he would not budge on his opinion of Becca. Was this the end of his relationship with his parents?

His heart sank. He would miss talks about life and medicine with his father. And in spite of his mother's direct and strong opinions, he knew she loved him. He disliked having to ask them not to visit him, but he would not change his mind.

He retrieved his doctor's bag and headed to his practice. How would Becca take the news about his father's rejection of her? He did not want his parents' objections to their courtship to come between them.

Matt left his horse and buggy with the liveryman and walked to his office. Inside, Dorothy and Becca were giggling. He put his bag on the floor and approached Dorothy's desk, tore off a piece of Becca's apple bread, and popped it in his mouth.

Dorothy handed him a cloth napkin and a large piece of the bread. "Do not steal hers. Get yourself a slice. We are laughing because Becca is not used to our corsets. Not something we can discuss with you."

Matt chuckled and snatched the bigger piece of bread. "I do not know anything about corsets, nor do I want to."

Becca followed him into the treatment room and straightened the sheet on the exam table. Matt turned her to face him and circled his arms around her. To spoil her good mood with his bad news saddened him. "I visited my father yesterday."

"Do you have good news?"

"No, I am afraid not. He and Mother are convinced I should choose a daughter of one of their friends to court. I told him I do not agree. Please understand my father disapproved of my mother offering you money to stay away from me. Nonetheless, I told him they are not welcome here or in my home until they accept you in my life."

She held on to him. "You've always been close to your daed. It bothers me to be the reason you'll no longer communicate with your parents."

"Put them out of your mind. They are the ones being simpleminded. I am hoping my father will mull over our conversation and reconsider accepting you. If he does, then maybe he will talk some sense into my mother."

Ruth burst through the exam room door. Her face was pale.

Startled, Becca rushed to her. "What's wrong?"

Her voice shaky, she grasped Becca's arms. "I found Margaret on the floor in the supply room, and she will not respond or wake up. I left Benjamin with her."

Matt grabbed his bag. Becca pulled Ruth with her as she ran to the mending shop.

Benjamin sat cross-legged beside Margaret with tears streaming down his cheeks. "Please help her."

Matt knelt and listened to the woman's heart with Becca by his side. He placed two fingers on her neck and checked for a pulse. He found none. He breathed air into her mouth and did chest compressions. Again, he checked for a pulse. Her lips were blue and her skin pasty white. She was unresponsive with no pulse. He repeated the actions several times then stopped. It was no use. Margaret had died. He covered Benjamin's hand with his. "Little one, there is nothing more I can do for Margaret. She is gone."

Ruth reached for Benjamin. He jerked away and placed his head on Margaret's chest with his arms stretched over her body. His little body shook with each heartbreaking sob. Becca pleaded with him to come to her. "Benjamin, please." She pulled him close.

Matt rubbed the child's back. "I am sorry, Benjamin. I know how much you loved her." He draped a quilt over Margaret's body and then wrapped his arms around Becca, Ruth, and Benjamin. He stepped back and cleared his throat. "Becca, you and Ruth take Benjamin home. I will alert the sheriff, reverend, and undertaker about Margaret's death."

Benjamin hugged Matt, wiped his tears, and clasped one hand in Becca's and the other in Ruth's. The three of them walked home.

Matt waved good-bye to them. He spotted the sheriff across the street and approached him. He explained what happened. He remained patient as the sheriff directed two deputies to take Margaret's body to the funeral parlor. He chatted with the sheriff a few more minutes then went to the chapel and informed the reverend about the woman's death. They set a time for the funeral then he informed the undertaker of the details. "I will pay for the funeral. Margaret did not have any relatives."

The undertaker stepped out from behind his desk. "You are a kind man. I was friends with Margaret, and the couple who lived next door to her bought her place some time ago. They treated her like family. They allowed her to stay on and pay them a small sum each month. I will ride out there and tell them the unfortunate news. They will clear out her belongings."

Matt patted the undertaker on the back. "I appreciate your help and theirs. I do not want Ruth and Becca to have to pack and donate her things."

The undertaker shook his head. "Benjamin has suffered a lot of pain for such a small child. He sure did bring a lot of joy into Margaret's life. She loved the child as if he was her grandson."

"He has brought such joy to all our lives. Margaret

was like a grandmother to him. He is taking her death hard, but over time, he will adjust. We'll take good care of him. Thank you for your help." Matt bid him farewell and closed the door behind him.

Benjamin had endured way too much pain and sorrow at such a young age. He would spend time with him, listen to him, and do what he could to make life better for the child. He'd ride horses and fish with him. Benjamin's happiness and feeling of security were important to him. He wanted him to feel loved and protected.

Chapter Ten

Two days later, Becca held Benjamin's trembling hand. She listened to the reverend's words about God's love and Margaret's kindness toward others. She observed the sky. Gray clouds moved across it and covered the sun. The wind blew her dress against her legs and threatened to remove her hat. She gazed at the bundle of white roses tied with a pink ribbon on top of Margaret's coffin. They were the woman's favorite flowers. Matt stood close on her other side. Ruth stood quietly on the other side of Benjamin. Margaret's friends huddled together holding handkerchiefs.

Benjamin's little sobs escaped as he leaned against Becca. He tightened his grasp on her hand. She wished she could erase his pain. Margaret had played such an important part in his life. The lovely woman had taught him how to play games, baked his favorite treats often, invited him to stay overnight at her house at least once a week, and read him his favorite books. She had loved him unconditionally.

Marked gravestones in uneven rows caught her

attention. The dash between the dates of Margaret's birth and death would represent her life on a tombstone. It would hold all her years of innocence, youth, and adulthood. The older woman had been like a mamm to her and Ruth. She was wise, dependable, and loving. Her laughter would no longer ring in their ears. Her hugs and words of wisdom were gone. Memories were all they had left.

The service ended and everyone turned to leave the gravesite. Ruth stopped to talk to some of Margaret's friends. Benjamin tugged on Becca's hand. "Wait." His shoulders slumped and tears trailed down his cheeks. He dragged his bony legs to Margaret's coffin. He paused and pulled out a note from his shirt pocket.

He tucked the folded paper under the flowers on top of Margaret's coffin. "You'll probably miss me, so here's a picture of you and me for your pocket quilt in Heaven to take with you. I'll ask God to give you a real pretty quilt." He wiped his nose with his shirttail. "I miss you already." He cried, covered his face, and fell to his knees.

Becca rested her hand on her heart and prayed, "Dear Heavenly Father, please spare Benjamin a long mourning period. Please give him peace and wrap your loving arms around him. I praise you and thank you. These things I ask and pray in your name, Amen."

Ruth joined them and put her hand on the child's back. Red splotches dotted her cheeks. She wiped her watery eyes. "I listened to what he said to Margaret, and I watched him hide the picture he drew for her. What a sad and sweet picture to witness."

Becca circled her arm around her sister's waist. "Benjamin wanted to share our tradition with Margaret, like she did with him. He's compassionate and loving like Margaret."

Benjamin leaned into Ruth, and she kissed the top of his head.

Matt bid farewell to Margaret's friends and joined Becca, Ruth, and Benjamin. He scooped Benjamin into his arms. "You and Margaret shared a special friendship. It is tough to lose someone you love. It is hard to understand, but the sadness you feel for Margaret's loss today will get better over time. Then you will be able to remember your happy times with her without tears."

"I can't stop crying."

Matt held him tight. "You will in time, little buddy. In the meantime, you can cry on my shoulder for as long as you need."

Benjamin nestled his face in Matt's shoulder as he carried him to the buggy.

Matt passed him to Ruth. He then faced Becca. "Are you having guests?"

She shook her head. "We didn't invite anyone over after the funeral because we wanted to concentrate on Benjamin. Several of our friends delivered food last night. We're going to warm potato soup for dinner. Would you like to join us?"

"Yes. After I drop you off, I need to stop by the office and pick up paperwork I would like to review at home later."

"We'll have everything ready by the time you get back."

Benjamin lay asleep in her sister's arms. She combed his hair with her fingers. "He's worn out."

Ruth caressed his cheek. "Maybe I can cheer him up with a few games of tic-tac-toe after dinner."

"He loves playing games with you. What a great idea."

Matt stopped in front of Ruth's house and secured his horse. He then carried Benjamin inside and lowered him onto the bed.

Becca removed his shoes and socks. She kissed his cheek. She closed the curtains and covered him with a quilt. They tiptoed out and closed the door.

Matt kissed her forehead. "I will be back soon."

In the kitchen, Ruth stood stirring the soup over the fire. Becca removed bowls from the cupboard and placed all but one on the table. "I talked Matt into having dinner with us. He went to his office to pick up some paperwork and will return soon."

A few minutes later, neighing horses caught her attention. She peered out the window. Her mouth flew open. The bowl slid from her hands, clanged on the floor, and shattered.

Ruth rushed to her side. "Becca, what is it?"

"Gertrude."

Ruth moved past her and peered out. "Oh no, what are we going to do?"

"I have no idea."

Becca opened the door. The dreaded day had come. Benjamin's mamm had come for him. The woman had not written or visited her son in months. Why would she come now?

Gertrude stomped in and bumped into Becca. She searched the room. "Where's my boy?"

Becca grabbed the door handle and steadied herself. "Why, after all this time, are you here?"

The red-haired robust woman put her hand on her hip and straightened her tall feathered hat on her head. "I came to fetch Benjamin to work on the farm me and my husband bought in Kentucky. My man's waitin' in the buggy. We're goin' to make money growin' tobacco."

Becca glanced at Ruth. Her sister's lips were drawn in a thin line. She hoped Ruth wouldn't say anything to Gertrude. She needed everyone to stay calm until Matt arrived. He should walk in the door any minute. Her mind raced on ways to stall them. He would know what to say to Gertrude to stop her from taking Benjamin. "Bring your husband in. It's too hot for him to wait in the buggy." He would get impatient and bored sitting outside, and she needed him comfortable.

Gertrude waddled to the buggy with her hips swinging from side to side. She waved to her husband. "Scutter, get yourself on in here. I want ya to meet my boy."

The man was short, fat, and bald, and his suit fit snugly. His short legs hurried to keep up with Gertrude. She guessed him to be the same age as Gertrude. He entered the house and tipped his hat. "I'm Scutter Grossman. You can call me Scutter." He pointed to Gertrude. "And this here's my pretty new wife."

Becca ushered them inside and motioned for them to sit at the kitchen table. Sheltered from bold and crude people like this couple, she wasn't sure how to deal with them. She wanted to shout and tell them to leave, but she didn't for fear they would take Benjamin with them right then. She didn't want to make things worse. She needed time for Matt to return and help her reason with Gertrude and Scutter. "Ruth, this is Benjamin's mamm, Mrs. Gertrude Grossman, and her husband, Mr. Scutter Grossman."

Gertrude put a hand on her hip. "I told you to call me Gertrude. Callin' me by my last name makes me sound old." She pointed to Mr. Grossman. "Call him Scutter. When you call him Mr. Grossman, it sounds like I married me an old man. Besides, he likes bein' called Scutter better anyway. Don't ya?"

He bowed and tipped his hat. "Yes, Gertrude. You may have these fine ladies call me whatever you would like."

Ruth clenched her fists and harrumphed.

Becca grabbed her arm. She leaned to her ear. "We need to stall them until Matt arrives. He'll know what to do." She filled glasses with lemonade and served the couple.

Benjamin walked into the room. His eyes widened, and he ran to Becca.

She gasped and scooped him in her arms.

Gertrude patted his back. "Benjamin, come and hug your ma."

He paled. "No. Go away. I want Becca."

Holding him tight, Becca pulled him onto her lap. She suspected Gertrude had not bothered to hug her son most of his life, if ever. Why would she suggest such an act now? It was ridiculous. He buried his face in her shoulder. "Back away from him. He's scared."

Gertrude lunged forward. "Don't tell me what to do." She tugged at the child's sleeve. "Benjamin, I want you to meet your new pa."

Slamming a plate of fried apples on the table, Ruth raised her voice. "Leave the child alone."

Gertrude waggled her finger. "You have no legal right to my boy, and he's comin' with me. Benjamin, fetch your things and we'll be on our way."

Benjamin tightened his grip on Becca's neck. She willed herself not to yelp. She clung to him. The woman was right. They had no legal right to him, but it didn't matter. She had to do something. "Gertrude, wait."

Matt entered the room. "What is going on here?"

A wave of relief flooded her chest. "Gertrude has come to take Benjamin."

He directed his attention to Scutter. "Who are you?"

"I'm Gertrude's husband, Scutter Grossman. Call me Scutter. We came to fetch her son, 'cause we need him to work on the farm we bought in Kentucky."

Becca gritted her teeth. How could a mamm be so indifferent to her child? She had made it clear she wanted to use her son for free labor and nothing more. She could not imagine what kind of life he would have with these two.

Matt waved the child over to him. "Benjamin, come to me."

The child ran into his arms.

Gertrude pulled at Benjamin's sleeve. "Gimme my boy. This ain't none of your concern, Dr. Carrington."

Matt stepped back. "Mrs. Grossman, how much money is it going to take for you to leave Benjamin and never return?"

Gertrude scowled at Matt. "Are you offerin' to buy my son from me, Doc?"

Scutter put his hand on Gertrude's back. "Maybe you oughta consider Dr. Carrington's offer. Frankly, I would rather have the money."

Becca sucked in her top lip and held her breath.

Gertrude stared at the ceiling for a moment with a look of cold greed on her hard face. "I would say a hundred dollars oughta do it."

Becca searched Matt's face. A hundred dollars was a lot of money. Gertrude was obviously taking advantage of the situation. It was no secret how much Benjamin meant to them. Becca was sure Gertrude could tell this by their actions. The greedy woman knew she had them at a disadvantage. What would Matt do?

He passed Benjamin to Ruth. "Please take him to his room. I need to talk to Mrs. Grossman."

Becca listened as Matt directed his attention to Gertrude.

"The judge has an office beside the bank. We are going there first, and you are going to sign documents giving Becca and Ruth legal custody of Benjamin. If all goes well there, we will go to the bank where I will hand you a bank note with the understanding you are not to step foot in this town ever again."

Gertrude held out her hand to Matt. "You got a deal, Doc. Time's a wastin'. Let's go."

Matt ignored her hand. "Becca, would you like to join me?"

She passed Gertrude and grasped his hand. Benjamin's mamm was a coldhearted woman. She sold her son. What a heartless act. At least the woman had accepted Matt's offer. Because of him, Benjamin would be safe and legally theirs. He had come to her rescue again, but it wasn't over yet. Anything could happen. Gertrude was unpredictable.

Matt held Becca's hand. His heart pounding and anger hard to control, he stared at Gertrude and Scutter. Their greed and cold attitude toward Benjamin was disgusting. The boy was no more important to his mother than a poker chip in a winning hand. He could not wait to be rid of them.

Gertrude faced them outside. "You can ride with us."

"Becca and I will walk and meet you there." Matt waited until they were out of earshot "You have had such a horrible day, and now this. Don't worry. Once she signs the paperwork, she will have no reason to remain in Massillon."

Becca squeezed Matt's arm. "Before you came, I didn't know what to do. I wanted to jump out of my chair and shout hooray when you came through the door. It's hard to believe they're accepting your money for Benjamin. One hundred dollars is too much to ask you to pay. Is there some other way?"

Matt gently squeezed her hand. Her concern for him was touching. "I am happy to pay them the money, if it means Benjamin will not have to worry about living with his mother ever again."

Matt gently pulled Becca along with him. He brushed past Gertrude and Scutter at the law office. He opened the door and greeted the distinguished judge. "Hello, Judge Mitchell, do you have a few minutes to spare? I am sorry to barge in on you like this, but I have an urgent matter I would like handled."

"Yes, of course. Come in. How may I help you today?" He frowned at the Grossmans.

Matt and Becca stood, while the odd pair sat. "Judge, I would like you to meet Miss Yost, she is Ruth Smith's sister."

"Yes, I know Ruth Smith. She is a kind woman and an excellent seamstress. She does all my mending."

"It's nice to meet you, and thank you for seeing us on such short notice."

Judge Mitchell squinted at the Grossmans. "And who might you be?"

Gertrude squirmed in her chair and shook her ample chest at him. "My name's Gertrude Grossman and this here's my husband, Scutter." She pointed to Becca. "I'm givin' her and her sister custody of my boy."

Matt studied Gertrude. The woman had no shame. She had announced her intention to give up her son as if she were talking about the weather. Her indifference toward Benjamin sickened him. Matt would not relax until Gertrude signed the documents. There was no telling how difficult she might make this transaction.

Judge Mitchell removed paperwork from his desk drawer and explained the legal details to Gertrude. She listened and then signed on the dotted line.

Becca accepted a pen and dipped it in the ink then signed.

The judge signed the papers. He handed Gertrude one to keep. "You no longer have legal custody of your son, and you have waived your rights to visit him. Do you understand?"

Gertrude waved her paper in the air. "Yeah, I got it, Judge. We gotta be off, 'cause we got some business at the bank. Ain't I right, Dr. Carrington?" She didn't wait for an answer and pushed past him.

The judge passed a duplicate to Becca. "You have full custody of the boy. I don't see the need for your sister to sign unless you would have a disagreement about Benjamin's care."

"Ruth and I are close. I don't foresee any problems."

"Congratulations on your legal adoption of Benjamin."

Matt was relieved Gertrude had signed the documents and had not made any more demands. He shook hands with Judge Mitchell. "I appreciate you letting us meet with you on the spur of the moment."

Becca clutched her skirt. "Yes, Judge Mitchell, thank you for helping us today. You've made us and Benjamin very happy."

"After meeting those two, I am happy to do it. No little boy should be subjected to a mother like Mrs. Grossman."

"I feel the same way." Matt and Becca waved good-bye and found the couple pacing in the bank.

His hand on Becca's back, Matt approached the bank manager. "Hello, Mr. Campbell. I would like to withdraw one hundred dollars from my trust account."

"Yes, Dr. Carrington. I will be happy to oblige. How would you like the money?"

Matt raked a hand through his hair. He had never used his trust account. His father set it up when he went into practice and had continued to make periodic deposits since then. He had protested, but his parents had insisted. They would receive an account of his transaction through the mail in about three weeks. He had never cared about them receiving this statement, until today. No matter. Once he explained the situation to them, he was sure they would understand and be glad he used the money to help a child. Or would they? He did not have time to ponder this at the moment. He would worry about their reaction to how he spent this money later. "In the form of a bank note, please."

The man left and returned with the bank note. He handed it to Matt. "Is there anything else I can help you with today?"

Matt accepted the paper. "This should do it. Thanks, Mr. Campbell."

Gertrude yanked at Matt's sleeve. "I believe this here's mine."

He jerked his arm free and tightened his grip on the note. "Outside."

The woman frowned and stomped out with her husband on her heels.

Matt and Becca followed and faced them in the hot sunshine. He handed Gertrude the note. "I don't ever want to find out you are in this town again. Understood?"

She grabbed the paper and waved it in the air. "Pleasure doin' business with ya."

Matt turned his back on the couple and put his arm around Becca. "I am glad we are rid of them. We must tell Benjamin and Ruth the Grossmans are no longer a threat to him. They must be wondering what is going on." His heart warmed. She had trusted him to solve this problem with Gertrude. Every trial they faced had brought her closer to him.

They hurried to Ruth's. Benjamin was curled up on Ruth's lap clutching a corner of the small quilt Margaret had made him.

Matt knelt and put his hand on the little boy's arm. "Your mother and her husband have left town. She signed a paper giving you to Becca and Ruth. Your mother will not be bothering you anymore."

Benjamin's mouth stretched into a wide grin. "Did you hear what Matt said? She's gone. I don't have to worry about her coming to get me anymore. Matt said so."

Ruth wiped her tears with her fingertips. "We have reason to celebrate. Let's have potato soup and strawberry pie."

Matt tossed Benjamin in the air and carried him

to the kitchen. He was happy to help them. He loved them, as if they were his family. Unspoiled and kind, they had taught him how unimportant material things were in life. He hoped Benjamin wouldn't grow bitter or angry from this experience. He would spoil Becca, Ruth, and Benjamin with dinners out, fishing, and anything else they wanted to do to help aid in the child's recovery.

Six weeks later, Matt sat in his favorite chair at home reviewing kidney research. A rap on his door caught his attention. He peeked out the window and groaned. His parents stood on the porch. Their faces looked stern. They must have been traveling and returned to find his trust fund statement in the mail.

They marched in the moment he opened the door. His mother sat, and his father remained standing. "What is the meaning of the large sum of money you withdrew from the bank?"

Matt motioned for his father to sit. "Would either of you like something to drink?"

Horace shook his head. "No."

"Answer your father."

Matt told them how Becca and Ruth came to know Benjamin and why he paid the boy's mother to give them legal rights to him.

His mother got up, reached for a glass, and poured water from a matching pitcher on Matt's table. "I cannot believe you let yourself get involved in this mess. Benjamin is not your son. You should have stayed out of this situation."

"Your mother is right. You should not have interfered."

Matt pinched the bridge of his nose. Their disapproval of Becca was bad enough, but to not want to help this little boy, after what he told them, was mean and selfish. "When did the two of you become indifferent toward those less fortunate? You donate money to help those in need in your community. Why are you opposed to helping this one sweet child? Is it because you are not handing a bank note to someone at one of our fancy parties in front of your friends? I am ashamed of you."

His mother slammed her glass on the table. Matt expected it to break. "You mind your tongue. You are letting Becca ruin you and turn you against us. The issue is not whether we wanted to help this child or not, it is your involvement with this Amish simpleton and the urge to solve all her problems. You made a fool of yourself bringing her to our party. She was at a loss about how to dress or act or what to say to our friends. Worse, she has gotten mixed up with a saloon trollop. Stay away from her and mind your own business. She is trouble."

Matt rose. "You could both learn a lesson from her on how to treat people. Benjamin is a defenseless little boy who is fortunate to have Ruth Smith and Becca Yost to take care of him. I don't regret my decision to pay Mrs. Grossman to sell her child and go away, and nothing you say will change the way I feel about Becca."

His father placed his hand on Matt's shoulder. "You have a big heart. Life is not fair and Benjamin had a bad mother. I understand why you helped the child, but you need to reconsider choosing this Amish woman as a potential wife. We don't want you to make a mistake you will regret someday. When you have children, you will understand our actions in trying to protect you."

"Your father is right. Parents are needed to guide their children at all ages. Your father and I shall stop your trust fund until you come to your senses and cease to involve yourself in this woman's life."

He searched his father's eyes.

"I agree with your mother."

Matt raised his voice and fisted his hands. His parents had crossed the line this time. "I resent your interference in my life, and you can do what you want with the trust fund. I never wanted it in the first place. I am going to continue courting Becca Yost, whether you like it or not." He was through listening to their insults and moved toward the front door.

Horace Carrington reached inside his coat pocket and pulled out his pipe. He filled it with tobacco and lighted it. "We will not make any changes to the trust fund, but you are to use it as it was intended."

His mother straightened. "As for Becca Yost, what trouble will she get into next? Do yourself a favor. Let me find someone else for you to court."

Matt clenched his teeth. "I am done with this conversation." He opened the door and stepped aside.

His father puffed on his pipe and sat. "Sit. Nothing is worth sacrificing our relationship. I am sure you agree."

His mother opened her mouth to speak, but his father put up his hand.

"I expect the two of you to welcome Becca into your lives. This is nonnegotiable if you want a relationship with me."

His mother faced him. "You cannot force us to like her because you do. I do not understand your attraction to her, but as your father stated, we will not go on about this. You have made your decision. We will see what the future holds."

Matt rubbed his chin. Had his mother finally listened to him? Was this a positive or negative statement coming from her?

Chapter Eleven

Becca dried the last dish and reflected on her time with Benjamin and Ruth at the pond earlier. The child had chased squirrels, ducks, and butterflies until he tuckered out. Since Margaret's death and his mamm's stressful visit, he had bounced back to his happy self these last few weeks. Earlier, she had thanked God for answering her request for a quick recovery for the little boy.

What was Matt doing right now? Reviewing his research? She hadn't wanted to insist he spend the day catching up on his paperwork but knew it was for the best. He would relax once he did. She missed him and couldn't imagine her life without him. She bowed her head and prayed. "Dear Heavenly Father, forgive me where I have failed you. Thank you for bringing Matt into my life. These things I ask and pray in your name, Amen."

Becca approached Ruth and Benjamin as they entered. She tickled Benjamin and giggled. She gently tapped his nose. "It's time for bed, little one."

Following him to the bedroom, she noticed he had grown a little taller. What was life like before Benjamin? It seemed like he had always been a part of their lives. She tucked him in, read him a story, and kissed him on the forehead.

She went to the kitchen and prepared two cups of hot tea and joined Ruth in the living room. "What would we have done if Matt had not persuaded Gertrude to leave Benjamin with us? It's been a while, and it seems like yesterday when she and her husband were here. I'm not used to dealing with people like them. Neither are you. I respect Amish order when it comes to sheltering us from people like them."

Ruth pulled her legs up under her and blew the steam off her tea. "Yes I, too, am grateful to have been raised by Amish parents. Matt rescued us and Benjamin." Ruth sipped her tea. "Matt is going to make a great father. He is patient and loving with Benjamin."

"I agree, but his mamm doesn't seem like the grandmotherly type."

Ruth chuckled. "She cannot be all bad. She raised Matt to be a gentleman."

Becca set her mug on the table. It was true. Matt had integrity and honorable values, and he cared about others. Mrs. Carrington didn't strike her as having any of those traits, but the woman had obviously done something right. Maybe she would get a glimpse of Matt in his mamm as time progressed, but she doubted this would come true. "I dread meeting Mrs. Carrington again. I'm convinced she won't leave me alone, no matter what Matt has told her. The woman is determined to destroy any chance of a future I may have with him."

"She is callous. Too bad his visit with his father did not go well. It would have been good if he had agreed to intervene on Matt's behalf concerning you."

Becca wrinkled her nose. "I didn't have high hopes his daed would lend his support after the way he frowned when we met for the first time. It was no surprise when Matt told me he agreed with Mrs. Carrington that I was not a suitable potential wife for their son. I'm bothered Matt is estranged from his parents because of me. It must make him sad."

Ruth picked up a needle and thread to sew a button on a shirt for Benjamin. "Matt made his choice. They are being stubborn by not accepting you in his life. Put them out of your mind and enjoy your time with Matt."

Becca held up a button. "You're right." She reached over and lifted squares of material. "I'm collecting Matt's old shirts to stitch a keepsake pocket quilt for him. I've already written a letter to him to tuck inside the pocket. I can't wait to surprise him with it."

Ruth fingered the fabric. "What a great idea. I regret not finishing the pocket quilt I was making for Margaret before she died. I had written a letter of gratitude and hid it to put inside the pocket."

"She knew we loved and appreciated her." Becca sighed. "I wish Mrs. Carrington was kind like Margaret. I had hoped for a loving mamm-in-law who would welcome me into her life."

Ruth used her authoritative tone. "If they do not

accept you, you will have to settle for a life of love with Matt and your children. Not all parents are accepting of their child's choice for a mate."

The next day, Becca sat in church next to Matt. What a relief Matt's mamm and daed attended the Methodist church and not here. Awkward would not begin to describe how uncomfortable it would be to sit next to his parents considering Mrs. Carrington's behavior toward her.

The reverend delivered his sermon, prayed, and dismissed the congregation. She waited while Matt retrieved his buggy and horse.

He stopped and she climbed in. She studied Matt as he talked about patients. What compassion he had for them. The townsfolk were blessed that he took care of their medical needs. She didn't think she'd ever stop learning from him. He read and studied the latest medications and treatments for diseases and injuries often.

When they arrived at his house, she stepped inside and ran her hand along the many books lining the shelves. She paused and pulled out the book titled *The Open Boat and Other Tales of Adventure* by Stephen Crane. "Did you enjoy this book?"

"He is a great author. Take it."

Matt sat on the piano bench and patted the other side for her to join him.

She slid in and warmth from his body ignited a fire in hers. His shoulder touching hers added to the magical moments. His big hands and long fingers glided along the keys as he played church hymns. They laughed and paused for kisses in between songs.

Hours passed and Matt rested his hands in his lap. "Come to the kitchen with me. We need to find something to eat. I am starving."

Becca rolled her shoulders and relaxed. She trusted him. He was more than someone she was falling in love with, he was a close friend. She could talk to him about anything with confidence and rest assured that he wouldn't judge or betray her. He had taken the time to teach her about many things, such as music, medicine, and world history. She admired him. "Thank you for today. I'm enjoying being here with you and listening to the music."

"I have enjoyed this as much as you have."

"Amish aren't allowed to have pianos in our community. The bishop considers them a form of worldly entertainment. The only time I heard piano music was in town when I passed by the saloon going to the general store with my parents. This type of music was more enjoyable."

He kissed her eyes and caressed her cheek. "I love playing the piano. It relaxes me and lifts my mood when I am upset. My mother taught me how to play. She plays beautifully."

"Enough about music. What are we going to eat?" She scooted off the bench.

"We can make something together." He motioned for her to follow him.

"Chicken sandwiches with fresh tomatoes would be great." She held up a ripe tomato from the basket on his sink. "Do you have some roasted chicken in your icebox?"

"Yes, I do." He stood beside her and helped slice bread and tomatoes. "I like having you in my kitchen."

She faced him as he set the knife on the table and pulled her close. Strong and gentle hands wrapped around her. She closed her eyes as his lips pressed on hers. She leaned in closer to him and got lost in the kiss. The knife Matt placed on the table fell to the floor and jerked her out of the moment. She pulled back. A gasp escaped her mouth. "Whew, we better stop."

He touched the tip of her nose. "You do not have to worry. You can always trust me."

The heat in her cheeks subsided. They placed their plates, silverware, and cloth napkins on the table. Matt seated her then sat in the chair opposite hers. He lowered his head and prayed his thanks to God for the food.

Matt cut his sandwich in two. "I have something we need to discuss. My parents visited me at home two weeks ago."

A sharp knock at the door interrupted them. Matt and Becca peeked around the corner. Mrs. Carrington stepped inside.

Becca stared at her. She opened her mouth to speak but shut it. Maybe it was best if she kept silent.

"Mother, what are you doing here? Why did you not wait for me to answer the door?"

She rolled her eyes at Matt and ignored Becca. She placed her hat on a nearby chair. "If you had a butler, I would not have to let myself in. Besides, the door was unlocked."

"Unless you are here to apologize to Becca for

your ill-mannered behavior toward her, you need to leave."

Becca stared stunned as Mrs. Carrington walked in the room and demanded control. *How brash.*

"Becca, you do not mind if I join you for dinner, do you?"

She shook her head and left the table. She went to the kitchen and fixed Mrs. Carrington a sandwich and poured her a glass of water. Becca returned to the table, placed the plate and glass in front of Mrs. Carrington, and sat next to Matt. The woman had no intention of apologizing to her like Matt had asked her to. It was obvious by the way she had talked down to her.

Matt sat quietly with his mouth in a tight line. "Mother, you have not done what I have asked of you."

Mrs. Carrington ignored him. "Becca, I am direct with people and speak my mind. I am sure you can forgive me for looking out for my son's best interest." She flattened her palm on the table toward Matt. "I am having a few of the surgeons your father works with at the hospital over for dinner at our house this Wednesday, and I would like you to come." She set her sandwich on the plate and waited.

"No. I told you, I am not going to associate with you or Father." He straightened. "Why did you come here?"

"Becca understands how important a meeting like this is for your career. She would want you to attend." She patted Becca's hand and used her most condescending tone. "Right, dear?"

Could she be more condescending? Mrs. Carrington had plowed ahead with her invitation to Matt and didn't allow her to even respond to the woman's offensive words, and there was certainly no apology. What was she supposed to say to such a rude remark? She had to get out of there. Instead of answering Mrs. Carrington, she rose. "I should be going." She grabbed her reticule.

Matt rose. "Becca, wait." He faced his mamm. "I am not going to attend the dinner meeting at your house. I meant it when I said you are no longer welcome here. It is time for you to leave."

His mamm stared at her folded hands on the table for a moment. "All right, you win. Becca, I am having a few friends over for dinner Saturday. I would like it if you and Matt would come at two. We will enjoy good company and delicious food. What do you say?"

Matt held Becca's hand. "No, Mother. We will not attend."

She closed her eyes for a moment. What should she do? Was this Matt's mamm's way of apologizing? Maybe this would be a new beginning. She wanted to get along with Matt's parents more than anything. She had to find out. "If it is all right with you, I would like to accept your mamm's invitation."

"No, I do not think it is a good idea."

"We must give them another chance."

Mrs. Carrington patted Becca's arm. "Thank you, dear. I will see you both Saturday." She walked briskly to the front door and left.

He guided her to the sofa. "I hope you did not

feel pressured by her to accept her offer. We should not succumb to her wishes."

She sighed. "I'm not used to such prejudice and blatant rudeness as she displays against me. I have my doubts about how she will behave at this dinner, but I must go and find out. This time, I hope she is sincere in wanting to mend fences with us."

"If they are impolite to you, we will leave."

"Yes, I agree. I want to return to the conversation you and I were having before your mamm interrupted us. You were going to tell me why your parents visited you a couple of weeks ago. What did they want?"

Matt rose and poured water in two glasses from a pitcher sitting on a side table. He passed one to her. "They receive a statement in the mail from the bank every month concerning my trust fund account. I did not care about this before because I have not used any of the money since my father set it up for me at the bank several years ago. They wanted to know why I withdrew such a large sum of money without consulting them first. I told them about Benjamin and why I chose to pay Gertrude off. They disapproved of my decision. I told them it was none of their business and we would have to agree to disagree on the matter."

She pushed her back against the chair. "It was a large sum of money, but I thought once you explained the situation, they would understand."

"It did not matter to me what they thought about my decision to help Benjamin. I did not waver in my stance or apologize. After a few minutes, my father softened and said he understood why I had to help the child. Furthermore, I told them I am courting you and, until they are ready to welcome you with open arms, to stay away from us. I should have asked her to leave on the spot today. She knew better than to show up unannounced."

Becca bit her upper lip. "Did your mamm let your daed do the talking, or did she voice her concerns on this matter too?"

"She let my father do most of the talking. She was angry when they arrived but seemed calm when they left."

"From what you've told me, they don't appreciate me dragging you into my problem with Gertrude." She bit her lip. "I'm surprised your mamm invited us to their house for dinner." She didn't trust Mrs. Carrington. She hoped this dinner didn't turn into a disaster.

"It is not too late to decline her invitation."

"No. I want to go. We need to fix things with them."

On Saturday, the morning of Matt's parents' party, Becca sorted through the dresses she had bought and the ones Ruth had made for her. She chose an elegant soft pink dress with puffed sleeves with buttons lining the thick cuffs halfway down each arm. She loved the high neck in the front. The lines of lace on the dress from her neck to her waist added an elegant touch. She twisted her hair in a bun and put on a hat with flowers and ribbon matching the dress. She blew out a breath. Matt would be arriving soon to take her to the party at his parents' house.

Ruth straightened the back. "You look beautiful. Matt's parents will approve, and he will be breathless at the sight of you. This afternoon, hold your head up with confidence. Stay by Matt's side and do not let him out of your sight. Then his mother will have to behave, or she will get an earful from Matt." Ruth held her chest and grabbed the dresser to keep from falling.

Becca wrapped her arms around her sister and eased her onto the bed. "What's wrong? Are you sick?"

"No. I do not know what came over me." Ruth steadied herself.

She touched her sister's cheek. "You're warm and flushed. When Matt arrives, I'll ask him to examine you. I'm going to stay home. You shouldn't be alone."

"You will do no such thing. I will be fine. Please do not concern Matt with my little bout of dizziness. Promise me. You are fretting over me for nothing."

"Has this happened before?"

"No, and you are making too much of this. What woman has not experienced a little dizziness now and then?"

Becca studied Ruth from head to toe. "Have you lost weight?"

Ruth shoved her hand aside. "Maybe a little, but with Margaret gone, I have been working harder at the shop."

She made a mental note to keep a closer eye on her sister. "Take it easy while I'm gone. Take advantage of the fact Benjamin is visiting with our wonderful neighbor, Hattie. The woman loves that child.

She has helped us a bunch offering to watch him now and then. Read the newspaper and relax."

Matt arrived to escort her to his parents' home. He twirled her around. "You look exquisite."

She curtsied and laughed. "Why thank you, kind sir." His black top hat and suit fit his frame nicely. Determined to make an effort with his parents, she looped her arm through his.

They waved good-bye to Ruth and stepped outside to his buggy. On the way to his parents' house, they chatted about patients and work.

Matt handed the reins to the stableman and walked Becca to the front door of the white two-story house.

A butler greeted and ushered them to the parlor where he offered tea. She enjoyed the piano music. Chatter among guests came from the living room. She touched the staircase rail. How many rooms were on the second floor? Mrs. Carrington gave her a cold stare. Did she misread Mrs. Carrington's face? If not, this was going to be a long night.

Mrs. Carrington approached them. "I am glad you are here. Come in and meet our guests." She appeared to be sincere.

Becca hooked her arm through Matt's and followed his mamm. Mrs. Carrington introduced them to her new friends, Mr. and Mrs. Zimmerman. The elderly couple engaged them in friendly conversation. She enjoyed talking to them and relaxed.

Mrs. Zimmerman touched Becca's collar. "Your dress is beautiful. Who designed it for you?"

Comfortable in the dress Ruth made for her, she stood straight. "My sister, Ruth Smith. She owns a mending shop in town. She designs and sews dresses for several of her regular patrons. I'm sure she would be glad to do the same for you. Stop by her shop and meet with her."

Mrs. Zimmerman's eyes sparkled. "I will visit her shop sometime this week."

Matt pulled her aside and guided her into another room full of people.

The gentlemen were handsome and confident and sported formal long-tailed jackets. Animated conversation buzzed throughout the room. Matt introduced her to his friends, but she had a hard time remembering all their names. Several ladies engaged her in polite conversation about the weather, complimented her dress, and inquired about how she liked working as Matt's nurse.

Matt conversed with the men but stood close to her.

Becca caught Mrs. Carrington's eye on several occasions, and when she did, Matt's mamm's eyes darted away first each time.

The butler rang a bell and jerked her out of her thoughts about Mrs. Carrington. "Dinner will be served in the dining room. Please make your way to the table and take your assigned seat. You will find your name on a card in the center of your plate."

Matt held Becca's elbow and guided her to the table. He leaned close to her ear. "I heard several ladies commenting on how much they liked your dress. Ruth did a marvelous job on it, and you look splendid."

Becca sat. The table settings at the massive table presented a beautiful picture. Mrs. Carrington knew how to entertain. One thing they had in common was their preference for soft colors. Mrs. Carrington had chosen light pinks and creams for flowers, table covering, and matching cloth napkins.

The woman next to her held out a gloved hand. "Hello. I am Beatrice Bloomingdale. Please call me Beatrice. I understand you are Becca Yost. You are here with Matt, right?"

Becca wanted to say she knew exactly who she was. The woman Mrs. Carrington had brought to town to introduce to Matt. "Yes to both questions." Tension pulled at her shoulders.

"I am surprised Matt and you are courting."

"Why?" Becca wanted Matt to hear their conversation, but he was concentrating on the gentleman next to him.

Beatrice removed her gloves while staring at Becca. "It is no secret Matt's parents disapprove of him courting you."

"If they do, it's no concern of yours." Becca sat erect. Now she understood why Mrs. Carrington pushed Miss Bloomingdale on Matt. The two women were alike in their dress, attitude, and rudeness. Attractive with her brown hair, green eyes, and medium build, she ruined her beauty with her arrogance.

The woman chortled and tilted her head. "None of his friends, me included, can understand why he is interested in a plain and unsophisticated girl like you."

She was not going to be humble with this woman. She would stand up for herself. "I don't need your approval and, as for the others, I'll wait until they speak for themselves."

Miss Bloomingdale leaned closer. "He can dress you in the proper clothes, but he cannot teach you all you need to know to support him in our society. In my opinion, with your Amish background, you are too simple and lack the proper upbringing to be an appropriate hostess, which is what he needs in a wife."

"Matt had nothing to do with what I am wearing. My sister, Ruth, made this dress. Many of the women here have asked about the design. Matt teaching me anything or how I was raised is none of your business."

Miss Bloomingdale placed her hand over Becca's. "Do not be naïve. Here by his side, you are already hurting his reputation. Matt's father's friends provide Matt with unlimited opportunities for getting involved in research. Without those relationships, Matt limits himself to being a small-town doctor. If you care for him, you would let him go."

Miss Bloomingdale had stared at her with cold eyes and spoke unkind words in a condescending tone. She was definitely prejudiced against her, but was the woman right? Was she hindering Matt's research support from other doctors and companies? If it was true, she must consider the woman's advice. She glanced at Miss Bloomingdale. The woman was manipulative. She wouldn't act in haste. She must ponder this before jumping to conclusions.

Chapter Twelve

Becca dabbed her lips with the white embroidered napkin. When would this dinner end?

Horace Carrington pushed his seat back and rose. He tapped his glass with a spoon. "The men are invited to my study for coffee. Mrs. Carrington will escort the ladies to the living room for tea."

She stood and moved away from Beatrice. She and Matt would be separated. *Not good.* She would stay as far away as she could from Beatrice and Mrs. Carrington.

Matt headed toward her. "Are you all right with joining the other women?"

Friends stood behind Matt waiting to talk to him. She didn't want to ruin his evening. She could handle staying a little longer. She would tell him about Beatrice later. "Yes. You enjoy yourself."

"I will not be long." A man pulled him aside.

She stepped to the living room. Mrs. Carrington and Beatrice were huddled in a corner. What were they whispering about? She moved behind them, but not too close. She strained to hear them and stared out the window.

Mrs. Carrington placed her hand on Beatrice's. "Tell me about your conversation with Becca."

"You should have seen her face pale when I told her she was hurting Matt's chances for participation in research. It was priceless. Our circle of friends and dinners like this make her squirm. After the conversation I had with her tonight, I am confident she will decide this is not a life she wants." She patted Eloise's hand.

She smirked. "I hope you are right, but the girl is not as timid as you might think. I offered her money to stay away from him, but she would not take it. She is determined to hang on to my son."

"She will go away eventually if we keep working on her."

Eloise chuckled. "We need her out of the way so Matt will concentrate on you."

Becca moved to the other side of the room and sat. Mrs. Carrington and Miss Bloomingdale seemed too engrossed in their conversation to notice. Mrs. Carrington was a devious woman. Should she confront her? What would she say? *No,* she would tell Matt what she overheard this afternoon. He would know what to do.

Mrs. Pines touched her arm. "Are you here with Matt?"

"Yes, he is in the library with his daed and friends."

"Are you courting?"

Becca blushed. "Yes."

Mrs. Pines grinned. "He is a lucky man. Matt's a wonderful doctor, but it is nice to have a nurse

present when I visit. You are a delightful person and
a talented woman. My friends have told me how you
have helped them when they have visited the office
too. Mrs. Carrington must be delighted Matt and
you are courting."

Becca licked her lips. How should she answer
Mrs. Pines's question?

Mrs. Cooper joined them before Becca could
answer. "Becca, how nice to find you here."

Mrs. Pines circled her arm around Becca's waist.
"Becca and Matt are courting."

Mrs. Cooper beamed. "What good news. How is
Ruth? I'm visiting her shop Monday to buy one of
her keepsake pocket quilts for my niece. I've written
a letter to tuck in the pocket, and I'm afraid I'll mis-
place it before I buy the quilt. My niece is visiting
and goes home to Canton Wednesday."

Becca's shoulders relaxed. *Good*. Mrs. Cooper
had changed the subject. "Don't worry. Ruth told
me yesterday she has two left. If you go Monday, you
should be fine."

Mr. Pines and Mr. Cooper approached their wives
and the two couples bid Becca farewell and left. She
didn't want to leave. The two women had provided
a ray of sunshine in her nail biting evening. She
glanced at Beatrice and Mrs. Carrington.

Miss Bloomingdale stood and kissed Mrs. Carrington on both cheeks before she left.

Becca stiffened. Why was Mrs. Carrington walking toward her? She had nothing to say to the
woman. Where was Matt? "Sit, Becca. My son will
join us soon. In the meantime, you and I can chat.

Miss Bloomingdale is quite charming. I am sure you agree." She moved her chair close and stared at her.

"I don't know her." She scooted her chair away.

Mrs. Carrington tilted her head. "Of course you do. You spoke to her tonight. I have told you what a perfect wife she would be for Matt. Look around. We live in a world you know nothing about. I am sure you understand Miss Bloomingdale fits in Matt's life much better than you. Do yourself a favor and leave him alone."

That does it. She had had enough of Mrs. Carrington's rude behavior. "Matt doesn't need your help to find a woman to court. He has chosen me."

Eloise crossed one leg over the other and folded her arms across her chest. "I do not care how hard you try. You cannot make yourself something you are not."

Becca dug her nails in her hands. "Matt likes me the way I am. As far as learning about how to fit into your world, I can learn what I need to."

Mrs. Carrington laughed. "I doubt that is true. I observed you tonight. You lack the most basic social graces and had no idea what utensil to use as you were served each course of the meal. You made little effort to engage in conversation with anyone. You are ignorant."

She was ignorant? *No,* ignorant was judging someone without getting to know them first. "You are the most difficult woman I have ever met. You insult me over and over again. I am done defending myself to you. Matt and I came here hoping you and your husband wanted to make amends for how you've treated me. Your son will be disappointed when I tell him what you've said to me, and I dread passing this information along to him. He told me if you misbehaved, he would no longer associate with you. In spite of what you might think, I don't want him to separate himself from you or his daed." Becca stood.

Mrs. Carrington rose. "If you would leave him alone, he would not distance himself from us."

"If you would honor his request to accept me, you could have your son in your life. You haven't bothered to ask one personal question about my life. You have judged me based on my dress and upbringing. Why won't you take the time to talk to me with an open mind? Matt and I are happy together. We want to have a relationship with you and your husband."

"I have no desire to know you. The sooner you are out of his life, the better off he will be. I will not stop finding ways to discourage you and my son from being together until you are out of his life."

Her heart hurt. She didn't want to have harsh words with Mrs. Carrington. She wanted the woman to put her prejudice aside and have a nice conversation with her. No matter how much she pleaded with Mrs. Carrington, the woman wasn't budging on her mission to cause trouble for her and Matt. Becca backed away as Matt entered the room with his daed. She moved to his side.

Eloise held her hand out to him. "I hope you and your father had a pleasant chat. Did you enjoy dinner?"

"You outdid yourself on the menu. It was exquisite, and I am stuffed."

Mrs. Carrington patted Becca's arm. "Your guest is tired and ready to go."

He kissed his mamm's cheek and shook his daed's hand, then stepped to Becca and reached for her hand. "Thank you both for a nice afternoon."

Becca cringed. Mrs. Carrington pretended harsh words hadn't been exchanged between them once Matt entered the room. Matt's daed ignored her. This party was a disaster. How would Matt react to her news?

On the ride home, Mrs. Carrington's and Miss Bloomingdale's cruel words spun in her mind. How did Matt turn out to be such a fine gentleman after being raised by such a coldhearted mamm? He told her to tell him if his mamm said anything to upset her. She had to tell him about her conversations with his mamm and Miss Bloomingdale, but she was tired. Maybe she should wait to discuss it at another time.

"Did you have a good time tonight?"

She groaned and bowed her head. She couldn't get the bad experience out of her mind. Maybe she should talk about it. "I sat by Beatrice Bloomingdale." She recounted to Matt her conversation with Miss Bloomingdale.

His jaw clenched. "I did not notice her next to you. I am sorry I did not pay more attention to you at dinner. You should have nudged me or something, and we would have left. We will not be visiting my parents again. This was their last chance to make things right with you and me. I want nothing more to do with them."

Becca rested her hand on his arm. "You love your

parents. We have to fix this somehow. You not communicating with them will hang over our relationship like a dark cloud."

"You wanted to give her another chance to reconcile with you, and she did not. Mother has gone too far this time. I am not going to allow her or my father to come between us. We are not going to accept any more invitations from them, and if she comes to my house or the office, I will ask her to leave. Please respect my decision."

She bit her tongue. She would honor his request, but she wished there was some other way to resolve the problem with his parents, especially his mamm. He was an only child. It would be hard for him to not interact with them. She would pray about it.

He stepped outside and caressed her cheek. "You are the most important person in my life." He kissed her hard on the lips.

A warm tingle settled in her stomach as she held her lips on his. His kisses ignited a fire in her every time. As he stepped off the porch, she went inside.

She gasped, dropped her reticule, and knelt beside her unconscious sister and Benjamin. She shook Ruth's shoulder. "Open your eyes." She pressed her fingers to Ruth's neck. Her pulse was weak. Tears streaming onto her cheeks, she said, "Benjamin, run and tell Matt to come inside."

Benjamin threw open the door. "Matt, we need you! Something's wrong with Ruth."

Matt rushed in and threw open his bag. "Did she fall? What happened?"

Benjamin followed behind him. "I don't know."

Becca's eyes darted to Benjamin. "Do you know what happened to Ruth?"

"Hattie got sick, so I walked home. Ruth told me to play in my room. I heard a thump. I ran in here, and she was flat on the floor." His eyes filled with unshed tears. "I shook her, but she won't get up, Becca."

Terror gripped her. How long had she been like this? Did she get dizzy, fall, and hit her head? Then it hit her. Ruth had been dizzy before she left with Matt. She couldn't bear it if her sister had a serious life-threatening illness. She needed her. Wiping her tears, she watched Matt tend to her Ruth. She bowed her head. *Please let her be all right, Heavenly Father. Please.*

Matt pushed the tips of his stethoscope in his ears. He listened to her chest. He removed the tips from his ears and examined her for broken bones. "Nothing is broken." He placed his hand on her forehead. "Her body is warm. Her fever must be high."

Becca grabbed a thermometer from Matt's bag and slipped it inside Ruth's dress and under her arm. She waited a few moments. "Matt, her fever is 104 degrees. Before we left tonight, she stumbled and looked pale. I questioned her about how she was feeling. She assured me it was nothing. I should not have left her alone. I'll never forgive myself if something happens to her. She's guided me through our childhood and my transition from Amish life to the world. I just got her back in my life. I can't stand the thought of losing her."

Benjamin tugged at Becca's skirt with moist

brown eyes straying to Ruth's still form. "Will Ruth be all right?"

Blinking back tears, she swallowed around the lump in her throat. She must be strong for Benjamin and not frighten him. "She's sick, but Dr. Matt will help her." She held Benjamin's shoulders and forced him to meet her eyes. "You must stay away from Ruth. I don't want you to get sick too. You go and play in your room." She hoped Benjamin hadn't been infected already.

Benjamin hesitated, glanced at Ruth, then Matt, and then padded out of the room. Matt scooped Ruth's small frame in his arms and carried her to her bed. Becca followed. She poured water from a pitcher into a bowl on the dresser and wiped Ruth's forehead with a wet cloth.

He put his hand on hers to stop her. "I do not want you or Benjamin around Ruth. We don't know if whatever she has is contagious. I will stay and take care of her. You and Benjamin pack your things and stay with Dorothy until Ruth is better."

"I'm not leaving my sister." Becca held the wet cloth tight.

"I wish you would do as I ask, but I know better than to argue with you. I know how stubborn you can be." Matt frowned and rooted through his bag. "I do not have the medicine Ruth needs with me. I will go to the office and get it. It will not take me long. Keep Benjamin away from her."

"Don't worry. I will."

Matt left.

If anything happened to Ruth, she didn't know what she would do.

Her sister was a source of strength and wisdom she had come to depend on.

Ruth's eyelashes fluttered. "What happened?"

Becca held the cool cloth to her forehead. "You fainted in the living room. You're sick with a fever. Matt went to his office to get some medicine to make you feel better."

Ruth talked slowly. "I did not eat much today. It is my fault I fainted. Where is Benjamin?"

"He's playing in his room. Don't worry about anything. Close your eyes." Becca prayed Ruth would be all right. She secured the cool cloth on Ruth's forehead and left to check on Benjamin.

He ceased rolling his wooden train across the floor. "I'm scared. I don't want Ruth to die like Margaret did."

"Don't worry. Matt and I will do everything we can to take good care of Ruth. Do you need anything?"

He shook his head.

"You stay in your room and play with your toys. I'll check on you again in a little while."

"All right, Aunt Becca." Benjamin chose another train and rolled it across the floor.

She returned to the bedroom. Ruth moaned and groaned and moved her head on the pillow from time to time but stayed asleep. She checked her sister's face and forehead. Her body was cooler than before. The tension rolled out of her shoulders.

Matt tapped on the door frame and entered the room. "I checked on Benjamin. He was asleep on the floor. I put him to bed. How is she?"

"Thank you for putting Benjamin to bed. Her

fever has lowered for the moment. She's resting right now."

"Please take Benjamin and go to Dorothy's tonight. Let me take care of Ruth."

Becca shook her head. After all Ruth had done for her, she would not leave her sister's side, even if it meant she might get sick. "No. You have patients tomorrow. I'll be fine. I would appreciate it if you would ask Dorothy to care for Benjamin."

Benjamin entered the room rubbing his eyes. "Can I talk to Ruth?"

"She is sleeping. How would you like to come home with me? We will get up early and do a little fishing then I will take you to work with me. Dorothy loves to piece together puzzles, and I am sure she would like you to help her with one."

Benjamin whimpered. "I don't want to leave Ruth. She might need me."

Becca's heart swelled. The child had such compassion for her sister. "I'll tell Ruth you're with Matt, and she'll be excited to find out you're going fishing with him. Go to your room and pack your clothes, shoes, and a few toys."

Benjamin walked toward the bed, but Becca stopped him. "I have to kiss her before I go. She would want me to."

"You can't touch her, because I don't want you to get sick. Ruth knows you love her, and I'll tell her you wanted to kiss her good-bye. You go with Matt and be a good boy."

He cupped her face in his small hands. "What about you? I don't want you to get sick."

She rubbed his back. "I'll be fine. You take care of Matt and Dorothy for me."

He puffed out his chest. "All right. I will, but can I see you and Ruth tomorrow?"

Becca kissed his nose. "Not tomorrow. You'll need to stay with Matt for a few days. Don't worry. Matt will bring you home to stay when Ruth is better."

Matt put his hands on Benjamin's shoulders. "Take your tic-tac-toe game. We will play it at my house. Bring your tiddledywinks game too."

Her stomach fluttered at his affection for the little boy.

He kissed her forehead. "I will come by in the morning. These pills should reduce her fever, and I hope help her sleep."

She rose and bid them farewell.

Darkness fell. Becca stayed with Ruth. Her sister's fever spiked and lowered for the next few hours. With heavy eyelids, Becca leaned from her chair to rest her arms and head on the bed and dozed. She woke with a start, straightened, and touched her sister's cheeks. Hot and red, Ruth's skin was clammy. She hustled to the kitchen, pumped water into a bowl, and returned to Ruth's side to wipe her face and arms with the cool water.

Ruth coughed and mumbled, but Becca couldn't make out her words. She lifted her with one arm, put a pill in her mouth with her free hand, and coaxed her to swallow water with it. She blew out a breath, relieved Ruth had swallowed it without choking.

Two days later, the fever broke and Ruth slept.

Exhausted, Becca climbed in bed next to her and closed her eyes. She woke to a noise. Benjamin and Matt stood beside the bed.

The little boy poked her shoulder. "It's time to get up. How's Ruth?"

Matt touched Ruth's forehead. "Her head is cool. How did the two of you do last night?"

Becca sat up and threw her legs over the side of the bed. "Thanks to you dropping by yesterday and bringing us a different medicine, she did better and I got to rest. We've been asleep for a few hours."

He touched Becca's cheek and put his fingers to her throat to examine her neck for swollen glands. "Do you have any symptoms?"

"No. I am tired but fine. What time is it?" Becca blinked and smoothed her hair.

He glanced at the clock. "It is eleven-thirty."

"I was up several times through the night wiping her face and arms with a wet cloth." She yawned and got out of bed. "I'm such a mess. My clothes are all rumpled. Ruth scared me with her fever rising and falling."

Matt sat next to her and put his arm around her shoulders. "You should go back to bed."

"I will. Benjamin can stay here, since Ruth's on the mend."

Benjamin held Matt's hand. "I'm having a fun time with Matt. May I stay with him a little longer?"

Matt stood and picked up his medical bag. "I will take Benjamin with me. Dorothy takes him to school and picks him up. She is enjoying him. He minds her well. We have had an enjoyable time reading and talking. We went fishing again this morning, and he caught two little blue gills but we threw them back in." He tousled Benjamin's hair.

Becca blew a stray hair from her face. Her sister hadn't wakened in spite of the conversation going on around her. "Let me make us something to eat before you go."

He tugged at her lopsided ponytail. "I brought chicken and biscuits from Dorothy for us. I have already made coffee. All you need to do is walk from here to the kitchen."

She stood on her toes and kissed his nose. "What would I do without you? You are always prepared and looking out for me."

With his hand on her elbow, he guided her to the kitchen. "You make spoiling you easy."

She sat. Benjamin chattered about the book Matt read to him before bed and fishing this morning while they finished dinner.

Benjamin walked to Matt and leaned against him. "When do we leave? I can't wait to go to work with you today." He crammed a bite of biscuit in his mouth and pulled his chair closer to Matt.

"As soon as I finish my coffee."

Becca slumped in the chair and sipped her coffee. The three of them at the table warmed her heart. She imagined them as a family one day. Then Matt's mamm as part of their family came to mind, and a knot formed in the pit of her stomach.

Chapter Thirteen

The next day, Becca walked Benjamin to school and bought a newspaper on her way home. She opened the door and stepped inside. She glanced at the clock. She had a few minutes before she had to go to work. Ruth sat on the sofa. "I'll make us coffee, and we can share the newspaper." She made fresh coffee and carried a mug to Ruth. She unfolded the newspaper and handed Ruth a section. She read the first page. The Carringtons were mentioned in this article. She read further. President McKinley and First Lady Ida Saxton McKinley had dinner in the Carringtons' home with a few other guests. What an honor for the Carringtons. Did Matt know about this? He hadn't mentioned it. Would he have been invited if he was speaking to his parents? She was sure he would have wanted to be there. She would have wanted to meet President McKinley and the First Lady.

"I found an article in the paper you might find interesting. It's the one about Matt's parents on the first page. President William McKinley, First Lady

Ida Saxton McKinley, former secretary of state John Sherman, Senator Marcus Hanna, and their wives, and Dr. Gary Morrison and his wife and daughter visited the Carringtons. Matt isn't speaking to his parents, but I'm surprised Mrs. Carrington didn't find a way to tell him about this."

Ruth put a hand to her throat. "The president visited the Carringtons? Eloise Carrington must be elated. I cannot believe they would keep this news from him."

"He has not said a word to me about his parents having the president for dinner. I'm certain they didn't tell him. He would have said something to me about it if he knew. I suspect he's reading it in the paper as we speak." Becca groaned. "I'm the reason he wasn't invited. He's missing important dinners and parties because of me. He enjoys mingling with his friends at these parties, and he meets other doctors who ask him to review their research. He isn't working with his daed any longer on research projects because they're not communicating. I'm hurting his professional life and ruining his relationship with his parents."

"Listen, Matt did not have any choice but to distance himself from his parents after the way his mother treated you when you went to dinner at their house. I believe, in time, Matt and his parents will reconcile. They love each other. Be patient."

A rap on the door interrupted their conversation. Becca answered the door. Kate Paulson, who worked for Ruth, stood on the porch. "Welcome, come in."

Ruth patted the cushion next to her. "Kate, come sit with me."

"I came to drop off samples of fabric a salesman delivered yesterday. They are beautiful. I cannot decide which ones I like best."

Ruth fingered one of the samples. "I like this one the best. The fabric is nice, and the flowered print is lovely." Ruth and Kate discussed which fabrics to order.

Kate rose. "I do not want to rush off, but I better get back and open the shop."

Ruth followed her to the door. "I am coming back to work tomorrow. I'm feeling much better and sitting at home is boring."

"What great news. Your color has returned to your cheeks and you seem much stronger. Your regular customers will be happy to see you. They have been asking about you."

Ruth chatted with Kate then bid her good-bye. She joined Becca on the sofa. "I appreciate you and Matt finding Kate Paulson to take Margaret's place. She keeps me up to date, and I have been happy with all the decisions she has made with regard to the business. I consider her a close friend. She and I have a lot in common, with both of us losing our husbands at such young ages. She had been married for three years when her husband died of a heart attack. She was pregnant when he died, but she lost the baby a few months later. She is a delightful and capable woman."

Becca curled her legs under her skirt. "I'm glad you're happy with her. Matt suggested I ask her to manage the shop while you were sick. She is a new patient of his. I trusted his judgment. It was better than closing the doors until you returned. I am glad you like her. Matt never mentioned she was a widow.

She's pretty with her dark blond hair, long face, and petite frame. She has the greenest eyes I have ever seen."

"She did not tell me about her husband or losing her child until a few days ago. She is quiet and shy. After we met a few times, she opened up to me." Ruth adjusted the pillow behind her back. "Kate mentioned her brother is on his way here soon from Houston, Texas. He sold his cattle ranch there and bought Mr. Brown's farm located near his sister's house. Kate said he is a talented carpenter and handyman."

Becca had to find out if Kate's brother was married. "Is Kate the same age as you? How old is he?"

"She and I are the same age. Her brother is two years older and unwed."

Becca lifted a pillow and pressed it to her chest. "Maybe we should invite him to dinner when he arrives to welcome him to town." If Kate's brother was as nice as his sister, he might be a good match for Ruth. "It would give us a chance to know him better."

The next day in the office, Becca waved their next patient into the exam room. Clad in a flannel shirt, denim blue pants, shiny boots, and a black Stetson hat, he had a rugged but handsome face and callused hands and walked bowlegged.

"Hello, I'm Becca Yost, and this is Dr. Matt Carrington."

Matt held out his hand. "Have a seat on the exam table. How can I help you today?"

He held up his arm. "I lost my footing and fell on

my box of tools. I cut my arm. My name is Isaac Kelly. Maybe you know my sister. She works at Ruth's Mending Shop in town."

Matt jotted the man's name on paper. "Welcome to Massillon. Ruth Smith owns the mending shop. She and I are friends. Becca is her sister."

Becca helped Isaac remove his shirt. She hung it on a hook. She then untied the cloth Isaac had wrapped around his arm and disposed of it.

Matt cleaned the wound and stitched and bandaged the cut. Matt asked him a few health questions and jotted notes in his chart. "How old are you?"

"I am twenty-four."

Matt penciled the information on his paper. Finished, he offered his hand to Isaac. "It has been a pleasure meeting you. Do you have any questions?"

Isaac shook his head. "No, you've taken good care of me. Thank you."

She passed him his shirt. "Will you miss Texas?"

"I don't mind moving here. I liked living in Texas, except for the hot weather in the summer. Kate and I have always been close. I've missed her, and I worry about her living alone in Massillon. It will be good for us to live near each other again."

"Your sister is joining me, Becca, and Ruth for supper tonight at Lizzie's Restaurant. Would you like to join us? Is six all right with you?"

Isaac buttoned his shirt. "Six sounds good. I will meet you there."

Becca liked Isaac. He had a strong but kind voice. He was not arrogant but confident. She was glad

Matt had invited him to supper. Her sister would like him. "See you tonight."

After he left, Becca readied the room for the next patient. "I'm excited to tell Ruth about inviting Isaac to supper with us. I hope they like each other. It could be the start of something wonderful."

Matt pulled her in his arms and swayed her back and forth. "He does seem nice. It would be great if they liked each other." He kissed her cheek. "I can handle things today. You go and tell Ruth and Kate about Isaac joining us for supper tonight."

A rap on the door startled them. Becca stepped away from Matt.

Ruth peeked in. "I hope I am not bothering you. I wanted to let you know Hattie has agreed to watch Benjamin tonight while we go to Lizzie's. She came and got him an hour ago. She is fixing shepherd's pie and bread pudding. She plans for them to work on a puzzle together. She bought him a new one last week."

Becca approached her. "I'm glad you stopped by. Kate's brother, Isaac Kelly, was a patient in our office today. He left moments ago. Matt invited him to join us at Lizzie's tonight for supper. I can't wait for you to meet him."

Ruth blushed and tilted her head. "What does he look like?"

Becca used her hand to show his height. "He is quite handsome. He is medium build and height. He has light brown hair and blue eyes."

"I better go home early. I will need time to select the right dress to wear for tonight."

What a relief. Her sister was interested in finding love again. This was encouraging news. "Wear your green and white printed collar dress, the one with the covered buttons from neck to waist. He will not be able to take his eyes off you."

Ruth tapped a finger to her lip. "I do like your suggestion, but do not get too excited. We might not even like each other."

"You are beautiful, talented, smart, and sweet. Why wouldn't he like you?"

"Maybe I will not like him."

Becca shut the door behind her sister. This was going better than she had planned.

Later in the day, Becca walked to Lizzie's with Matt on one side and Ruth on the other. Balmy and warm, leaves fluttered in the light breeze. "What a pleasant evening."

Matt squeezed her hand. "You two ladies look lovely, as always." He chose a table and motioned for Isaac and Kate to join them when they arrived.

Matt introduced Ruth.

Isaac held his hand out to her. "It is nice to meet you."

Ruth's cheeks pinked. "Your sister helped me in my time of need. I recently recovered from a fever and exhaustion. She did an excellent job taking over the shop for me. In such a short time, we have become close friends."

Covering Kate's hand with his for a moment, Isaac said, "She is a strong woman and a diligent worker. I am proud of her."

Becca leaned into Matt. "I have a positive feeling about these two."

He put his lips to her ear. "Yes, they do appear to like each other."

Lizzie shifted her overweight hip to the side, penciled their orders, and left to wait on another table.

Matt and Becca listened while Isaac talked about the farm he'd purchased and his love for carpentry. Ruth's eyes danced with excitement. She laughed at his stories and answered his questions.

Becca was encouraged by Ruth's obvious comfort with Isaac. It was the way she hung on his every word. They were off to a great start. If things progressed between Isaac and her sister, he and Kate could possibly end up family one day. She liked the idea. Maybe she and Matt should give them some time alone. She pushed her plate aside. "Would you excuse us? Matt and I are going to take a walk. Take your time and chat."

"I am ready to call it a night, too." Kate yawned and stood. "It has been a long day. Thanks for paying for supper, Matt." She waved to Ruth and Isaac. "Have a nice evening, you two."

Matt and Becca walked Kate to the livery to get her horse. Later, on their way to Ruth's, Becca linked her fingers through Matt's. "Ruth and Isaac didn't have any problem finding things to discuss. I'm interested to see what the future holds for them."

"I believe he is interested in her. He could not keep his eyes off her, listened to her, and seemed at ease. Ruth talked more than usual. It would be nice if they courted. They do not have anything standing in their way."

The evening stagecoach stopped a few feet away from them. A striking woman with shiny auburn hair in ringlets and an elegant dress stepped out.

He gasped in obvious surprise. "I know her." He pointed at the woman. "Her name is Laura Morrison."

Becca stared at the striking woman with an angelic face and a perfect frame walking toward them.

Laura outstretched her arms as she raced forward. "It is wonderful to see you."

He wrapped his arms around Laura and twirled her around before letting her go. "What are you doing here? It is nice to see you, too. It has been years since we last laid eyes on each other."

"I attended the dinner at your parents' home honoring President McKinley. I was disappointed you were not there. Your mother suggested I come and surprise you. You are as handsome as I remember." She brushed a thread from his shoulder. "I hear you are a fine doctor."

Oh no. Mrs. Carrington suggested she visit Matt. How convenient. His mamm was quick to devise yet another plan of attack on them. She had barely had time to recover from her ordeal with Miss Bloomingdale. The familiarity between Matt and Laura was more than a little unsettling. His face showed his happiness to see her. Jealousy reared its ugly head at their display of affection. She wanted Laura to step back in the stagecoach, go home, and forget about Matt.

He dropped his arms from Laura's waist and grasped Becca's hand. "You are too kind. This is

Becca Yost. She works with me in my office, and we are courting. Becca, this is Laura Morrison. We were childhood friends. I have not seen her since I left for medical school."

"Hello."

The beautiful woman didn't move her eyes off Matt. "It is nice to meet you, Becca. Matt, we have to get together and catch up. Right now, I have got to get some rest. Traveling here has worn me out."

Becca sighed. Would their talk rekindle feelings he might have had for her in the past?

"Are you staying at the Massillon Inn?"

Laura batted her lashes. "No, I am staying at the Rose Inn. I will visit you at your office tomorrow and set up a time to meet." She blew him a kiss and left.

"I am glad Laura came to visit. It will be good to catch up on what has been going on in our lives since we last met. Her father and mine were colleagues. They had practices in Columbus until her father moved his to Washington, DC. Mrs. Morrison was not fond of my mother. She tolerated Mother because their husbands were close. You will like Laura. She can be quite amusing."

Becca doubted she would agree, but she was glad to learn she wasn't the only one who disliked Eloise Carrington. Matt and Laura shared a past. Would Matt fall for Laura's charm? Worse, Laura was Mrs. Carrington's type for a daughter-in-law. The way she dressed, talked, and acted. "Did you know President McKinley came to your parents' house for dinner before Laura mentioned it to you?"

He raked a hand through his hair. "Yes, I read the

article about it in the newspaper, but it does not matter. I would not have gone if they'd invited me. I am serious about not talking to them until they have a change of heart toward you."

They arrived at Ruth's house.

They'd had such a nice evening with Kate, Ruth, and Isaac. She didn't want to upset him further by discussing his mamm or her insecurities about Laura. She would end their night on a positive note. "I would like nothing better than to see Ruth happy with someone."

"I agree. It will be interesting to find out what she has to say about him."

He kissed her full on the lips before leaving. She loved him. Laura's face flashed in her mind. Laura and Matt had a history. She was afraid life was about to get interesting and not in a good way.

The next day, Matt flipped through a patient chart while Dorothy poured him and Becca coffee. "Did you enjoy your days off, Dorothy?"

"I caught up on my chores. I ran into Lizzie on my way to work this morning. She told me all the latest gossip. I understand Kate Paulson is working for Ruth. Lizzie mentioned Isaac, Kate's brother, joined you, Becca, Kate, and Ruth for supper last night."

"Isaac came to the office yesterday and needed stitches for a cut. I liked him and invited him to supper. He and Ruth got along well, and Becca liked him too." Matt put the chart on the desk.

Becca sipped her coffee and put her mug on the table. "Dorothy, the office runs much smoother when you're here. You were missed. As far as Ruth and Isaac go, I'm delighted to see her interested in a nice man."

The door chimed and Matt rose to greet Laura Morrison. She flew into his arms. Matt glanced at Becca over Laura's shoulder.

Giggling, Laura separated herself from him but kept her hands on his arms. "I did not sleep a wink last night. I was anxious to spend time with you today."

He stepped back and gestured to Becca. "Laura, you remember Becca Yost." Dorothy frowned and he shoved his hands in his pockets to keep from fidgeting.

Laura ran her finger along Matt's cheek. "Of course I remember. Hello, Becca. I am sure you will not mind if I steal Matt for a while. You would be bored listening to us prattle on about our prior history together and chatting about people you do not know."

He waited for Becca to answer, not sure what she would choose to do. Laura was right. She would be bored, but he would welcome her coming with them.

Becca ran her hand along her braid. "You're right. I'll stay here. I've got paperwork I need to catch up on. You two go ahead and have a nice visit."

He kissed her on the cheek before donning his coat and shutting the door behind them.

Laura looped her arm through his. "We had a great time playing games and chasing each other as children, then things changed between us. I remember the day you kissed me like it was yesterday."

Matt patted her hand. "You broke my heart when you went off to college and ended things between us."

Women who were friends with Ruth and Becca, sitting at tables in the restaurant, frowned. With his focus on Laura, he avoided Lizzie's questioning gaze. Glad she was not waiting on them, he relaxed. "I am surprised you are not married with children."

She sipped coffee. "I was with someone for two years, and he developed a drinking habit. When he refused to do anything about it, I ended our courtship. I needed a change of scenery, and here I am. Your mother said you were not courting anyone, but she must not know about Becca."

"Mother is quite aware I am courting Becca. Mother has been on a mission to convince Becca to have nothing to do with me. My father agrees with her, so I no longer communicate with them."

Laura leaned into Matt. "Your mother is right. She is an awful choice for you, and I do not understand your attraction to her. What could you have in common with her? Do not let her ruin your relationship with parents who love you."

Matt bristled. "I assume my mother has shared her negative opinions about Becca with you from what you have said today. I am grateful my parents supported and put me through medical school. I love them, but Becca is my first priority. I am serious about her, and I will not let them destroy what we have together. Furthermore, Laura, my private life is none of your business."

Her mouth tightened. "Calm yourself. We are
friends, remember?" She twisted her mouth. "You
can have her as your little nurse, teach her social
graces and how to carry on an intelligent conversation, but she will not be happy in your world. As far
as your parents are concerned, you will be miserable
without them. They *are* your family."

In their past, he remembered the lighthearted
Laura but also her sometimes shrewish nature and
biting tongue. He sighed. Laura had obviously given
in to her more manipulative and snarly side. He was
sorry she had come to visit him. "You sound like my
mother."

Laura put her head back and laughed. "You are
such a naïve man. Even if you do not socialize with
your parents, you will be invited to dinners at your
friends' homes. Becca will be an outcast. She will
never be accepted by your parents or your friends.
People you have known all your life will distance
themselves from you because of her. You will eventually resent each other."

He stood and scooted his chair back. "This conversation is over. I need to return to the office."

Laura grabbed her reticule and rose. "I am sorry
I wasted my time coming here. You have turned into
a weak and unattractive man. I will walk myself back
to the hotel. You go on back to your little Amish
girl."

Matt waited until she left before heading back
to the office. Laura had become a spoiled and self-
centered woman. Her good nature and ability to
make him laugh were no more. Laura was the same

kind of manipulative woman as his mother. No wonder she sent Laura to do her dirty work. Soon, she would find out from Laura that her plan did not work.

He hoped Becca would not encourage him to reunite with his parents. It was the one thing he would not do.

Chapter Fourteen

Becca finished her chicken broth and crackers and hoped they would steady her nerves. She was having a hard enough time keeping her anxiety in check without Dorothy's comments about Laura. "Please change the subject." She couldn't stand to hear Laura's name one more time.

Dorothy filled her mouth with a spoonful of oatmeal and it dribbled down her chin. She caught it with a napkin. "I cannot help it. I do not like the way Laura flirted with Matt. She is here to snatch him away from you. He practically fell over the way she jumped into his arms."

"Matt will tell her we're courting, and she will have no reason to pursue him." Becca rinsed her bowl under the sink pump then sat next to Dorothy.

Dorothy threw her a sideways glance and bit into a slice of apple bread. "Women like her do not care. They go after a man with a vengeance. You need to stand up for yourself and put aside your Amish humbleness. Do not let her walk all over you."

"I have faith in Matt." She hid her doubt from Dorothy. She was concerned about Matt and Laura's prior history together.

Dorothy shook her finger. "Men can be ignorant when it comes to women like Laura. You may have to set him straight. If you do not, I will."

The door opened. Matt returned alone. Becca and Dorothy stopped talking. He strode over to Becca and kissed her on the forehead. "How many patients stopped into the office while I was gone?"

Dorothy stood and brushed at her skirt. "I need some flour from the store. I will be back in a little while." She whispered in Becca's ear, "Be frank with him."

"None, it's been a quiet day thus far. Where is Miss Morrison? How was your time with her?" Becca washed her hands.

Matt raked his hand through his hair. "At first, I thought she was here to visit me as a friend, but she talked nonstop about how wrong you and I are for each other. I told her I was serious about you and not interested in hearing anything negative she had to say concerning you or us. We quarreled, and she is on her way back to Washington."

"Dorothy suspected she came here with bad intentions. I told her I had faith in you to set Miss Morrison straight if she had."

"She has changed and not for the better. She has become way too forward and opinionated."

"Dorothy pegged her right away."

Matt snorted. "She would be my mother's choice for a daughter-in-law. They are very much alike. It angers me Mother told her I was available and coaxed her to come and visit me under false pretenses."

"Your mamm's a persistent woman."

"She is. I had no idea she would send another woman to plead her cause to me. Even though I have had nothing to do with my mother, she will not stop finding ways to interfere. I do not know what else to do to discourage her from doing these types of things."

Becca gripped the edges of the sink behind her. She had been praying about God's will for her life concerning Matt and all the turmoil they were enduring from his mamm. She had hoped Mrs. Carrington would miss her son and would have a change of heart toward her. His mamm wasn't going to give up. Matt had sacrificed too much to be with her. He no longer reviewed research with his daed. He no longer met with influential people who supported his ideas for research, because he refused to attend their dinner parties. And most importantly, he no longer had a relationship with his parents. Her heart sunk. She knew what she had to do. "I'm always dreading your mamm's next move against me, and I won't stand in the way of your research career. All this turmoil cannot be God's will for your life or mine. Your mamm has won. I can't do this anymore."

Matt's face paled. "Please do not do this to us. I prefer not having my parents in my life with the way they are acting. I do not want you to worry about my mother. Nothing she has done to break us apart has worked, and nothing will. I love you."

"I must do this." She let tears drip onto her cheeks and did not bother to wipe them away, grabbed her reticule, and ran outside.

She rushed across the street and entered Ruth's shop. Benjamin was occupied with Kate. Customers selected fabrics to purchase, and Kate accepted their money. Ruth removed different fabrics off the wooden shelves and showed them to two ladies.

Becca met Ruth's eyes.

Ruth pointed to her office. Becca hid from Benjamin and shut the door to Ruth's private space. She sat in a chair across from the desk. What had she done? She loved Matt. It didn't matter. Their courtship had to end because otherwise, their lives would always be subjected to torment from his mamm.

Ruth stepped inside and broke her train of thought. "What is wrong? I could tell you were upset when you avoided Benjamin." Ruth faced her.

"I shouldn't be here. You're busy with customers. We can talk later. I came to talk to you in the heat of the moment."

"No. You stay put. You are not leaving until you tell me what is wrong. Benjamin is playing, and Kate is helping the customers."

Becca shuffled her feet from one side to the other. "Last night, I told you about Laura Morrison coming to town to visit Matt. I can't get over Mrs. Carrington telling Laura that Matt isn't courting anyone."

"Matt introduced you to Laura and made it clear you are the one he is interested in. Why do you seem upset?"

"Today, she and Matt went to Lizzie's and chatted. Matt told me Laura had romantic intentions toward him. She voiced his mamm's concerns about me. They argued, and Matt left in a huff."

"Good for him. He set her straight. What will Mrs. Carrington think of next? She needs more to do with her time, rather than spending it devising ways to separate you and Matt."

Becca hung her head. "Since Matt told his parents to stay away from us, his mamm is finding other ways to cause trouble." She paused for a moment. "I can't believe God would want us together with his parents opposed to us courting. It was time I separated myself from Matt. Mrs. Carrington won't stop causing trouble for Matt and me until I do."

"No, you must reconsider. You and he are meant to be together. You have weathered more storms than most couples have in a lifetime. Matt sent Laura away. His mother will find out soon enough that her latest plan did not work. You are making a mistake letting him go."

Becca opened her bag, pulled out a handkerchief, and dabbed her eyes. "My mind's made up." She had to remain firm on her decision, no matter how bad it hurt. Would this pain in her heart ever end?

Ruth gripped Becca's shoulders. "Do not let Eloise Carrington rob you of Matt."

"Our being together shouldn't be this hard. Mrs. Carrington is never going to accept my Amish upbringing, nor will she ever leave us be."

Ruth sat in her chair with a thump and tapped her foot on the floor. "He chose you, and he is happy with you the way you are. He does not communicate with his parents. What else can Matt do? He has done everything he can to prevent anyone from coming between you. It is not fair for you to make this decision alone."

"None of it is fair, but I am doing it because I love him. He is sacrificing too much to be with me. If I'm out of his life, he will reconcile with his daed, and maybe his mamm, and continue reviewing research. God would not want me to come between Matt and his parents."

"Pray about this. Do not make any rash decisions."

Prayer was something she would do. If God wanted her to be with Matt, He would find a way. There was nothing more to say on the matter.

Ruth got up and placed her hands on Becca's shoulders. "I know how much you love him. Please reconcile with him."

"Please understand. I must leave him be." She caressed Ruth's cheek. "I'm going home. You go back to your customers. I'll be all right."

Her body weak and her heart heavy, she left. Gray clouds shielded the sun.

She stepped out the door and her eyes widened. *Matt.* Matt reached for her hand. "I followed you to Ruth's, but waited outside. I did not want to talk inside the shop. Please come back to my office. We can weather this storm. Please do not end our relationship. Nothing else matters if I do not have you in my life."

Heart pounding and knees buckling, she gripped his hand. "I must do this. I'm sorry." She stared at her feet.

He gently pulled her to him. "Marry me."

Overwhelmed with joy then sadness, she dropped her hand from his. She had longed for this day and wanted to say *yes,* but she couldn't forget why she ended things with Matt in the first place. "I want to marry you, but I must do what I think is right." She whirled around and ran home, ignoring his plea for her to come back.

She refused to answer his repeated knocks on the door. Her temples throbbed. Climbing into bed, she couldn't remember anything hurting this much, not the shunning, not the separation from Ruth, not Gertrude showing up and threatening to take Benjamin, and not Margaret's death. The pain of losing Matt was unbearable.

Later, she listened as Ruth and Benjamin whispered outside her room. Her door opened. She curled in a tight ball under the quilts and pretended to sleep. It was no use burdening Ruth anymore on the subject.

The next morning, Ruth peeked around her bedroom door. "Becca, I am worried about you. Please talk to me."

"You can come in. Sit here next to me." Becca sat up and patted the bed. "I ran into Matt after I left the mending shop. He asked me to marry him." She pushed back her hair from her red blotched face. "I refused."

Ruth scooted closer. "He asked you to marry him? You cannot say no. You will regret it for the rest of your life."

Becca smoothed the bed quilt. "It pains me to say

no, but I must. Even if Matt and I married, his mamm would devise ways to break up our marriage."

Ruth stood erect. "I cannot believe you let this woman win. Matt has stood up to her. You need to do the same."

Becca paused and fidgeted with the corner of a quilt. "There is nothing more he or I can do. None of this is his fault or mine. His mamm has worn me out. I give up." She would never forget Matt's fresh scent, his laugh, his kiss, his touch, or the way he raked his hand through his hair when nervous.

"You will be miserable without him. He has become such a big part of your life. You are sacrificing too much not being with him." She stalked off.

Becca buried her face in the pillow and wept. His handsome face wouldn't leave her mind. She touched her mouth. How she missed the feel of his lips on hers. The man had all the qualities she wanted in a husband. She loved him. If only there was a way to make it work. After Ruth and Benjamin left, she got up, dressed, and headed to work in Ruth's Mending Shop.

Two weeks later, Becca had enjoyed doing seamstress work, but she longed to shake the heartache of separation from Matt. She missed his scent, his voice, his lips on hers, and every little thing about him. She missed working by his side. Walking home, she couldn't push thoughts of him out of her mind. A gust of cool wind caught her off balance. A hand grabbed her elbow and stopped her from falling.

Matt stepped in front of her. "I have missed you. I waited for weeks before coming to the shop, but every time I came by, you either waited on customers or hid from me. Do not deny it. Ruth admitted it was true when I asked her. Please talk to me."

"Talking will not change our situation." She fought putting her arms around him and holding him tight. Her knees weakened and her heart sunk. Nothing had changed. She must remain strong. God would intervene if He wanted them together. She turned and hurried home. Her shoes crunched the small stones on the boardwalk's weathered wooden planks, as she hurried to get away from him. She didn't trust herself around him. In her dreams, he approached her and she fell into his arms. In real life, she was miserable running from him.

Arriving home, she stepped inside. Benjamin squealed and wrapped his arms around her hips. "You look sad." He tugged on her sleeve. "Let's go see Matt. He'll make you happy again."

Becca glanced at Ruth and Benjamin. "Matt was outside. I stumbled, and he caught me. He asked me to reconcile."

Benjamin pulled on her hand. "Come on. Let's go find him."

Ruth handed him an apple. "Becca does not want to visit Matt. You finish your puzzle and leave us alone for a bit."

Benjamin shrugged and chomped on his apple. He returned to his puzzle on the floor and picked up his next puzzle piece.

Ruth pulled Becca to the kitchen.

Before Ruth could speak, Becca held a finger to

her sister's lips. "We're not going to discuss Matt and me. There is nothing left to say on the matter."

Ruth poured water in two glasses and passed one to Becca. "I am not happy about your decision, but I will not comment on it further." She removed a piece of thread from Becca's collar. "Isaac is taking me to the chapel picnic. Everyone has been asking about you. Please come with us."

Becca sighed. "I'm not in the mood to socialize. You go and enjoy yourselves." Matt might be there. She wouldn't be able to take her eyes off of him if he was. It would be too painful.

Ruth stood. "I wish you would reconsider coming with us. It's not healthy for you to do nothing more than go to work and come home and mope."

Becca shrugged and lifted a box she had tucked away a few weeks earlier. She opened the lid and closed it quick. She'd forgotten. The box was where she stored the fabric pieces she'd collected from Matt's old shirts. The ones she had planned to stitch together to make a memorable pocket quilt for him. Her words she would write on the letter remained the same. She loved him with all her heart and wanted to spend the rest of her life with him. Now, she would never have the opportunity to give it to him. His mamm's attitude toward her had shattered her dream of marrying Matt.

Her chest tightened. Reminders of Matt were everywhere. When would the pain of loving him end? Never, she was afraid. Love for the office, patients, and medicine also left emptiness. She longed to have those things back in her life too, but she dismissed the desire. Without Matt, patients and medicine meant nothing.

Ruth removed the box from Becca's grip and tucked it away on a shelf. "Are these fabric swatches from Matt's old shirts?"

"Yes. I couldn't wait to stitch him a pocket quilt. Now it makes no sense."

Ruth knelt beside her sister. "You miss him and your work as a nurse. Two big losses in your life are going to make you sad for a long time, unless you change your mind."

Becca's cheeks heated. "Please don't argue with me about this matter."

Ruth held up her hands. "I am not going to argue with you. I can tell your mind is made up. Maybe a change of scenery will take your mind off things. Go and visit Hester. If you help deliver babies, then Grace wouldn't have to shun you while you all three work together. The bishop would find this acceptable. Visiting Mamm and Dacd would be another matter. You'll have to wait to visit them until they come here."

She had missed Hester and Grace. What a great idea Ruth had. She could birth boppli again. At least she would be helping people. Maybe she would sneak over at night and visit her parents. No, Ruth was right. She didn't want to cause any trouble for her parents with the bishop. Ruth's idea to visit Grace and Hester was a good one. Yes, she would do it. "I'll leave tomorrow."

* * *

A few days later, Matt visited Ruth at her shop. His face twisted with worry. He rubbed his brow and paced. "Is Becca here today?" He looked around the room.

Ruth crossed her arms. "Becca went to visit her friend Hester, the midwife."

"Is she coming back?"

"Yes. She has left her Amish life behind whether the two of you end up together or not. She needed some time away. I told her to marry you in spite of your mother, but she will not listen. A small part of me understands her decision."

He needed Ruth on his side. Becca listened to her. "You and she are close. Give me advice. What can I do to get her back?"

Ruth went to the small kitchen and opened up a container of coffee. "You have done all you can. I have pleaded in your favor numerous times."

He lifted two mugs and handed them to Ruth. Becca was too stubborn. Her strong will would cost them a future together. "I have not seen this side of her before, and I do not like it."

Ruth poured the coffee and pressed her lips in a tight line. "As much as you and I do not agree with Becca, we have to honor her commitment to God and her belief she is doing His will."

Matt placed his mug on the table with force. "I believe God brought us together. Becca is keeping us apart." He left with those angry words hanging between them. His life had turned into a nightmare.

He arrived at the office. His mother was waiting.

"You are not welcome here. How many times do

I need to say it for you to respect my wishes?" He walked into his office and sat at his desk.

She followed and pounced like an angry cat. "You should be ashamed of yourself. You have ignored our letters and have not visited for weeks. Your father is upset because you have been returning his research unread." She slid her gloved hand along a bookshelf. "This place is filthy. Everything is a mess. Your supplies are strewn all over the place and your books are scattered on your desk. The trash is overflowing. You kept a neat office until Becca came along."

He rose from his chair and slammed a book on the desk. "I will not listen to you insult Becca. She is a neat and orderly person. I am too. I have not been the same since she left. She is no longer working here or in my life because of you." He could not stand the sight of his mother. She had ruined his life, again.

Her nostrils flared. "You should thank me. In a few years, you would have been sick of her. She would embarrass you over and over with her inability to carry on a decent conversation. Someone with your education needs more stimulating conversation than to talk only about the weather or chapel."

"You are wrong. The sound of her voice and the way she carries herself without an arrogant bone is what attracted me to Becca in the first place. I found her refreshing because she is not worldly."

She threw back her head and scoffed. "You do not get it. She is interested in your trust fund, not you."

He lifted his stethoscope and slapped it against

his thigh. "This shows how little you know about her. You could learn from her humbleness, kind heart, and true faith in God." Instead of his mother teaching Becca worldly things, his mother would be better off learning kindness and humility from the woman he planned to marry.

She peeled off her gloves and waved them in his face. "I go to chapel and believe in God. I cannot believe you would insinuate otherwise."

He doubted she learned anything from the sermons. Her actions did not portray that she did. "It is one thing to go to chapel, and it is another to put your faith into action. I doubt God is happy with the way you have treated Becca."

She clicked her boots as she stepped back from his desk. "You will realize in time I have done what any mother would do for her son when he has chosen the wrong woman for a wife."

Matt stepped close. "Most mothers respect their children and do not meddle in their lives. You have crossed the line with me, and I do not want to see you for a long time, if ever. I have patients coming soon. Please leave and do not come back."

She gasped, turned on her heel, and slammed the door as she stormed out.

He shook his head. The woman was exasperating. He was ashamed to call her his mother.

Chapter Fifteen

Two days later, Becca rode in the stagecoach to Hester's house. As she traveled to Berlin, Ohio, her mind flooded with memories of times she had spent birthing boppli with her friends. The snow had melted, but the air remained cold. She covered her legs with one of the blankets the driver left inside the stagecoach for passengers. Then she pulled a bag of butter cookies and a jar of water from her bag. Glad to be the only passenger, she opened her King James Version of the Bible to read but dropped it on her lap.

Matt was probably at Lizzie's ordering his usual bread and eggs. A vision of his long legs, broad shoulders, handsome face, and dark hair sent a thrill through her. She loved him. She always would. Part of her wanted to return to Massillon, run inside Lizzie's, and agree they should be together. The other part said no when Mrs. Carrington's face flashed in her mind.

She opened her Bible and thumbed through the pages until she found the Book of John. She read for a few hours and then ate two cookies from her bag. Two wild horses ran alongside the stagecoach. They didn't have a care in the world. She wished the same were true for her and Matt. She read a few more chapters and then the stagecoach halted in Berlin. She breathed in the cold, fresh air and pulled her burnoose tight around her. She headed to Hester's home. The barn door was open, and Hester sat on a stool milking.

"I thought I would surprise you with a visit." She loved her friend's dark black hair and eyes and her rail-thin frame. She admired the woman's willingness to help mamms birth their boppli day or night.

Hester rose, wiped her hands on her apron, and circled her arms around Becca. "What a wonderful idea! You wrote me you were working as a nurse and in love with a handsome doctor. How did you find time to come and visit me? Don't get me wrong, I'm delighted to have you."

"I needed some time away, and I've missed you. If you don't mind, I would like to stay with you for a few days and help you and Grace with birthing boppli."

"I could use the help, and you are always welcome here. Grace is meeting me here in the morning. She will be thrilled to see you. You look pretty in your yellow calico dress." She touched the ribbon in her hair. "I like your locks fixed this way. The ribbon is a nice touch."

"Ruth's a stickler for ringlets and does them for me. I prefer soft curls or a braided bun, but I never turn down her offer to fix my hair." She ran her hand over the buttons lining the front of her dress. "I do enjoy wearing colors and buttons."

Hester lifted her pail of milk and went inside the house. She poured the milk into two jars and put them in the icebox. She extended her arm. "Hand me your burnoose. I put a fire in the iron stove. Go warm your hands. The weather's cold outside."

Becca stretched her fingers in front of the warm stove. Soon, Hester had hot apples in one pan and vegetable stew simmering in another. Coming to Hester's lifted her spirits. Her house was cozy and diverted her attention away from Matt at least for the moment. "I'm hungry." She glanced in the pan. "Warm cinnamon apples are one of my favorite dishes."

"Mine too. I'm surprised you would leave work and your beau." Hester scooped the food onto plates.

"Matt and I aren't courting any longer. I had to quit working as his nurse, and I have been helping Ruth in her mending shop. It was too awkward to continue working in the office with him, under the circumstances."

"Did you have an argument?" A loud bang startled them. The door blew open from the wind. Hester used her foot to close it.

Becca tested the heat of the apples. "No, it was because of his mamm." She recounted her story regarding Matt's mamm and why she ended things with him.

Juice from the apples dripped from Becca's spoon onto her skirt. She wiped it with a cloth napkin. "My biggest concern is doing what God would have us do, and I believe it's ending our courtship."

"It sounds as if Matt's done all he can with his parents. You should not allow them to disrupt your lives like this."

Setting her spoon in the bowl, Becca licked her lips. "Even though I don't agree with his mamm on most things, I do agree he would be better off with a wife who fits into his society."

Hester poured water over the dirty dishes in the washbowl to soak. "I don't agree with you. Mrs. Carrington sounds like a selfish and high-minded woman. You pay her no mind and go reunite with your man. God doesn't promise us life will be easy."

Hester threw her wet rag over the washbowl and wiped her hands on her flowered apron. "Take it as it comes from his mother and deal with each incident. She'll give up in time." She sank on the chair and clasped her hands across her stomach. "Take a load off and put your feet on this stool next to mine. You love helping others more than you do working as a seamstress. Don't let your skills as a nurse and midwife go to waste."

"I enjoy working with Ruth, but I had never been happier than when I was treating patients and spending time with Matt. He's everything I could have ever hoped to find in a man for a potential husband."

A coyote howled. Hester flinched. "I'll never get used to those varmints." She sighed. "Think about what you want. You better not let him go. He sounds like a rare find. Marry the man."

A yawn escaped Becca. "You make it sound easy."

"It can be." Hands on the edge of the cushion, Hester pushed her body to the edge and rose. "I'll leave you alone about Matt's mother for now. Let's go to bed and get some sleep. I spoke with Irma's husband at the general store today. He told me Irma's been having pains. I need to check on her early in the morning."

Becca bid Hester good night, changed into a gown, and crawled into bed. Unable to sleep, she stared at the ceiling and pictured Matt's face. Memories danced in her mind. Their first kiss, the way he held her, and working side by side in the office with the man she loved. She buried her face in the pillow and moaned.

The next morning, coffee aroma and the sizzle of eggs in a skillet beckoned her. She chose a simple pink and white Gibson Girl dress and headed to the kitchen.

Grace sat at the kitchen table. "I'm thrilled you're here." She hugged her friend. "Hester told me you and Matt are no longer courting and why. I'll pray for God's will in your life concerning Matt and you. I'm sorry. I know you love him."

"I appreciate your prayers. I pray Matt's parents will have a change of heart and accept me. In the meantime, I'm working at Ruth's shop. She suggested I visit Hester and deliver boppli with the two of you. I miss helping people. It will be good for me." She picked up a mug filled with coffee.

Grace swallowed a bite of egg. "You help Hester with Irma. I'll go along and do what I can. I'm just thrilled to spend time with you."

"I've missed you, too. I'm anxious to practice my

midwifery skills again. I haven't birthed too many boppli since I've worked for Matt."

Hester cut an egg on her plate. "As soon as we finish with breakfast, we'll head to Irma's. I'm worried about her."

Thirty minutes later, Hester pushed her plate aside. She checked her bag for supplies. "We better get going." She threw on her burnoose and hoisted her bag over her shoulder.

Becca wiped her mouth, grabbed her heavy burnoose, and followed Hester and Grace outside.

At Timothy and Irma Lantz's house, a shrill scream rang out. Timothy gestured for them to come in. A look of relief was on his harried face. "I was going to kumme and fetch you, but I was afraid to leave Irma."

His wife was writhing in pain. Water soaked the bed. "Please get this boppli out of me."

Hester threw her burnoose over a chair. She examined Irma to assess the infant's progress. "This is Becca Yost. You know Grace already. They are going to help me deliver your baby. Timothy, you can wait in the other room."

His eyes lit with relief. He didn't hesitate and headed for the door.

Hester winked at her friends.

Becca stifled a chuckle and went to the kitchen. A large pot of water warmed on the iron stove. She wiped her forehead with her sleeve and placed the large pot on the floor next to Hester in the bedroom. After pouring water from the pot into a second bowl, she set it aside. She dipped a cloth in the water and sponged Irma's face to calm her.

"Timothy is scared to death and worried sick about you. He must love you a lot."

Grace handed Hester what she needed.

Irma bit her lip and scrunched her face. "Timothy is a wonderful husband. I am frightened too. I have never had pain like this in my life. It is awful. When this boppli is born, I am not having any more kinner." Her nose wrinkled. "Here comes another pain." She yelled at the top of her lungs and held her stomach. Sweat dripped from her face onto her neck.

Crouched at the end of the bed next to Hester, Becca watched the boppli's head crown. The sight was a miracle. Soon, Irma would be holding her boppli. She rose and arranged the second bowl of warm water and towels to wash the newborn.

Irma gripped the bedsheets. "I'm tired. I can't stand this pain."

Becca rushed to her side and grasped Irma's hand. "It will be all over before you know it."

Hester wrinkled her nose and peered close. "Becca, come here. I may need you."

Irma cried out. "The boppli is coming! The boppli is coming!"

The midwife positioned herself on one knee and held her hands out to catch the boppli. "Push, Irma. Push now."

Irma did, and the infant's head popped out.

Becca marveled as Hester rolled the little one's shoulders and eased the rest of its body free.

The boppli squalled and trembled.

Becca cut the umbilical cord, and Grace tied it off.

Hester finished with Irma, and Grace handed her what she needed.

Becca lifted the boppli girl and placed her on a table next to the bed. She cleaned her tiny body and marveled at the tiny face, hands, and feet. Wisps of black hair stood straight up on the newborn's head. Becca giggled as the newborn's legs kicked and arms stretched as she struggled to clean her. She would never tire of witnessing the miracle of birth. The little one was precious with its small mouth and full cheeks. She swaddled the infant in a blanket and handed her to Irma.

Irma cuddled her dochder. "As horrible as the birth was, the pain was all worth it. I can't believe I'm holding her. Her name is Esther. Nine months was a long time to carry her inside me. She's even more beautiful than I imagined. Timothy must be anxious to see her. Can you ask him to kumme in?"

The door creaked and Timothy peeked inside. She gestured for him to enter.

He sat on the edge of the bed next to Irma.

Irma handed him Esther. "We have a dochder."

He cradled her in his arms. "She's almost as pretty as her mamm." He kissed Irma's forehead. "We're parents and on to the next chapter of our lives. Life with you keeps getting better."

Becca stood by Grace and Hester and watched the new daed. Timothy holding Esther reminded her of Matt when he held sick infants he treated. He told her he never tired of birthing boppli. She guessed he would react much like Timothy when he held his boppli. Her dream to be his wife and the mamm of his children had been shattered thanks to Mrs. Carrington.

"Timothy, would you mind holding Esther in the other room for a few minutes, while Grace and I help Irma change into fresh clothes?"

He kissed his wife on the forehead and left.

Timothy didn't hesitate to leave with the boppli. He appeared rather comfortable with Esther, unlike most daeds she encountered who held their boppli for the first time. Becca bathed Irma and watched as Grace changed the new mamm into a fresh new cotton nightgown. She helped her to a chair, and she and Grace changed the bed linens.

A snap rang through the room when Hester closed her bag. "Irma, send Timothy to fetch me if you need anything. You enjoy your daughter."

Becca dropped the bloody rags in a flour sack and tied it in a knot. She put on her burnoose, slung the bag over her shoulder, and joined her friend and Hester. They bid the happy couple good-bye and stepped outside.

Out of nowhere, an Amish woman ran toward them flailing her arms and yelling, "Kumme quick. My neighbor has fallen. I don't know her name. I moved here from Lancaster, Pennsylvania, a few days ago. My other neighbor told me to come to you if I was ill or injured." She gestured toward Hester.

The distressed woman guided them to Becca's parents' house. Becca's pulse rate shot up. She ran inside.

Hester and Grace followed close behind her.

Her daed was pale as he sat on the floor beside her mamm. Hope lit his face. "Becca, I'm surprised you're here. Please help your mamm. She fell. I don't know what to do."

She knelt next to him. She examined her mamm's head. "I can't find a cut or bleeding, but she is sure to have a goose egg on her head for a few days. I can feel one forming." She caressed her mamm's face. "Mamm, it's me, Becca."

Mamm's eyes fluttered. She touched her head. "Is it really you? I fell and hit my head. Everything went black for a moment. I've got an awful headache." She gripped Becca's arm. "I have missed you."

Sitting on the floor, Becca covered her mamm's hand with hers. "I'm relieved you're all right. You scared me."

Joseph reached for his wife's hand. "I found you sprawled on the floor. You wouldn't answer me. You were unconscious. I was afraid you'd had a heart attack or something."

"I should've been more careful. I climbed on the chair to lift a bowl from the cupboard. I lost my footing. It was an accident." She touched Becca's cheek. "What brings you here? Is Ruth all right? Is anything wrong?"

Her parents' faces, her chair at the table, and the oval white plate filled with her favorite butter cookies hurt her heart and were too painful to look at. All things she had missed. "I'm here for a few days to visit Hester. Your new neighbor found us outside and asked us to help someone who had fallen. I was surprised when I discovered it was you."

"I feel better already with you by my side."

Becca helped her sit up. "I wanted to visit you and Daed but didn't want to run into my friends or the bishop and cause you any trouble. I didn't want to experience being shunned or put you in an awkward position with them. It's better if you visit us in Massillon. Your fall provided me with a good reason for coming to your house. No one will be upset with me for helping you."

Daed raised his hand. "It's gut to see you. Your mamm and I have missed you." He gestured to Hester and Grace. "I'm sorry. I didn't mean to ignore you."

Grace waved a dismissive hand. "We understand. You were upset about Mrs. Yost falling. We are glad we can help."

Becca and Grace helped her mamm to a chair. Hester stood close by. They sat with her at the kitchen table. Becca made hot coffee and served them.

Mamm and Daed chatted with Hester and Grace about the boppli they helped enter the world.

Grace patted Becca's shoulder. "Becca was able to help us since she is a midwife. The bishop or our friends wouldn't argue about her helping someone in need in our community. I have never understood shunning our friends for leaving." She squeezed Becca's fingers. "It was gut to birth a boppli with her again."

"Yes, it brought back fond memories of our times together. I am happy to be here, but I do miss Benjamin. He's such a delight. You will have to meet him."

Mamm pushed a stray hair into her kapp. "How is Benjamin? I was shocked when I got your letter about how you came to know him."

Becca addressed her parents and friends. "He is a delightful little boy. At the end of a long day, it is nice to come home and enjoy one of his big hugs. He loves to bake cookies, work puzzles, and play with his wooden train set. He makes us laugh when he asks questions like 'Do fish have lips?' I don't remember what life was like without him."

They laughed.

Mamm pressed a hand to her heart. "I can't wait to meet the child. He sounds adorable."

Daed patted her hand. "I can't get used to your new look."

Hester leaned forward. "She may be dressed differently, but she is the same sweet woman you raised."

Grace kissed her friend's cheek. "I agree."

Her friends had accepted her change in dress in a positive way. Her parents hadn't been aware she had discarded her Amish clothing. English clothes on her must be hard for them. She hoped her clothes would not cause an argument. "I missed my plain dresses at first, but now I like wearing colorful dresses."

Mamm caressed her cheek. "I like this soft pink dress on you."

Daed squeezed her hand. "I must agree with Hester and Grace. You look beautiful."

"I'm glad you're not angry with me. I realize Ruth and me living in Massillon is not easy for you. Please be assured we love God and have not abandoned our Amish values when making decisions."

Mamm pushed a stray hair from Becca's face. "We love you and Ruth. We're not happy our dochders have chosen to leave the Amish community but realize we must accept your decision. In your last letter, you wrote that you and Matt are no longer courting. Why?"

Becca recounted to her parents why she and Matt were no longer courting.

Mamm covered her hand. "Pray for guidance. God may surprise you."

Becca had learned Mamm was a good judge of character. No doubt Mamm would rather she marry an Amish man, but she suspected Matt had made a good impression on her when she met him.

Hester glanced at her timepiece. "We better get going. I need to check on my animals."

Becca hugged her parents and bid them farewell. She followed her friends outside. Arm in arm, the three women walked to Hester's house, huddled against the cold. She wished Grace could have visited her at Hester's a little longer, but she understood her friend had chores to tend to. After they reached Hester's, Grace readied her horse in the barn and bid them farewell.

Inside her tidy house, Hester threw wood in the iron stove and stoked the fire. Heat radiated throughout the room. Hand on the kitchen pump, she filled the teapot and waited for it to heat. A few minutes later, Hester added tea to the kettle, let it steep for a few moments, and filled two mugs. She handed one to Becca. "You rest while I check on the animals. I'll be right back."

Becca sipped the tea. Ruth would be excited to hear about her visit with their parents. She wished she could tell Matt about her visit with them too.

A coyote howled and interrupted her thoughts. She threw open the door. Her heart raced. Hester stood several feet away from a coyote.

Her heart thumped against her chest. The coyote growled and bared its teeth. What should she do? She reached for the shotgun hanging on the wall inside the door. She got into position, cocked the gun, aimed, and fired. The coyote fell and lay lifeless.

Hester put a hand to her neck. "I was afraid to yell out to you. I thought it might cause the animal to lunge at me. I'm glad you came to my rescue." She stepped to the animal and kicked it. "It's dead. Good shot."

Becca held out her trembling hand. "I was terrified the coyote was going to attack you." Hanging the gun on the wall, she glanced over her shoulder at Hester. "I'm relieved the gun was loaded, or you might have been in big trouble. You should take a gun with you when you go out at night."

"I'm a little shaken up too. I most often do. I forgot to grab my shotgun on my way out the door. I won't forget again after this bad experience. I didn't know you could shoot. I'm grateful you can and did."

"Daed taught me how to use a shotgun. I liked to go turkey hunting with him."

Hester slumped in a rocking chair. She pushed it back and forth with her foot. "Thanks for your help. I thought this might be my last day on earth for a minute. Life is short. You never know when your life might end. You need to enjoy it with the one you love. What does Ruth have to say about Matt's mother?"

The house grew dark. With a shudder, Becca turned up a lantern and helped Hester light candles. She rubbed her arms. "Ruth is fond of Matt. She's upset we are no longer together. She wants me to ignore Matt's mamm and reunite with him."

Hester threw her another blanket. "Listen to your sister. How is she?"

Becca recounted to her the story of how Isaac and Ruth met. "I hope they will marry one day. I didn't tell Mamm and Daed about Ruth's new beau. She'll write and tell them about Isaac when she's ready."

"I'm happy for Ruth. Isaac sounds like a good man." She rose and pulled potato soup from the icebox for supper.

Two weeks later, Becca packed her things, then joined Hester for dinner. A tear escaped her eye. She touched the keepsake pocket quilt she had given Hester. What a precious time she had had laughing, telling stories, and sharing meals with Hester and Grace during her visit here. They were good friends.

Hester came alongside her and wiped the tear from Becca's face with the pad of her thumb. She patted the letter tucked inside the pocket quilt. "I read your letter at least once a week. I never tire of the words. They always make me smile and warm my heart when I feel sad and alone." Hester wiped a tear from her cheek. "Enough of this sappy talk. Time to eat. Sit."

Becca laughed and obeyed.

Hester served her rabbit stew. "We had better have supper and get to bed, because you've got an early start home tomorrow since the stagecoach carries the bank's money on the early morning run. I wish you were leaving on the later one. There is less chance of trouble."

The next morning, Becca kissed Hester's cheek. "Thank you for the advice and hospitality."

Grace rode her horse to them and dismounted. "I was afraid I'd miss you. I had to feed the animals this morning. Daed usually does, but he had to help the neighbor find a horse that got away from him." She hugged Becca.

Becca hoisted her bag on her shoulder. "I'm glad you're here. Thank you both for the help with my mamm and your friendship. I'll miss you. Write to me."

Hester engulfed Becca with her strong arms. "When you get back, straighten things out with Matt and put those nursing skills to use working in his office. Good men are hard to find. He sounds like a keeper. Don't let his mean mother ruin your life." She winked.

Grace wiped a tear. "I miss you already. I expect a letter from you soon. I pray everything works out for you and Matt."

Becca waved and headed to the stagecoach. She had enjoyed her visit with Hester, Grace, and her parents. Her friends had listened to her problems and provided wise advice. A wave of nostalgia passed through her. The three of them had spent a lot of time together over the years. She would miss Hester and Grace. Visiting her parents had been unexpected but a welcome surprise. They appeared healthy and happy. It was a little easier to leave them knowing this. She would miss them, too.

Two kind-faced men greeted her. "Welcome aboard, miss. I am Frank Stone and this is my brother, Lester. We will be taking you to Massillon. Let me take your bag. You may get cold along the way. Blankets are inside if you need them." He tied her bag to the top of the coach and held out his hand.

She accepted Mr. Stone's help. She stepped inside and her body tensed. She blinked twice. Becca's heart pounded. No other passengers besides her and Mrs. Carrington were riding in the stagecoach? This was not a good situation. Should she step out of the coach and take Hester's advice? The later stagecoach would've been a better choice considering the company if she remained in this one. The next one wasn't for another two hours. No, she wouldn't be intimidated by Matt's mamm. She sat across from Mrs. Carrington and acknowledged her with a polite but curt nod.

Eloise Carrington rolled her eyes and folded her hands in her lap. "What are you doing on this stagecoach? Did you run to your Amish friends and family when my son stopped courting you?" She pointed to the door. "Do me a favor. Get off this stagecoach. Go home to your little Amish community and stay out of Massillon."

Teeth on edge, Becca seethed and pushed her body into the side farthest away from Mrs. Carrington. She wouldn't let this woman's harsh words weaken her. "I visited friends. Like it or not, Massillon's my home."

The coach jostled them on the bumpy road. Mrs. Carrington pressed her hand into the bench. "If I had known you would be riding with me, I would have chosen a later time."

Blood boiling, Becca focused on her Bible. Minutes passed in strained silence. Slamming the book shut, she focused on Mrs. Carrington. "Matt and I love each other. I would like nothing better than if you and I could have a nice conversation."

Mrs. Carrington dropped her scarf, and they both bent to recover it. They banged heads. The thump resounded inside the coach like a heavy wooden bowl. She rubbed her forehead. "Get away from me, you bumbling simpleton. You are too ignorant for my son." She huffed and shifted in her seat. "I will have a headache soon, thanks to you."

Becca's face heated. Book in hand, she pretended to read but couldn't concentrate on the words. Anger welled in her like a fire out of control. "I've been nice to you and have made every effort to get along with you, but you will not even consider accepting me. Since Matt and I are no longer courting, there is no need for you to insult me. Please be quiet."

With a click of her tongue, Mrs. Carrington pointed a finger. "If you do not entertain any ideas to try and win my son back, you will not have to deal with me. If you do, I will give you no peace until I am sure the two of you are through. I refuse to have a poor, uneducated woman for a daughter-in-law."

Fists clenched, Becca counted to ten under her breath. "I'm not poor. My parents provided for our family quite well, and I have been both educated and trained in many areas. Ruth and I have no financial concerns. Our knowledge and skills help many people. Your accusations are unfounded."

"You do not even understand what I am saying to you. You are ignorant when it comes to socializing in the world. The things you know to talk about are dull and boring. Two words I use to describe you perfectly. Stay away from him. Understand?"

To see Matt again would be stressful. Her heart spilled over with love for him. She had even considered heeding Hester's advice to return to him, but Mrs. Carrington's reminder of her disapproval changed her mind.

A loud clap sounded. Becca jerked her head up and glanced at Mrs. Carrington. She shifted her weight on the bench.

"Answer me, you country bumpkin."

A surge of fury spiraled up Becca's spine. The rudeness, the insults, when would they end? "I will talk to Matt whenever I choose. He and I are friends." Mrs. Carrington's badgering tested the strength of her character to the limit.

"Matt does not need friends like you. He will have women clamoring after him in no time. When he marries, his new wife will not want you around.

Besides, it would not be proper for Matt to have women friends once he is married."

"I'm not interested in anything you have to say. Please leave me alone." A pang of guilt stabbed her. God would not want her to act this way. She must turn the other cheek. "Let's call a truce and ride in silence."

As silent as stone, Mrs. Carrington threw her shoulders back in a huff.

A gunshot rang out. The stagecoach skidded and bumped to a grinding halt.

Becca heard a thud and pressed her hand on the bench to keep from falling. Heart pounding, she looked out the window. Two men, with scarves up to their eyes, circled their horses alongside the stagecoach. They wore big brimmed hats and brandished guns. Lester Stone lay lifeless on the ground. Blood pooled around his head.

The heavyset outlaw stopped and pointed his gun in the direction of the driver's bench. She backed away from the window but not too far so she could still see the men. "Throw the bank's money chest to the ground or the next bullet goes in your head."

Becca quailed and covered her mouth with her hand. Would the bandits shoot Frank Stone? What should she do?

Mrs. Carrington screamed and held her fists to her face. "What is happening?"

Becca held a finger to her lips. "Be quiet and don't move." The coach shook, as Frank Stone's feet hit the ground. Outside the window, he came into her view. Would they leave? If not, what was going to happen to Frank Stone, Mrs. Carrington, and her?

Frank raised both arms and dropped his rifle. "You did not have to shoot my brother. He would have cooperated." Frank shook his head and hoisted himself to the side of the stagecoach, right by her window. He threw the iron reinforced wooden chest to the ground, stepped down, and faced the robber. "Let me help my brother."

The outlaw laughed and shoved Lester's body on the ground. "He's dead."

Frank Stone tilted his head to the bank box. "Take it and go."

The heavyset bandit dismounted and shot the lock. A bang sounded. The chest burst open. The other bandit kept his rifle pointed at Frank. "Clanton, we're rich. A load of money is in here." The man still on horseback circled Frank and shot him in the head with his rifle.

Becca gasped and trembled as she fixed her eyes on the men. Frank Stone lay still on the ground near his brother. Blood oozed from his head. She ducked inside the stagecoach and swallowed the bile rising in her throat.

The robber dismounted. "Hey, Gus, let's find out who's inside."

Fear pounded like bullets in Becca. She pushed her back against the bench, out of sight. She glanced at Mrs. Carrington. "Don't speak, no matter what they say."

Mrs. Carrington's book teetered in her hands, fell, and slapped the floor. "We are going to die."

Becca put her finger to her lips.

Gus thrust the door open and barreled inside. He plopped down hard next to Becca. His foul breath blew in her face. "You're a pretty one." He caressed her cheek with the back of his coarse, calloused hand.

Her pulse raced as she inched away from him. She had never fought anyone. Should she kick and slap him? She couldn't stand the thought of him touching her again. *Yes,* she would kick, punch, scream, and fight with all her might if he put his hand on her again.

He leered at Mrs. Carrington. "Expensive necklace you're wearing, old woman." He snatched it from around her neck.

Mrs. Carrington yelped and cowered. "Get away from me, you scoundrel."

Dangling the jewelry, he yelled out, "Clanton, open the door. I got us something worth some money."

Clanton snorted and opened the door wide but didn't enter the stagecoach. "What did ya find, Gus?"

Mrs. Carrington shrieked, "Ahk!" She threw her book at him. "Stay away from me."

Becca shoved Gus away from Mrs. Carrington. Both of the men had been shot by these two. These men had no problem killing anyone. Would they be next?

Growling an evil laugh, Clanton ogled them from the doorway. "I like feisty women."

A guttural grunt erupted from Gus. "We're gonna have us some fun with these two." He pushed Becca out of the way and put his dirty hand on Mrs. Carrington's covered knee. "This one needs to learn I'm the boss."

Mrs. Carrington flailed her arms and legs. Her boot connected with his head, and the color drained from her face. She cowered as far back in the corner of the stagecoach as she could.

He howled and kneaded his head. He reached and grabbed Mrs. Carrington's hand and savagely ripped her wedding rings from her finger. He passed them to Clanton. "These will bring us more money than the necklace."

Mrs. Carrington kicked him again, and he pointed his gun at her head. "You're gonna git yourself killed if you're not careful, old lady. Lucky for you, I'm not through with you yet."

Becca scooted close to Mrs. Carrington. Gus pushed Becca to the floor and grabbed Mrs. Carrington's leg.

Mrs. Carrington cried out, thrashed her feet, and caught him in the eye with her heel.

Groaning, he recovered and shoved the barrel of his gun to her throat.

She kicked and pummeled him off balance.

Clanton grabbed the back of his coat and yanked him out of the stagecoach.

Red-faced, Gus scowled and shook off Clanton. He pointed his gun at Mrs. Carrington.

Sweat beading on her face, Becca moved to shield her but stumbled. As she righted herself and fell on the bench next to her, a deafening shot rang out.

Mrs. Carrington screamed and grabbed her shoulder. Blood oozed and spread through the material on her dress.

Becca gasped and pressed her hand on the hole,

but blood flowed between her fingers. After yanking off her scarf, she pressed it against Mrs. Carrington's wound. "Keep pressure on it with the scarf to stop the bleeding."

Mrs. Carrington's face paled. She trembled and clutched the cloth as she pressed it to her shoulder.

Becca stared at the gun pointed at them. She couldn't stop her hands from shaking. What would keep these men from ending their lives? She shook and waited for the bullet to hit her next.

Clanton steadied his gun and snarled. "Let's take the money and leave. You said nobody would get hurt. We got one dead body already, and the other one don't look too good. Now you're fixin' to kill them. I'm not gonna hang for no murders."

Recovered, Gus scoffed at him. "It's too late to worry about hangin' for murder. Like you said, we already killed one of them, and the other one will most likely die. What's two more?"

Becca fisted her hands. This was it. She was going to die today. Well, not if she could help it. There must be something she could do. Becca cleared her throat. "This road's a straight shot to Massillon. The sheriff will come looking for the stagecoach when it doesn't arrive on time. You'll be caught if you don't leave soon."

She held her breath as Gus pointed his gun inches from her face.

Gus cocked his head to the side. "We're taking you both with us."

She blew out a breath. Mrs. Carrington would never make it. She would resist them, and they would kill her. They had no reason to put up with her. If she stayed still, the bleeding would stop. If not, she might bleed out. Was the bullet in her shoulder, or did it go through? If it was still in her shoulder, she might get an infection. If they left Mrs. Carrington here, the sheriff would find her and take her to Matt. She had to convince them to take her instead. "No. Leave her. She'll slow you down."

Gus paused and stared at her. "You might be right. We'll leave her and take you." He threw her a bag. "Fill it with any money and jewelry you're hidin'." He pointed his gun at Becca. "Hurry it up. Don't make me have to come in there, or you're both dead."

The heat rose in her body. She snatched the bag and flung Mrs. Carrington's purse in it, then leaned close to her ear. "Keep pressure on your shoulder. It's true what I told them. When the stagecoach doesn't arrive, the sheriff will come looking for it."

Becca pushed her water, cookies, and a blanket near Mrs. Carrington. She grabbed the two remaining blankets and stepped outside.

Gus grasped her arm. "Hand over the bag."

Becca passed him the valuables.

He brushed her fingers and winked.

Eyes wide, she pushed past him and stepped over Lester Stone's lifeless body. She knelt next to his brother, Frank Stone, who lay motionless on the ground. Blood oozed from the gaping wound in his head. She ripped the bottom of her skirt and tied the material around his head. Her hand on Frank's neck, his pulse was weak. He was alive! She covered him with both blankets.

The bandit jabbed her side with his gun. "Get on the horse behind him."

Becca gritted her teeth and mounted the horse. She gripped the sides of Gus's filthy coat and distanced herself from him as much as possible. The horse bolted, nearly throwing her off. Where were the men taking her? As the horses' hooves pounded the dirt, she contemplated her chances of escape if she rolled off the horse and ran. *No,* it was far too risky. They had more than enough time to shoot her before she could reach the surrounding woods.

Becca guessed about an hour had passed when the men reined in their horses not far from a farmhouse with smoke billowing from the chimney. Clanton pointed to the modest dwelling. "I'm cold to the bone, tired, and hungry. We need a warm place to sleep. Let's stay here tonight."

Clanton spat a vile slug of tobacco juice. He dug his fingers into his pouch and deposited a fresh wad in his mouth. "We'll pass this 'un off as our sister and play nice. I don't want no more trouble." Clanton dismounted and tied their horses to the hitching rail.

Gus gripped Becca's arm. "Don't you dare say one word to these people about who we are or what we have done, or I'll kill you and them."

Becca shivered and asked God to intervene and save her and whoever was inside. They proceeded forward. This poor family had no idea what they were in for. These men had bragged about robbing banks, and shooting and killing others before today on the way here. She considered running for the woods. No, they would shoot her in the back before she could hide.

Clanton knocked on the door.

A woman appeared. "Yes?" She studied them with suspicion.

He removed his hat and revealed his gleaming bald head. "Our sister isn't well and needs food."

The woman opened the door wide. "Come in, you poor dear." She clasped Becca's hand and led her to the table. "I have venison stew on the stove. We are about to have dinner. Please join us."

Becca shuffled her feet and didn't say a word. She wanted to warn the woman to shut the door. No, they would kill her and this family.

A man with a stocky build and handsome face held out his hand to Clanton. "My name is Dewey Grayson. And this is my wife, Nora." He tousled a young boy's light brown hair. "This is Luke who is six." He gestured to a little girl with auburn hair and big hazel eyes like her mamm. "Patricia is four."

Oh no, the Graysons had children. These men wouldn't tolerate them making noise or asking questions. This was not good.

Clanton ignored his hand and plopped in a chair at the kitchen table. Gus followed, and the two outlaws used spoons to slop food in their mouths. The noise of their piggish chomping made the children giggle. *Children, please keep quiet.*

Mr. Grayson wrinkled his forehead and then drew his mouth in a grim line.

Mr. Grayson's back stiffened. He knew something wasn't right with these men. *Good.* Becca moved to the warm wood-burning stove and held out her palms. He didn't understand how much danger they were in. She had to warn him, but how? If she wasn't careful, the bandits might hear her and no telling what they would do then.

Mr. Grayson joined her. "Are you ill? Is there anything I can do for you? You are afraid of these men. Am I right?" He passed her a cup of hot coffee.

Becca accepted the coffee and sipped it. She whispered, "I'm not their sister. I'm not sick, and yes, I'm afraid of these men. You should be too. They're dangerous. They robbed the stagecoach, killed two men, shot a woman, and kidnapped me."

Gus yelled at her. "You get over here and join us at the table. Now!"

She shook as she walked to the table.

Gus grabbed her arm and jerked her toward him and whispered in her ear. "You better keep your mouth shut, or I'll kill this family and make you watch. Their blood will be on your hands. Got it?"

She jerked her arm free and sat in the chair farthest away from him. Mr. Grayson's face reddened and he clenched his jaw. Would he find a way to defend his family? He wasn't near as big as these men. What could he do? She bowed her head and prayed a silent prayer for herself and the family's safety again.

Mr. Grayson headed for the door. "I am going to put your horses in the barn."

Gus chomped on a biscuit and didn't respond.

She chewed a bite of stew. Gus must not suspect Dewey Grayson had caught on that these men were no good. He didn't stop him. Maybe Dewey had a gun in the barn. Her spoon shook. It was their only chance of survival. She swallowed the food in her mouth and willed it to stay in her stomach.

Luke, the freckle-faced little boy, poked the fat man's arm. "You eat funny."

Gus yelled at the child, "Get away from me, and shut your mouth."

She threw her spoon on the table, flew out of her chair, and grabbed the little boy away from Gus. A click followed by a thunderous bang sounded. Becca trembled and pulled Luke to the floor. She wrapped her arm around him.

The room erupted with screams and the clatter of overturned furniture. She raised her head. Mr. Grayson had shot Clanton in the chest.

Clanton fell with a thud. Blood pooled around his upper body.

Gus dumped the table over for cover, drew his pistol, and blasted Mr. Grayson in the arm.

Mr. Grayson lost his footing, and his gun skidded across the floor, hit the wall, and landed a short distance from him. He reached for it, but it was just out of his grasp.

Before Becca could stop him, the young boy jumped to his feet. She grabbed him quick and hugged him to her. Gus laughed and pointed his gun at Luke. He stared at Mr. Grayson. "You make another move, and I'll shoot your boy." Gus moved, lifted the gun, and stuck it in his pants. He pointed the gun in Mr. Grayson's face. "Lay still."

Luke shouted, "Papa!" and held out his arms.

Becca whirled in front of the child and pushed him behind her. Her body tensed.

Gus moved the gun in her direction. "Boy, shut up."

Staring down the barrel of Gus's gun, she met his eyes. "Leave him alone."

Mr. Grayson struggled to remain on his feet but fell. He raised his head. "Do not harm my son."

Mrs. Grayson yelped and rushed to Becca and Luke, while holding Patricia.

Becca's knees knocked. She understood Mrs. Grayson wanted to protect her children, but she had made a bad situation worse by joining her and Luke. She herded the mamm and the children behind her. Maybe if Mrs. Grayson could take them to the bedroom, they could climb out a window and escape. Otherwise, she suspected this would be the last day any of them would spend on this earth. Gus was getting angrier by the minute. "Let them go in the other room."

Gus nudged her with the gun. "You get over here and patch my friend up. They're not going anywhere. I'm keeping an eye on all of you. It makes no difference to me who I shoot." He pointed the gun at Patricia. "I mean it. One wrong move and you're all dead."

Mrs. Grayson shuffled the children over to her husband.

Gus shifted the gun to Mrs. Grayson. "Lady, weren't you listenin'? I said stay put. You move again, and I'm shootin' you in the head. Got it?"

Mrs. Grayson whimpered and bobbed her head up and down.

Becca thought her heart would burst out of her

chest. She had to concentrate. Their lives depended on it. Mr. Grayson had blood flowing from his gunshot wound. She had to act fast. "I'm going to the washbasin to get a towel for Mr. Grayson."

Gus narrowed his eyes. "Make it quick."

Becca moved to the table near the washbasin and threw Mrs. Grayson a towel. "Apply pressure to your husband's injury." She pumped water into a bowl and grabbed several towels, then knelt next to Clanton. Her skin crawled to be near him. Blood gushed from the gunshot wound. His face was colorless. Eyes glazed over, he looked dead. She glanced at Gus who was peering out the window. She hurried to check for a pulse. There was none. She quickly closed Clanton's eyelids before Gus discovered his friend's demise.

Goose bumps lined her arms and crawled up the back of her neck. What would Gus do if he knew Clanton was dead? She had to convince him otherwise. She needed time for the sheriff to find Mrs. Carrington and discover she had been kidnapped. He would come looking for her. Would the sheriff find her in time? Mr. Grayson came in too soon with his gun to have had time to put the bandits' horses in the barn. Maybe the horses would alert the sheriff. He would surely question why the horses weren't in the barn. Wouldn't he? She glanced at the dead bandit. His blood pooled on the floor and stained her dress.

Gus nudged Clanton with his gun. "Hey, wake up, ole buddy." Face fierce, he pointed the gun at Becca. "What did you do to him?"

She hurried and put two fingers to his wrist to pretend to find a pulse. "He's breathing but knocked out cold. He probably won't wake up for a while." She put her hand to her throat and stared at the floor.

"What are ya waitin' for, do something!" Gus towered over her. "If he dies, all of you die."

Chapter Sixteen

Matt bid farewell to his patient. He shut the door. The door burst open. He stumbled and the sheriff grabbed his arm. "Sheriff, are you all right?"

The sheriff bent to catch his breath. "Sorry, Doc. The stagecoach is late. I'm worried. There have been recent robberies of other stagecoaches. This coach was carrying the bank money. Will you come with me to retrace the coach's route in case someone is found injured? Last week, two people were killed near Canton by robbers."

Matt accepted his bag from Dorothy. "Yes, of course." He glanced at Dorothy. "Close the office. Take the day off."

She patted his arm. "You men be careful."

Matt followed the sheriff and climbed in his wagon. They rode for miles. He spotted the stagecoach. Two men were on their stomachs on the ground. Were the men alive? Blood stained the ground surrounding them. A voice rang out. He jumped out of the coach. "Check the bodies on the ground. I will check inside the stagecoach." He opened the door. His eyes widened. "Mother, what happened to your shoulder? What are you doing on the stagecoach? What happened?" After removing the soiled scarf, He examined the wound. "Who shot you?" Hand behind her back, he eased her forward and evaluated her shoulder from behind. "The bullet went straight through."

Eloise pushed his hand away, cried, and touched his face. "Never mind why I am here or that I have been shot. Becca and I ended up on the same stagecoach. She boarded the stagecoach in Berlin. We were the only two passengers. Two men attacked us and shot the driver, the guard, and me. They stole the bank money and kidnapped Becca. Patch me up quick. The sheriff must go find her, now!"

"Wait here a minute." Matt jumped out and hurried to the sheriff.

His heart raced. The love of his life was in danger. Had the robbers harmed her? Where was she? "Becca was on the stagecoach with my mother. The outlaws kidnapped her. My mother has been shot. She will be fine, but I have to apply sutures to her injury before we leave. I will hurry. We have got to find Becca!"

The sheriff's voice heightened, as he held out his palms. "We have to take your mother back to town and bring some deputies with us. Frank and Lester Stone are both dead. I'll tie them to your horse and take them with me. You drive the stagecoach. Leave her with Ruth. We need to tell her what happened to her sister, and then join me at my office. After I drop these two off at the funeral parlor, I'll join you. Then we'll head out to find Becca."

Matt raked a hand through his hair. They had to move fast. "These men are killers. We don't have much time if Becca is going to survive." He trembled hearing his words out loud. He stepped inside the stagecoach and prepared what he needed to tend to his mother's wounds. He applied sutures and a bandage.

The sheriff poked his head inside the stagecoach. "Let's get a move on and find them before dark. The bandits will want a warm place to sleep and something good to eat. They'll choose a house and take over. Let's hope we find them and Becca before these outlaws harm anyone else."

"I agree." Matt told his mother they were leaving right away.

Matt stopped the stagecoach in front of Ruth's. He opened the coach door and offered his hand. His mother went rigid. "I cannot stay here. Take me home. Horace is out of town, but the maid and butler can take care of me."

"I do not have time to take you anywhere. Ruth deserves to hear from me and not someone else that her sister has been taken hostage. There is no time to make two stops. You must make the best of this. When I return, I will take you home." He lifted her out and carried her to the front door. He banged it with his foot.

Ruth opened the door and gasped. She stared at Mrs. Carrington and opened the door wider for them to enter. "What in the world happened to your mother?" He lowered his mother to the sofa.

Matt put his hands on Ruth's shoulders. "The stagecoach was robbed. Mother has been shot, and Becca has been kidnapped. I am sorry to put you in this position, but I had to bring her here. I had to tell you what happened, and I do not have time to take her somewhere else. I have got to go with the sheriff and find her."

Ruth put a hand to her heart. "Please bring her back. I do not know what I would do without her. Be careful." She grabbed his arm.

He hugged her and left.

Matt found the sheriff in his office with two deputies. "Have you sent anyone to notify Isaac Kelly of what has happened? He would want to come. Besides, he is an excellent marksman." Matt knew Isaac was a good shooter from previous conversations they'd had.

"I ran into him at the livery and told him about the robbery and Becca. He should be here any minute." The sheriff handed Matt a gun belt with two Colt revolvers.

The idea of Becca alone with outlaws made his jaw tighten. If they harmed her, he would go crazy. He pushed the thought she may be dead out of his mind as he wrapped the gun belt around his hips.

Isaac joined them. "Matt, how are you holding up? You must be sick with worry."

"I am. Thanks for coming. We are going to need all the help we can get."

The sheriff deputized them and addressed the men. "We'll track them from the stagecoach. I suspect they will stop at a homestead to find food and shelter. Let's hope they won't harm the family they choose to intrude on. Be careful and remember they've already proved they're armed and dangerous. Let's go."

Matt put his hand on Isaac's shoulder. "Isaac, I do not know what I will do if anything happens to her."

"She is going to be all right. We are going to rescue her and bring her home. Becca is like a sister to me and you have become a good friend. I am right with you every step of the way. It is time to show these men we mean business." He patted his rifle.

Matt rode alongside Isaac and the other men. He scouted with them for signs of the bandits. After a while, the sheriff raised his hand and pointed to a house half hidden by trees. "This is a perfect place for them to stop. It's out of the way."

The sheriff guided his horse to a position where he could face them. "I'll go on foot and see what I can find. I'll wave you over if they're there. Secure the horses and stay hidden in this brush until I signal. Deputies, go around back. Matt and Isaac, you keep low and make your way close to the front." He dismounted and handed the reins to one of the deputies.

The sheriff approached the house and crouched below the window. The men were ready to move on his signal; they focused on the man in charge.

The sheriff knocked on the door.

A woman appeared. The two spoke for a few moments, then she shook her head and shut the door.

The sheriff walked toward them. "They're not here. Let's keep going." They untied the horses, mounted, and resumed their search.

Matt anticipated each house would be the one where they would find Becca. As more time passed, his mind cast doubt on finding her before dark.

The sheriff reined in his horse and pointed to a small ranch where smoke billowed from the chimney. Two horses were tied to the hitching rail. "Dewey and Nora Grayson live here. They have two small children. It's not like Dewey to leave horses tied out front. The barn's in the back. Whenever I visited, he always insisted on taking my horse to his barn. I have a gut feeling about this one."

Matt straightened his shoulders. "Let me scout out the house this time."

The sheriff dismounted. "No. I'm going, and you're staying here. Tie your horses to a tree and watch for my signal. I'll wave my hand if they're in there, and then everyone duck and be ready with guns drawn. Line up behind me by the front door and keep low to the ground. When I point to the door, we'll barge in."

Matt squeezed his thumbs in his fists. There was no time for an argument. He prayed for God to protect the posse and Becca.

Slow and deliberate, the sheriff snuck to the house with gun in hand.

Matt held his breath. The sheriff waved.

Matt, Isaac, and the deputies sprang into action. His gun cocked, he readied himself.

The sheriff whispered, "Dewey's on the floor, along with another man. Becca's tending one of the outlaws. Blood is pooled around him. Another man is holding everyone at gunpoint. Nora Grayson and the two children are huddled in a corner of the room."

Matt could see his breath. Becca was alive, but this ordeal was not over yet. He edged closer and flattened himself next to the door. "This will be tricky."

Isaac sighed and kept his long gun tucked close to his chest. "We must be careful. Innocent people could get killed in the crossfire."

On the sheriff's command, Matt raised his leg and kicked open the door.

They rushed in. Furniture clattered. Nora and the children screamed. Shots rang out.

Matt's heart pounded as bullets whizzed by his head. He rolled to the ground and shot the big gunman in both legs. The man fell to the floor, screaming in pain.

Matt's heart plummeted. Becca lay flattened on the floor. Nora and the children sat huddled in the corner sobbing. The woman he loved didn't move.

The big man grappled with his gun in hand and aimed at Matt, but Isaac's bullet hit his hand. The gun skidded across the stone floor near the fireplace.

The sheriff kicked the gun out of reach and yanked the other gun from the man's holster. He rolled him on his stomach and pulled his arms behind his back. He slapped handcuffs on the stout and fat bandit's wrists. "You did a fine job, men."

Becca scrambled to her feet and ran to Matt.

He held her tight and pressed her head against his chest, then pulled her back. Her dress was splattered with blood. He searched her for any sign of injury. "Where is this blood coming from?"

"I'm all right. It's from the dead man on the floor. I'm glad to see you, but when shots rang out, I feared you would be killed. I couldn't stand it if anything happened to you. Hold me for a minute."

"I was sick with worry about you. You mean everything to me."

"I love you and have missed you."

Luke tugged at Matt's sleeve. "Can you help my pa?"

Becca stepped to the boy's daed and addressed Matt. "Mr. Grayson was shot by one of the robbers at pretty close range." When Matt moved to care for the injured man, she joined Mrs. Grayson and held her hand out to Matt. "This is Dr. Carrington. He'll help your husband."

Mrs. Grayson thanked Matt and hovered over her husband.

Luke knelt beside Matt. "Is my pa going to die?"

Matt removed his small hand still holding his sleeve. "Your pa is going to be fine. I will take good care of him." He used his knife and cut away the sleeve of Mr. Grayson's shirt to examine the wound. He lifted the man's arm to check him from behind. "The bullet went clean through."

Isaac put his hand on Becca's shoulder. "You scared us, little lady. I am glad you are all right. Your sister will be relieved too."

"You shot the robber in time to save Matt. We are fortunate to have you in our lives. Thank you. When you all came in the door, I was shocked and relieved. I'm anxious to hug Ruth and Benjamin. I

thought I might not see any of you ever again."
Tears stained her cheeks.

"No need to thank me. You're like family to me."
He leaned over to Matt. "Can I do anything?"

"Yes. My bag is tied to my saddle. I need it to
suture and bandage Mr. Grayson's wound."

"Consider it done." Isaac winked and hurried out.

Matt chatted with Mr. Grayson until Isaac returned and handed him the bag. He pulled out
everything he needed and tended to Mr. Grayson's
gunshot wound. He could not steady his hands. The
thought Becca could have died today would not
leave his mind. Pushing this aside, he focused on his
patient.

Mr. Grayson spoke to Becca. "God bless you, miss.
You risked your life to protect me and my family. You
are a brave woman. I was useless, but you kept your
wits about you. How did you do it?"

Becca pressed her hands to her heart. "God deserves all the credit. Without Him, I would have
fallen apart."

Matt finished with Mr. Grayson and moved to the
bandit motionless on the floor. He checked for a
pulse. "He is dead."

Nora whirled around to Becca. "Was he dead this
whole time?"

Becca blew out a breath. "Yes, but I feared we
would all be killed if I didn't convince Gus otherwise."

Matt slid his arm around Becca's waist. "You are
one courageous woman. You must be exhausted. It
is time for me to take you home."

The sheriff peered in the door. "Isaac has the

prisoner outside. Do you want to check his wounds before we leave?"

Matt headed for the door and raked a hand through his hair. "Yes. I will have a look at him."

Becca gripped Matt's sleeve. "Did you find your mamm? How is she? What about Frank Stone, the driver? I checked his brother, but he was dead."

Matt ran his finger along her worried brow. "We found them. Mother will recover, thanks to you. Frank Stone didn't survive."

Becca frowned and shook her head. "Those poor men didn't stand a chance. Lester was killed first. Frank passed them the bank money. They could have taken the chest and left, but they shot him anyway. They're coldhearted killers."

Matt left to examine Gus, glad the sheriff had gagged the man with a handkerchief. He ripped a towel and tied the strips around the three gunshot wounds. "The shots did not hit anything major. He will be good to ride back to town. I will bring what I need to the jail and take the bullets out then. I do not want him anywhere near my office."

The sheriff and deputy threw the moaning man over a saddle and secured him with rope.

Even though groans escaped the man, the gag prevented him from speaking. Matt shook his head. The murderer deserved to suffer. He waited until the sheriff and men left with the prisoner and then joined Becca.

Becca slid her arm through his. "I'll ride with you."

"I have missed having you close." He mounted the horse and reached for her hand. "Ruth must be beside herself with worry. I left Mother with her when I told her what happened. I did not want to inconvenience Ruth, but I did not have time to make other arrangements. I was frantic to find you. I hope it was not too awkward for Ruth."

Becca stepped back. "I can't imagine your mamm being nice to my sister. I hope she didn't argue with Ruth. You did put her in an awkward position."

"It was not the best idea, but time was of the essence. As soon as we reach Massillon, I will take her home. It was awkward for me, too. I have not talked to my mother for a while now. I wanted nothing to do with her."

Becca mounted the horse and rested her chin on his back. She wrapped her arms about him and didn't say another word.

Isaac followed the sheriff and deputies and rode alongside Becca and Matt. "How are you two holding up?"

Matt slowed the horse. "Glad Becca is safe, and none of us were shot. I felt better having you there, friend."

Becca said, "*Yes*, thanks again, Isaac."

The horses' hooves pounded against the dirt. They rode in silence.

Matt warmed at having her arms around him. She had been through a dangerous situation. The blood-stained dress and splats on her arms and face had scared him. Those outlaws had no conscience. She had protected others and shown courage and strength most women could not have mustered in such a terrifying situation. He loved her even more, if possible. She was too quiet. What was on her mind? Would she allow him to court her again?

His heart broke for Becca. She was exhausted.

He should have taken his mother to the office. Dorothy would not have liked taking care of her, but she would have done it for him. Becca was tired and weak. His mother was the last person she would have wanted her sister to have to deal with, let alone having to face his mother herself. He would get his mother out of their house as soon as possible. He was relieved his mother was all right, but he meant what he said. She had done enough meddling in his private life. He wanted nothing to do with her.

Chapter Seventeen

Becca, Matt, and Isaac, breathless and disheveled, stepped inside Ruth's house.

Ruth's tears stained her cheeks as she wrapped her arms around Becca. She stepped back and held her sister's shoulders. "I am happy to see you. Why is there blood on your dress? Were you shot?"

Becca hugged her sister. "Don't worry. It's the robber's blood, not mine. One's dead and one's in jail. I'm fine. It must've been horrible for you to wait and wonder about me, but the ordeal is over. I'm blessed Matt, Isaac, the sheriff, and his deputies rescued me." She missed Benjamin and couldn't wait to wrap her arms around him. "Where's Benjamin?"

Ruth's body relaxed. "He is at Hattie's. We will let him stay with her tonight. You can see him in the morning. You need to rest." She moved to Isaac and held him tight. "I am glad you are home safe. Thank you for bringing my sister back to me."

Isaac kissed her cheek. "I consider Becca my sister too." He rubbed his forehead. "Since I have had my hug, I must get home and catch up on my chores. You and Becca have plenty to talk about and will want some time alone. I will stop by your shop and see you tomorrow."

Ruth blushed. "Becca and I might take the day off from work. If I am not there, visit us here." She kissed his cheek, then closed the door behind him.

Matt clasped Becca's hand and led her to the chairs near his mother. Her eyes were closed. "Mother, I would like to hear your version of what happened." Eloise opened her eyes wide. "Do not be ridiculous. We can talk later. You need to take me home and let Becca rest. This ordeal has worn her out."

Mrs. Carrington must not have been sleeping. She was too quick to answer Matt's question. It was hard to tell if she had softened after what they had been through together. Maybe she would have a change of heart toward her since she had saved her life. If she did, at least something good would come of this horrific experience.

He shook his head. "This will take but a few minutes. Start talking."

"We were robbed, and you know the rest."

Matt shook his head. "Why did they take Becca and not you?"

"Becca suggested they leave me, since I was wounded, and take her."

Mrs. Carrington's voice was laced with regret. Becca liked this side of Matt's mother.

His eyes went from Becca to his mother. "Let me get this straight. Becca offered herself instead of you?"

"Yes, she did."

"After all the petty and mean things you have said and done to her, she saved you?"

Eloise put a hand to her heart. "Yes, and I appreciate what she did more than I can say." She spoke in a quiet voice and looked at Becca. "I would not be here if it was not for you. I do not know where you found the courage to stand up to those men."

Becca's eyes drooped from exhaustion, but her heart soared. Mrs. Carrington had spoken kind words to her in a sincere and genuine voice. "Your words mean a great deal to me, but God was with me, and He deserves all the credit. I'm happy Matt found you and tended to your wound before it became serious." Matt patted Becca's arm. "I have been thoughtless making you both talk about this now. It is time for us to leave. Mother, I will take you home. We can discuss the robbery tomorrow." He opened the door. "The sheriff and his deputy must have picked up the stagecoach. Ruth, do you mind if I borrow your buggy to take my mother home? I will return it tomorrow."

"No, of course not. Take it."

Eloise asked, "Will you take me to your house? Your father will not be home until around noon tomorrow. He went to a meeting."

"Yes." He draped her shawl over her shoulders. "I'll bring the buggy to the front in a few minutes." He went to the barn.

She supported her arm with her other. "Thank you for taking care of me."

Hand on her hip, Ruth stared at Eloise. "After what my sister did for you, I hope you will search your heart and accept Matt and Becca as a couple."

Eloise's face heated and she did not respond. Matt pushed open the door and helped Eloise from the sofa. He kissed Becca and Ruth on their cheeks. "Ruth, thank you for taking such good care of Mother. Becca, I'll check on you tomorrow."

Becca kissed his cheek. "You coming to rescue me meant a lot to me. I'll never forget it."

"I would not have had it any other way. Isaac was right. You and Ruth must want time alone to talk. Get a good night's rest."

Mrs. Carrington nodded and left with Matt.

Would Mrs. Carrington express her regret for her rude behavior and apologize to Matt for all the trouble she had caused them? Maybe this was God's way of bringing them together with his mamm's blessing. She shouldn't get her hopes up just yet. She must wait and find out what Matt had to say about his conversation with Mrs. Carrington.

Becca settled on the sofa. "I can't believe Matt brought Mrs. Carrington to your house."

Ruth sat next to her and covered her with a quilt. "He was in a desperate rush. He did not have time to take her anywhere else."

"Imagine my unhappy surprise to see Matt's mamm in the stagecoach and no other passengers. If I could've walked to Massillon, I would have."

Ruth fetched towels for her sister to wipe her face and hands. "How did she react?"

She shrugged and pinched her nose. "She insulted me as usual."

"Did she know you two were no longer together?"

"She did but wanted to make sure I didn't change my mind and attempt to win him back." Matt was the first person she wanted to behold after the robbery. In his arms, she calmed. She missed him every minute they weren't together. She'd considered having a change of heart concerning Matt, and then it all came rushing back as to why she ended their courtship in the first place.

Ruth sat in a chair close to Becca. "Do not let his mother steal another minute from you and Matt. You belong together."

Becca closed her eyes for a moment. She didn't see any way possible out of this situation. "I'm at a loss as to what to do. I wish there was a way, but there isn't."

Ruth sighed and raised her hands. "Maybe after she has time to reflect on how you saved her life, she will have a change of heart. Relax while I make us some tea." She rose and went to the kitchen.

Becca pictured Mrs. Carrington. She was quiet, reserved, and her facial expressions looked less harsh. She seemed different. Was it because she was injured and tired, or was it something else?

A few moments later, Ruth returned with tea and offered her a cup. "I am selfish to ask after all you have been through, but I must. Please tell me more about the robbery."

"It was frightening." Becca rubbed the dull ache in her forehead. "The robbers threatened to abuse us, stole our money and Mrs. Carrington's jewelry."

"How did she get shot?" Ruth's face flushed and she gripped her dress.

"She kicked one of the men and injured his eye. He recovered his balance and aimed his gun at her. I moved to shield her, but his shot caught her shoulder. The other bandit got nervous and wanted to leave. His partner suggested they take us with them. I convinced them to leave her behind."

"You are a better person than me." She waved her hand. "Mrs. Carrington did not deserve such kindness after what she has put you through. Where did they take you? Did they . . . touch you?"

Becca's hand shook as she sipped the tea. "No. They shoved me with their gun and pushed me around, but nothing like that. They stopped at a family's house outside of Massillon. Dewey and Nora Grayson are husband and wife. Their children are Luke and Patricia. Mr. Grayson joined me as I warmed by the stove. I told him the men were dangerous."

Ruth gripped the arms of the chair, her knuckles white. "Where were the children during this?"

"The Graysons' son, Luke, approached the robbers." Becca recounted how the child intervened during the time she and his family spent with the men. "It's a miracle he wasn't shot on the spot. I had no doubt they might shoot him to make a point. They proved they had no problem with killing people." She sighed. "There was never a dull moment through the whole ordeal." Becca pictured their leering and quivered. Their cold and scary eyes had frightened her. She was convinced they would have killed her and the Grayson family if she had not been rescued.

Ruth bolted upright and clutched her apron. "What did they do?"

She exhaled through her teeth and recounted the entire episode to Ruth.

Ruth held her face in her hands and wept. "I prayed God would bring you back to me unharmed. You have spoiled me. I never thought we would live together again after I left home. Yet, here you are. I treasure our time together. I do not know what Benjamin and I would do if anything happened to you."

Becca caressed Ruth's hand. She thought several times her life might end. All the faces of the people she loved flashed before her more than once when the robbers pointed their guns at her. She planned to shove this horrible nightmare out of her mind. "Everything happened fast. I didn't have time to panic. Besides, I learned firsthand, God does provide us with the courage and words to say when we need them. If I hadn't had my faith, I would've panicked."

Ruth wiped her face with the back of her hand. "You have always been the strong one. I had Caleb when I left home. You came alone. It is another reason I admire you. I wish I had one ounce of the strength you do."

Becca patted Ruth's knee. "Caleb dying young was much harder for you. You had to survive without help from anyone. We are both strong." She flexed her arms and giggled. "As for Mrs. Carrington, she's almost as bad as the bandits." They laughed. Becca slapped a hand on her mouth. "I shouldn't say such things, it's not proper."

Ruth giggled and reached to smooth Becca's messy hair. "It was at Mrs. Carrington's expense, but the remark caused us to laugh and we needed it."

She set her teacup on the table. "I never want to

experience anything like it again. Hester begged me to take the later stagecoach because it doesn't carry the bank's money. I should've taken her advice. Tell me about *your* time with Matt's mamm."

"She infuriated me when she insisted you and Matt were not right for each other. I let her know how much I detested her behavior toward you. I could not stand the sound of her voice and told her to stop talking. I told her if she did not, I would dump her off at the Inn."

Becca put her hand to her mouth. "I don't blame you for speaking what was on your mind. The woman brings out the worst in me, too."

Ruth sneezed and pulled a handkerchief from her apron pocket. "I have to admit she would be a terrible mother-in-law. Enough talk about Mrs. Carrington. How was your visit with Hester?"

Becca told Ruth about her time with Hester and Grace, delivering the young couple's boppli. Her eyes widened. "With all the bad news, I almost forgot my exciting news. I visited with Mamm and Daed." She recounted how she came to visit them.

Ruth's chin snapped up. "I am relieved Mother is all right. Were they worried their neighbors might see you there?"

She hadn't encountered the bishop or familiar faces while walking to their house. "No, they didn't mention it. It was understood I shouldn't be there, but Mamm's fall prompted the visit. The Amish mamm we helped had no problem with me assisting Hester. The other mamms we helped weren't Amish and lived outside of town."

Ruth put a hand to her heart. "I am thrilled you

told them more about Benjamin. I am anxious for them to meet him. I hope they visit soon."

"They're happy we were able to help him. They can't wait to meet him." She drew a breath and put a hand over her heart. "They want to come, but Daed told me it is hard for him to leave home because of taking care of the farm. He assured me they will visit in the near future."

Ruth scooted to the edge of her chair. "I understand. I am thankful we are a family again. I love receiving Mother's letters. When they do come here, Benjamin will light up their lives with his big brown eyes and sweet personality."

"Yes, and they will light up his life as well."

"Speaking of family, Benjamin has been asking about Matt. To him, Matt is already a part of this family. Where do you stand with him?"

She wanted to marry him, but she chose not to. She had shown Mrs. Carrington she was willing to do anything to protect her during the robbery. Would it mean anything to the woman? She had to put Mrs. Carrington out of her mind. There was no use guessing what the woman would or wouldn't do. She appeared to have a heart of stone. "You got a taste of Mrs. Carrington's manipulative personality. Nothing has changed there. Maybe now you understand my dilemma and why Matt and I can't be together. You must take Benjamin to visit Matt. It's best if I stay away from him."

Ruth crossed the room and selected a clean nightdress from the laundry. "Nonsense. You cannot let Mrs. Carrington dictate your life. After what you have been through, you must realize now more than ever, life is too short. You need to marry the man you love and honor Matt's request he not communicate with them. Do not coax him into trying to fix things with them. Let him be."

Becca lifted her arms and Ruth pulled her soiled dress from her. "I am going to pray and hope God intervenes in my situation with Matt." She winced. "Oh, I ache."

Ruth grimaced and touched Becca's side. "You have bruises the size of small plates." She slipped a clean nightdress over Becca's head. "I am praying God will find a way to bring you two back together."

"I need all the help I can get." She shifted to get into a comfortable position. "My bruises will heal. My heart is another matter." Mrs. Carrington had expressed genuine appreciation for what she had done for her during the robbery. Maybe by helping her during the robbery, Mrs. Carrington had gotten a glimpse of her character. If the robbery could bring them together, it was worth it. She better not get her hopes up yet. Once the woman healed, she might return to her arrogant self.

Chapter Eighteen

The next morning, Matt mixed batter for pancakes. Eggs crackled in the cast iron skillet on the stove. He placed bread and butter on the table and pulled milk out of the icebox. "How is the pain?" His mother entered the kitchen with one hand on her shoulder.

She gingerly sat. "I am sore all over, but the pain in my shoulder is diminishing. The whole ordeal was rather frightening. I am glad we are all safe."

He served her, then poured milk in their glasses. He had tossed and turned all night wondering what she said to Becca before the robbery. He was sure his mother had been unkind, given her history with Becca. Whatever she said to Ruth could not have been positive either, considering Ruth's stern face when they left. His mother was in pain, but it did not excuse her behavior. He could not wait any longer to find out what happened during her stay with Becca's sister. "I was surprised Ruth spoke in a harsh tone to you when we left. Did you say something to upset her?"

His mother drank her milk and wiped her mouth. "Becca had confided in her about our conversations. She is angry I do not approve of you and Becca courting."

He slammed the bottle of milk on the table. "I am too. Mother, if you do not do everything in your power to convince Becca you would be blessed to have her for a daughter-in-law after all she has done for you, I will never speak to you again. I would not want to be associated with such an ungenerous person."

"I am appreciative for all she did for me during the robbery, but it does not mean she is the right woman for you. All my concerns about her being a suitable wife for you remain true."

Matt raked his hand through his hair and grunted. "You make it hard for me to love you sometimes, and this is one of those times. You could have risked your life for hers, but you did not. You measure someone's worth by how much money they have acquired and not by their integrity, their honor, and how they treat others. Did you think only of yourself during the robbery? How important was your money when you thought your life would end? Becca offered to sacrifice her life for yours. Would you have done the same for her? No, I think not."

"You remind me of my father. People took advantage of his goodness too. He gave money to his friends when they were in need, even when our family was struggling and could not spare it. He could have worked as an accountant for a big company and made a lot more money, but he did not like the way they shunned the middle class. He said the worth of a man was not how much money he had acquired but his honor and integrity. My mother tried to coax him to no avail. He should have listened to her, and we would have had a better life."

She grasped his hand. "Again, I appreciate what Becca did for me. I admire her courage and admit I misjudged her. I panicked and could not think straight. She did. Like it or not, money is what bought the nice house you were raised in and the clothes you wore and paid for your education."

He jerked his hand away and stiffened. "You are shallow and selfish. Money and status are too important to you. They will not bring you happiness and have blinded you to what is important in life. Love and family are what should matter. You care about your needs ahead of everyone else's. I cannot be in the same room with you. Eat your breakfast while I go to the living room and read. When you are finished, I will take you home."

"Your father and I provided a good life and education for you. We continue to involve you with influential people to further your research with your father and open your world to other opportunities." She touched her shoulder, then rested her hand in her lap. "You are the selfish one. You want to add Becca to our family, but you have not thought about how unhappy she might be in our world. Maybe she would be miserable planning dinner parties, mingling with our friends, and forcing herself to speak properly."

Matt flared his nostrils. "You have pointed out

these same concerns over and over again to me about Becca. I am sick of it. You need to shut your mouth. Do not mention Becca's name again. You are not half the woman she is and could learn a lesson in kindness by observing how she treats others. I do not care about the things you mentioned." Dispirited, he shook his head. "You are going to live a lonely life if you do not change your attitude. I suspect your friendships are shallow and meaningless. If you lost your money and status tomorrow, those high society friends of yours would dwindle away. You can choose to be a better person. Do it for yourself, for Father, for me, and for Becca." He strode out of the room.

A few minutes later, his mother passed him, selected a book from the shelf behind him, *Virginia of Virginia* by Amélie Rives, and glared at him. "I am going upstairs to read until after one when your father should be home."

He moved his eyes to the medical journal he was reading. He had nothing more to say to her. *Go upstairs.* Out of sight would be good. He flipped through the pages and his eyes got heavy. He settled in the chair and closed his eyes.

A hand on his shoulder wakened him. He opened his eyes and straightened. His journal slid off his lap and slapped the floor. "Mother, what's wrong?"

"Nothing's wrong. The time is after two. Your father should be home by now. I am ready to go."

Her stern face and direct tone set his teeth on edge. Rest must have provided her with energy. She was not bent over and her wincing in pain had ceased. No doubt, she was a tough woman. He would give her that.

He walked outside to the barn, readied his horse and buggy, and guided it to the front of his house. He helped her into the buggy. "Once I have delivered you to your front door, do not visit my home or office. Do not bother sending me invitations to dinner in the mail or any other correspondence." He focused on the dirt road ahead. She had no retort. *Good.*

Matt stopped the horses in front of his parents' house and handed the reins to the stable hand. He must have seen them coming. He thanked the stable hand. His father approached them. The horse's neighs and squeak of buggy wheels outside the house must have alerted his father they had arrived.

Horace Carrington helped his wife out of the buggy. "Eloise, what happened to your arm?"

His mother fell against her husband's chest. Stroking her hair, his father held her with his other arm. "Please talk to me, what happened?"

"Walk me inside. I would like tea. I will tell you the whole awful story."

Dr. Carrington Senior gestured to Matt. "Come in, son."

Matt paused. He would oblige. He wanted to hear what his mother would tell his father. Would she admit Becca had saved her life? What would his father's reaction be? *Yes,* he would not miss this conversation for anything. He followed his parents inside and sat across from them.

Iris entered the room. She carried a tray of teacups to Matt and offered him one. "Thank you."

Iris passed Eloise and Horace Carrington cups of tea.

Horace waved a dismissive hand. "None for me, Iris."

She bowed to him.

Eloise sipped her tea. "Iris, this is not hot enough. You bumbling simpleton, bring me another cup."

"Yes, Mrs. Carrington. Right away, Mrs. Carrington."

She reached for Matt's cup.

He shook his head. "Thank you, but my tea is fine." His mother treated the house staff terribly. "Mother, be kind to your housemaid. You scare her with your direct tone."

"How I treat Iris is none of your business. I pay her to do her job well. If I am not strict with her, she will become lazy."

"I doubt you are right. When you treat people with respect, they want to do a good job for you."

Iris hurried into the room and passed his mother a cup of tea. She waited for Mrs. Carrington to sip it.

"This is much better, Iris. You may go."

Iris bowed and left the room.

"Mother, do you ever thank your staff or praise them for a job well done? I have witnessed your softer side. I suggest you show it to us and others once in a while."

Mrs. Carrington huffed. "Horace, are you going to sit there and stay silent? Why are you letting our son talk to me this way?"

Horace Carrington cleared his throat. "Enough,

you two. Eloise, I want to know this instant. What happened to your arm?"

Eloise recounted the stagecoach robbery, murder, and kidnapping story. "The robber shot me. Becca turned her body to shield me, but the bullet hit my shoulder. The robbers insisted on taking Becca and me with them. She talked them into taking just her. The bandits agreed and left me in the stagecoach. Becca risked her life for me several times during the horrible ordeal. I feel terrible for treating her so mean." She wiped a tear.

Horace circled his arm around her shoulders. "I am thankful you are all right. Is there anything I can do for you?"

Eloise shook her head. "No, Matt took care of my shoulder. I'm fine."

Matt scratched his head and leaned forward. Had his mother had a change of heart toward Becca since their talk at his house? "Mother, have you reconsidered your opinion of Becca? From what you have told me earlier and now your words to Father, I cannot tell where you stand on Becca."

Eloise rubbed the back of her neck. "I have mixed emotions. I'm grateful for what Becca did for me, but she is not the right woman for you."

Matt held up his palm and stood. "Stop talking. I have heard enough. Under the circumstances, I find it appalling. I am going to do everything in my power to convince her to marry me. What I said before the robbery about not communicating with you has not changed. Please honor my request."

His father rose and faced Matt. "I will visit you

soon. We need to have a heart-to-heart talk in light of what has happened." He frowned and rested his hand on Matt's shoulder.

Matt's shoulders straightened. "Do not bother me with further rebuffs about how I should not marry Becca. I have had it with both of you." He turned on his heel and left.

Becca woke early. Whose dog was barking? She nestled in the covers. She would sleep for a few more minutes. The dog barked louder. She threw back the covers and climbed out of bed. She took a deep breath. Ruth must be frying bacon. *Yummy, it smells good.* She dressed and ambled to the kitchen. "I'm starving this morning." She plucked off a piece and chewed it slowly. She edged her body into a chair and winced.

Ruth cut a hefty piece of cinnamon bread and dropped it on her plate. "What is your plan for today? I am going to stay home and spend time with you. I will cook for you, and we can chat about everything but the robbery."

She licked her fingers and grimaced. "You're sweet. Although sore, I'm doing well. I slept through the night. Do stay home but not to take care of me. Let's take Benjamin to Lizzie's for dinner later. I'm craving her famous shepherd's pie."

Ruth poured her a cup of coffee. "After we go to Lizzie's, I will bring Benjamin home with me. You should go and thank Matt again. The man risked his life to rescue you. It is the least you should do. By the way, when I went to the barn to do the milking, our buggy and horse were in the barn. Matt must have stopped by very early this morning."

"Matt can walk to his office from here. I suspect he stopped by the sheriff's office on the way to work and asked him for a ride home at the end of the day. The sheriff's office is close to the medical office and his house is close to Matt's. He and the sheriff are good about helping each other."

Her body tensed. She should express her appreciation again to him for putting his life in danger to rescue her. Her head told her to stay away. Her heart told her to take whatever Mrs. Carrington threw her way and be with Matt. "I will talk to him about it in a few days."

"Matt deserves to hear from you today."

The fire in the stove crackled. Becca poked it with a long piece of wood. "I'm anxious but afraid to hear what his mother had to say to him after they left here. I hope she will want to start fresh and want to know me, but we both know she might stand firm in her negative opinion of me as a potential wife for Matt." Ruth's account of her conversation with Eloise while she cared for her broke her heart. She had hoped Matt's mamm had softened toward her with all they had been through during the robbery.

"You need to fall into Matt's arms, tell him you love him, and ignore Eloise Carrington. I will get dressed. We have time to sew on our keepsake pocket quilt tops before Hattie brings Benjamin home. I cannot keep enough in stock. Our keepsake pocket quilts are my best-selling item. Gather your needles and thread, and I'll join you in the sitting room in a few minutes."

Becca went to her room to change clothes. Spending time in front of the fire and with her sister and Benjamin this afternoon sounded good. After she was dressed, she joined Ruth in the sitting room and dug out her needle and thread from her quilting bag. She enjoyed laughing and chatting with her sister. It was nice to forget her woes for a few hours.

Benjamin arrived. He wrapped his arms around Becca's waist. "I asked Hattie where you were. She said you'd been taken by robbers. We prayed you'd be all right. I cried and cried."

She kissed the top of his head. "I'm fine, but your hugs make me even better." He was even more precious than she remembered.

Hattie Roll hung her head. She wrinkled her weathered face. "I could not lie. Too many people knew the truth."

"You were right to tell him the truth, and thank you for taking such good care of him."

"He takes care of me. He is a well-behaved little gentleman. He beat me and my nephew at tiddledywinks a dozen times. My brother and his wife took my nephew back to Canton, Ohio, on the early train this morning. We had a good time."

Benjamin beamed as Hattie talked.

Hands on her small hips, Hattie chatted for a few minutes and left.

Later in the afternoon, in the backyard, Benjamin chased after the chickens and caught a chick. "Ouch, it pecked me." He lowered it to the ground.

Becca checked his hand. "It didn't break the skin. You'll be all right. Don't pick them up." She guided him over to a pile of leaves and threw a handful in the air.

He giggled and did the same until a squirrel caught his attention, climbing a tree. He stretched his neck to watch it clamber to the top. "Can I take the squirrel inside and keep it for a pet?"

"No, he's not meant to be a pet. He would bite you harder than the chick. You can look but don't touch wild creatures."

He frowned and rubbed his hands.

Ruth laughed and leaned close to Becca's ear. "I overheard your conversation with Benjamin about the squirrels and thought of Eloise."

Becca giggled. "She does resemble a wild creature when she gets angry."

The two sisters grabbed Benjamin's hands and they went inside, chatted, and mixed and baked oatmeal cookies.

An hour passed, and Becca's stomach growled. "I'm hungry for dinner. We can have these cookies for dessert later. Let's go to Lizzie's."

She gathered their things and on their way to the restaurant, she paused as one person after another stopped to congratulate her. News had traveled fast. The sheriff and his deputies were the worst gossipers. They had told everyone how she had risked her life for Mrs. Carrington and the Grayson family. God deserved the credit for saving them, not her. She hoped she had made this clear to everyone who spoke to her.

Benjamin held Becca's and Ruth's hands. "We are never going to make it to Lizzie's with all the people wanting to praise you. You are a heroine in this town. Is it uncomfortable? You look tense."

"I'm embarrassed. I'm not used to all this attention." Becca bit her lip. Ready to put it behind her, she didn't enjoy answering the townsfolks' questions.

Benjamin pointed to Matt's office. "Let's go see Matt. I miss him."

Before they could stop him, he ran, pushed the door, and bolted inside. When they entered the office, Dorothy engulfed Becca against her pudgy frame. "I am happy you are here. I was sick with worry when I heard what happened. When are you coming back to work? I do not like blood, stitches, and needles. I am begging you, please come back."

Ruth untied her hat and held it. "What a great idea."

Matt exited the exam room with Clyde. "Becca, Ruth, Benjamin, welcome."

Benjamin skipped to Matt. "We came to visit you. Hattie told me you and the sheriff rescued Becca. She told her friend, Harry, you shot a robber. Can you show me how to shoot a gun?"

Becca gasped and tousled the child's hair. "You have big ears, and you're not going to learn to shoot a gun yet."

Matt put his hands on Benjamin's head. "When you are old enough, I will teach you how to shoot. In the meantime, I will buy you a toy gun."

Benjamin stuffed one of Dorothy's sugar cookies in his mouth. "What a great idea."

Clyde removed his hat and held out his hand to Becca. "It's all over town what you did for Matt's mother and Dewey's family. You're one tough woman. You surprised me. Why if I wasn't fifty, I'd ask ya to marry me."

She laughed.

"All kiddin' aside, I'm glad you're unharmed. If I would've known, I would've gone with Matt to get ya."

"You're a good friend, Clyde. Thank you for thinking of me." She could hardly concentrate on Clyde's words. Her stomach fluttered at the sight of Matt. Standing in the familiar office and not working beside him made her heart plummet. She longed to have his arms around her.

Ruth put her hat on. "Matt, come with us to Lizzie's for dinner. Dorothy, you come too."

Dorothy touched her nose. "I have a cold and do not have much of an appetite today. You all go, and I will man the office. I brought my famous chicken noodle soup."

Becca pinched the back of Ruth's arm and whispered in her ear. "What do you think you're doing?"

Ruth shrugged her off and hustled Benjamin to the front door. She stayed ahead of Becca and Matt, swinging Benjamin's hand in hers.

Seething and nerves on end, Becca fumbled as to what to say. "How is your mamm?"

Matt put his arm around her shoulders. "Her wound should heal quite nicely. She was fortunate the bullet went straight through." He touched her arm. "I need to talk to you alone after dinner."

* * *

Matt finished his dinner and pushed the dishes aside. On a paper napkin, he drew pictures of animals for Benjamin and encouraged him to do the same. When everyone had finished eating, he touched Becca's hand. He could not wait another minute to speak to her alone. "Will you go outside with me for a few minutes?"

Ruth winked at Matt and hurried to get Benjamin out of his seat. "Benjamin and I are going to meet Isaac at our house. Before he left yesterday, he mentioned stopping by this afternoon."

He wanted Becca, Benjamin, Ruth, and Isaac as his family. She had to come to her senses for all their sakes. "I promise not to take much of your time."

"All right, but we do need to go to your office rather than outside. Otherwise, townspeople might overhear us as they pass by."

He held her coat while she slipped into it. He escorted her to his office. "Sit with me."

She sat next to him.

With his hand in hers, he met her eyes. He had prayed for the right words to say before bed the night before. He wanted to hear her say she would marry him. He was sure he would never love anyone like he loved her. They walked to his office. "My heart is about to come out of my chest. I have missed you and cannot stand the fact that you were taken. The possibility I could have lost you forever is still haunting me." He leaned close. "Marry me. I want to spend the rest of my life with you. I want us to have children and grow old together."

Becca's lip quivered. "I love you. I do. You are everything I would ever want in a husband. I have dreamed about having your children and sharing our future together. I had hoped my helping your mamm during the robbery would show her my character, but it did not change her mind one bit. She will never give us any peace." She looked away from him.

He missed her. She had spoiled him. The office was a mess. Patients asked about her all the time. Dorothy hated assisting him, and she was terrible at it. "I need you at the office. I want us to be together. I want to be a part of your family. Your parents have accepted we are together. It is not something you thought would happen. Someday, maybe my parents will too. Do not make their problem ours. Please reconsider." He reached inside his pocket to pull out the box with the ring in it.

The door flew open and a burst of cold air made them both squint. Ruth shouted, "I have been searching for you. Isaac's fallen. Come now!"

Matt pushed the box back in his pocket and grabbed his bag. Becca ran with Ruth to the house. He outpaced them. Isaac lay on the living room floor. Kneeling, he examined him. The bump on the man's forehead swelled. It was red and warm. "What caused you to fall, Isaac?"

Isaac groaned and pointed to the ladder turned over. "A loose board in the ceiling needed a nail. I lost my balance, fell, and hit my head. Everything went black for a moment."

Matt ran his hands over Isaac's body to check for broken bones. "No broken bones."

Isaac touched a bump on his forehead. "Other than a bad headache, I will be fine. Will you help me up?"

Matt offered his arm for Isaac, as the man settled into a sitting position. "Sit still for a few minutes. Did you experience dizziness or chest pain?"

"No, I was in a hurry and missed a step on the ladder."

Benjamin wrinkled his nose and turned to Matt. "There was a big cracking sound when Isaac hit the floor. I stayed with him like Ruth told me to. I told him you'd make him all better."

Matt put his hand on the boy's shoulder. The child was precious. He had a soft heart, much like Becca and Ruth. "You did the right thing staying with Isaac. I am sure he liked having you with him."

Benjamin got on the floor next to Isaac, as close as he could. "Ruth would be sad if anything happened to you. I would be too."

Isaac nudged Benjamin. "I need you as much as you need me."

"Did you ask her yet?"

Isaac reddened and shook his head no. He put his finger to his lips.

Benjamin nudged Isaac's arm. "What are you waiting for? Go ahead."

Matt glanced at Becca with raised eyebrows.

Ruth lifted one shoulder. "I do not know what Benjamin is talking about."

Isaac held out his hand to Matt. "I guess this is as good a time as any to ask Ruth my question. I will need to stand for this."

Matt helped Isaac to his feet. There was obviously

a secret Benjamin and Isaac shared. The interaction between them was touching. They had formed a meaningful bond. "What is Benjamin talking about?"

Isaac stepped in front of Ruth and lifted her hands in his. "I am in love with you. I have already asked Benjamin's permission, and he said yes to the question I am about to ask you." He pulled a box out of his pocket, knelt on one knee, and opened it. "Will you marry me?"

Eyes wide, Ruth lifted the ring out of the box and slipped it on her finger. "Yes!"

Becca squealed with delight and congratulated them. Matt did the same.

Benjamin clapped. "I'm Isaac's best man. Matt should stand with us too. What do you think, Isaac?"

Isaac placed his hand on Matt's shoulder. "I would be honored if you would stand with Benjamin and me when I marry Ruth."

"I accept." Isaac had become a good friend. The man was kind and funny and someone he could always depend on. He was honored to stand next to him at his wedding. His heart ached a little. A twinge of jealousy engulfed him. He wished Becca had said yes to his proposal. If she had, they would be the couple getting married. Nonetheless, he was happy for Isaac and Ruth. "I would be glad to. Do you have a date in mind?"

Isaac chuckled and shrugged his shoulders. "The bride can choose the date. I am ready tomorrow."

Everyone laughed. Ruth tapped her fingers on her chin. "Becca, is six weeks enough time to plan a wedding? Between you, me, and Kate, we should be able to make dresses. We can notify all our friends and send a telegraph to our parents. I will pencil out an announcement and we can hand them out." She winked at her fiancé. "Isaac can help deliver them."

Matt patted Isaac's shoulder. "Sounds like you are going to be busy."

"I will do whatever it takes to make this woman my wife. I love her."

Matt sat. Isaac had surprised them all. What a happy way to take Ruth's mind off the ugliness of the robbery. "She is a wonderful woman, and you are blessed to have found her."

Ruth giggled and clasped her hands together. "You better stop or my head will burst. We must get busy. We have a wedding to plan, and I cannot wait to marry this handsome man."

His hands on her waist, he twirled her around. "Six weeks sounds like a long time to wait. Tomorrow we could visit Judge Mitchell and ask him to marry us."

Becca pointed her finger at him. "Isaac, I insist you wait six weeks. The two of you are going to have a beautiful wedding. A day you'll never forget. It'll be worth the wait, and you'll thank me when it's over."

Ruth kissed Isaac's cheek. "Becca is right. Planning a wedding will be exciting, and I would like to share our special day with friends and family."

Benjamin intertwined his fingers in Matt's. "Why don't you and Becca get married with Ruth and Isaac? I'll carry the pillow with two rings on it. My friend, Otis, got to do it for two of his sisters when they got married at the same time. He said his legs got awful tired. Don't worry though, I'm tougher than Otis."

Becca gasped at the child's innocent words. Her face reddened, and she avoided everyone's eyes. "Matt and I aren't ready to get married yet."

"I still think it's a good idea."

Matt kissed Benjamin's head. "I agree with Benjamin."

Ruth faced Becca. "Isaac and I would not mind a bit sharing our special day with you. I agree with Matt and Benjamin. Will you at least consider it?"

Becca stifled the urge to run from the room. She understood they loved her, but it was painful having to tell them no to the question she longed to say yes to. Why wouldn't they accept her decision? She had told them over and over why she couldn't marry Matt. Why wouldn't they listen?

"I appreciate your offer, but it's not the right time for Matt and me to consider marriage."

Benjamin puffed his chest out and stared at Becca. "I don't understand why you won't marry Matt. Matt wants to marry you. You told Ruth you're sad without him."

The child's comments melted his heart. Matt could not have said it better. "Thanks, buddy. I appreciate your help. It is a great idea, but we have to wait until Becca is ready."

Benjamin wrinkled his nose at Becca. "When will you be ready to marry Matt?"

Matt held his breath. Did he have any chance at all?

She put her hand on his shoulder. "I don't know, Benjamin. Matt and I have some things to work out. You're too young for me to explain it to you. Let's concentrate on Ruth and Isaac's wedding."

Matt stared at the floor. At least she did not say it was not possible. Maybe there was hope. He would keep praying for God's intervention.

Becca headed for the kitchen. Isaac and Ruth chatted about who to invite to the wedding and created a guest list.

Benjamin played with his wooden horses and barn on the floor.

Matt accepted the plate of cookies Becca passed to him. He bit into one. "I am not going to give up on you accepting my proposal one day. I will wait as long as it takes to change your mind."

"I don't want to hurt you. Believe me, I'm hurt too. The situation is difficult and many sided. I'm praying about it."

Matt stood. Why did she have to make this difficult? They had treated patients, saved lives, rescued Benjamin, solved problems, and enjoyed doing it all together. They had formed a strong bond. One he did not want to lose. He had to have faith God would intervene and bring her back to him. "I am too."

She removed the plate from the table. "I'm tired. It has been a long day. If you don't mind, I would like to help Ruth plan her wedding."

Matt turned on his heel and approached Ruth and Isaac. He had received her message loud and clear. The tension between them had become uncomfortable. It was time to leave. "Isaac, how is your head?"

"I am fine. The pills helped."

He placed his hat on his head. "Congratulations to you both." He stepped outside. He would have to witness Isaac reciting his vows to Ruth on the couple's wedding day. Becca would be next to Ruth. It should be them getting married.

Chapter Nineteen

In Ruth's bedroom, Becca's eyes traveled the length of Ruth in her wedding gown. "You look beautiful. I can't wait to watch Isaac's face when he first sees you in this dress."

"I hope he likes it. I need to stitch another piece of lace along the neckline." Opening a box, Ruth handed Becca a light blue lacy bodice and full-skirted dress with a row of satin buttons in the back. "Maid of honor, this is yours. I received it yesterday from Sears and added lace at the bottom."

Becca gasped and placed a hand to her heart. "I love it. It's the perfect color. I'm honored to stand next to you on your special day."

"I had given up marrying again. Isaac is a kind, generous, and thoughtful man. I am thrilled to spend the rest of my life with him. I never thought you would be here living with me and in my wedding. My heart is about to burst, I'm so happy."

Becca slipped off her dress and put on the new one. "It means a lot to me to witness your wedding with Isaac. I love being a part of your life again." She tugged at Ruth's lace cuff. "You and Isaac make the perfect couple. I'm happy for you." She moved to the mirror. "I love this dress."

Ruth ran her hands over the sleeves. "Matt will love this on you. Have you talked to him?"

She wanted to see him, but then again, she didn't. Nothing had changed. Tomorrow she would be in the same room with him. Ruth would voice promises to Isaac she had imagined exchanging with Matt on their wedding day. How would she keep her wits about her through the ceremony with him standing next to Isaac? She pushed his face from her mind. "I haven't and as sick as I am about it, I have to accept we may not ever be together."

Becca changed out of her dress and helped Ruth do the same. "I have said this a dozen times, but I am going to say it again. Marry the man."

"Please, leave me alone about this matter."

"It should be you in a wedding dress tomorrow." She raised her palms. "I'll leave you alone about it for now because I have something else we need to discuss."

Becca didn't like the look of concern on Ruth's face. "What is it?"

"Is it all right with you if Benjamin lives with Isaac and me at the farm?"

She swallowed and worked to keep emotion out of her voice. She suspected that Ruth would ask if Benjamin could live with her and Isaac, but she had chosen not to dwell on it. They would visit each other, but it wouldn't be the same. He needed a mamm and a daed. "Of course Benjamin can live with you. I will spend time with him every day at the shop, and he can stay with me overnight when he likes." She hoped she had hidden her disappointment.

"You may have him over anytime you want." Ruth opened a drawer and pulled out a paper. She passed it to Becca. "This house is yours. I had the bank transfer ownership to you." She pointed to Becca's name on the deed.

Becca wiped a tear. "Ruth, this means a great deal to me. I love this house. I'll treasure it."

"I would not have it any other way, and I have ulterior motives. I want to keep you close, and I do not want to sell it. This house holds precious memories for me here. Consider it a thank you. I could not have accomplished the wedding plans in such a short time without you, and your help in the shop eased my workload tremendously." Ruth held a wedding announcement. "Do you think our parents will attend the ceremony?"

Becca prayed they would come and surprise Ruth tomorrow. It would be the best wedding present Ruth would receive, but she did not expect them to come. Maybe Ruth's wedding was a bit much for them to handle. "It's hard for them to leave the farm and animals. They would have to ask one of the neighbors to help out while they were away. They promised to visit, but your wedding day may not be convenient for them."

Ruth headed toward the kitchen, and Becca trailed behind. "I understand. Nothing would make me happier, though, except if you and Matt got back together."

Becca opened the cookie bin and handed one to Ruth. "Trust me. I'm doing the right thing." She had no idea what she was doing. Visions of a life and children with Matt ran rampant through her mind, and then Mrs. Carrington's face showed itself every time.

"Matt is not giving up, and I am glad you have to face him at the wedding."

The next day, Becca stretched her arms and sipped her coffee. No, today the pain still lingered. The ache in her throat when his face popped in and out of her mind refused to go away. She was silly to think life without him would get easier. A knock at the door interrupted her thoughts.

"Ruth, can you answer the door?"

Moaning, she remembered Ruth was getting dressed. Late for work, she did not have time to talk to anyone. Hand on the knob, she swung open the door. Why was Horace Carrington here? "Dr. Carrington, I'm surprised to see you here. Is something wrong?" Maybe Matt was ill or had had an accident. "Is Matt all right?"

"Matt is fine. I came to talk to you. It is important. May I come inside?"

What on earth could the two of us have to say to each other? "Yes. Come in. Would you like coffee?"

He shook his head, removed his hat, and sat. "Coffee is not necessary. Please come and sit. I will not be here long."

This was her first time alone with Matt's daed. Would he insult her like his wife had? Maybe she should not have let him in. No, she was curious to hear what he had to say. She waited for him to speak.

He paused, then leaned forward. "Eloise and I have been unkind to you. I apologize and hope you will forgive us. No more hateful words will be spoken. You will not have to worry about being uncomfortable with us anymore. I cannot thank you enough for what you did for Eloise. Please do not let our bad behavior stand in the way of you and Matt being together. We would be blessed to have you in our lives. We do not deserve it, but I am hoping you will give us another chance to show you a different side of us."

She swallowed and put a hand to her chest. Dr. Carrington had apologized and seemed sincere in his plea for her to forgive them. She couldn't believe it, but it was true. There he sat. But wait a minute. His acceptance without Mrs. Carrington's meant nothing, because she was the real problem. "Where is Mrs. Carrington?"

"I am confident she will talk to you soon."

"What changed your mind?"

"The courage and compassion you showed during the robbery. Mrs. Carrington told me everything. The whole town is buzzing about you and how you handled the harrowing situation. We were small-minded in our judgment of you. I have asked God to forgive me for how I have mistreated you, and I hope you will forgive me. Again, I am sincerely sorry."

This brilliant surgeon, this well-respected and confident man had humbled himself in front of her. She admired this side of him. Why hadn't Mrs. Carrington expressed her heartfelt apology? If she had, then she and Matt could finally be together. They could be a family. Horace Carrington's blessing wasn't enough. "I appreciate you coming here and apologizing to me more than you will ever know.

I have been praying for God's will in this matter. I do accept your apology, but without Mrs. Carrington's approval, I cannot accept Matt's proposal."

"I understand." He stood. "I am headed to Matt's office after I leave here. I will tell him what I told you today. Matt has never wavered in professing his love for you, despite our objections. I thought you should know."

Matt shone through in him. The sincerity in his eyes and voice today reminded her of Matt when he spoke about matters of the heart. He raked a hand through his hair. The same nervous habit Matt had.

"I'm glad you came here today. It's been nice to get to know you a little better." She escorted him to the door.

"Thank you for your time. It would be an honor to have you for my daughter-in-law. Soon, I believe I will." He winked and left.

She shut the door behind him and leaned against it. Matt's daed had said all the things she had longed to hear from him. If only his mamm would say those same words to her. Dr. Carrington said Eloise would approach her, but when? Could it be true? She bowed her head and prayed, "Heavenly Father, please forgive me of my sins. If it's your will for Matt and me to marry, please change Mrs. Carrington's heart. All these things I ask and pray in your name, Amen." She had prayed this prayer many times. She believed God had a plan for her. Was Dr. Carrington's visit today a sign Matt was a part of God's plan for her life?

* * *

At noon, Matt shuffled through a pile of papers on his desk. When the door opened, he glanced up. "What brings you to my office?"

His father appeared pale and nervous. It was unlike him.

"Is everything all right? Are you ill?"

Dr. Carrington hung his coat and hat on a hook and sat in a chair across from the desk. "No, son. I am angry with myself for the way I treated you and Becca. I visited her this morning and am here to tell you what I told her."

Matt's eyes narrowed. "Why did you visit her?"

"Calm yourself. I apologized to her for your mother's and my behavior, and I also expressed my approval of the two of you as a couple. I told her we would welcome her with open arms into our family."

"What did she say?"

"She thanked me, but she insists your mother must voice her approval of her before she will accept your proposal. I told her your mother would visit her soon."

"Mother will not apologize." Matt gripped the armchair. "She has made her opinion quite clear."

"I made it clear she has no choice and besides, she has waffled on the subject since the robbery. I can read her like a book. She wants to make amends with Becca but finds it difficult to humble herself to do so. I believe after my discussion with her this morning, she will have a heart-to-heart with Becca soon. She just needed a little encouragement from me."

His father wanted to restore their relationship. Visiting Becca was the best thing he could have done for him. If his mother followed in his footsteps, Becca might agree to marry him.

God was intervening and answering his prayers. "What changed your mind?"

"Becca proved she can handle any situation. I would be proud to have her for my daughter-in-law. Frankly, I am ashamed of how we have treated you both. I hope you will accept our apology."

He moved to his father and shook his hand. "Your apology is accepted and when Mother apologizes, I am going to propose to Becca again." He pulled open a drawer and removed a small box. He showed his father the engagement ring he had bought. Soon, he hoped to put the sparkling diamond ring on her finger.

His father rose. "The ring is excellent. I have no doubt she will love it." He patted Matt's shoulder. "I am happy for you, son. You and Becca are fine examples of two people who love God and show it through your actions."

This was the father he knew and loved. He had missed having him as a confidante and companion. Was his father right? Would his mother ask Becca to forgive her?

Becca admired the dress she would wear today for her sister's wedding. Isaac had gotten his way. They had thrown this wedding together in one week. In a few hours, she would witness her sister vow to love Isaac for as long as they both shall live. Isaac had been good to her, Ruth, and Benjamin. She couldn't ask for a better brother-in-law. The patter of feet alerted her. She straightened Ruth's veil. "You look lovely. This is your special day. How do you feel?"

Ruth stared in the mirror with Becca behind her. "I am a bundle of nerves but happy."

"We better go. Hattie has been kind to keep Benjamin for us. They will be at the church soon. He'll want to see you before the ceremony."

Becca readied the buggy and horse. Ruth climbed in. "Life is full of surprises. A year ago we had no idea Isaac would move here and ask you to marry him. Soon, I hope to have nieces and nephews." She giggled.

Ruth's cheeks pinked. "Isaac and I plan to have children soon."

They discussed names they liked as she guided the horse-drawn buggy to the chapel. She dropped Ruth off first then went to the stable next door and handed the reins to the stableman.

"You look lovely, miss. Enjoy the wedding."

She thanked him and hurried inside the chapel to find Ruth. "Guests are already here." She tilted her head. "Kate is playing the piano. She has been a big help with the wedding. I don't know what we would have done without her."

"She offered to play the piano when I asked her to stand with us. I am glad she did, because I forgot Matt would be next to Isaac and not able to play. She is a true friend, and I am thrilled to have her for a sister-in-law."

Benjamin walked in with Hattie. His eyes swept her from head to toe. "You look like a princess from one of my storybooks."

Ruth reached for him. "You're a handsome

young man in your Sunday suit. Do you have the pillow with our rings tied on it?"

"I do." He held it up for her to see then set it on a chair. He faced her, his face serious. "I asked Hattie a question, and she said to ask you."

"You can ask me anything."

"Would it be all right if I called you Mama and Isaac Papa?"

Ruth's voice caught. Her eyes watered. "Of course you can. Isaac and I hoped you would want to think of us as your mama and papa." She kissed his cheek.

Becca swallowed, threatening tears. Benjamin had such a tender heart, and his timing couldn't have been better. What a priceless wedding gift. She read Ruth's face, wanting assurance this would be all right with her. "Mama and Papa instead of Ruth and Isaac. I like it."

"And you will always be my Aunt Becca."

Becca dabbed a tear. "I love you, Benjamin."

He giggled. "I love you more."

She pulled him close and tears flowed.

Hattie waved to them. "I will take Benjamin and wait outside the door until it is time for him to walk down the aisle."

Benjamin wiped her wet cheek before he left. "See you soon." He took Hattie's hand and left.

Kate rapped on the door and opened it. "You both look beautiful. The guests are seated, and Isaac is in front with Matt by his side. When I start to play, Benjamin will go first, then you, Becca. Ruth, you then make your grand entrance."

Becca blew Ruth a kiss. "In a few minutes, you'll be Mrs. Kelly. Enjoy every moment of your wedding day."

She left Ruth in the room and stepped inside the church. She walked down the aisle. Her heart raced. Matt stood next to Isaac. The man she loved was stunning in his handsome suit. She met his eyes and glanced away. She clutched her bouquet of daisies, moved into position, and waited for Ruth to enter. Kate pounded the keys and guests rose, but there was no sign of Ruth. Where was she? Had something happened?

Becca's heart soared with joy when her parents appeared on either side of Ruth as they walked her sister down the aisle. She gasped. Grace sat in the back row.

Grace grinned and winked.

She winked back. She said a silent prayer. "Heavenly Father, thank you for making it possible for our parents and Grace to come and visit on this special day."

Becca's eyes traveled to Matt.

He flashed a bright smile.

Her face warmed. Not a word needed to be spoken. He loved her. She held his gaze for a moment, then turned her attention to her sister and Isaac. Isaac held Ruth's hands and faced her. The reverend asked them to recite their vows. Promises she could have made to Matt if his mamm had followed through on voicing her acceptance of their union.

Becca stole glances at Matt. Life without him had not gotten any easier with time. She bowed her head as the reverend asked everyone in attendance to pray.

Moments later, the reverend presented Ruth and Isaac as man and wife to the congregation. The couple and Benjamin headed to Mamm, Daed, and Grace.

Becca joined them. "I'm happy you're here." She drew the child forward. "This is Benjamin. Benjamin, this is our mamm and daed and my best friend, Grace Blauch."

He cocked his head in confusion. "Why haven't I met you before?"

Mamm patted his head. "We're sorry we didn't kumme sooner. We'll visit more often and then you will get to know us better."

Grace giggled. "Maybe Mr. and Mrs. Yost will bring me with them when they kumme to visit. We could play tiddledywinks. Becca tells me you're quite good at it."

"Oh, yes, you must come. We can play tic-tac-toe, too."

Isaac cleared his throat. "Mr. and Mrs. Yost, it is a pleasure to meet you. I love your daughter and will take good care of her. Will you be staying long?"

Her daed shook his head. "We are going home tomorrow. I don't like to impose on my neighbors. They are feeding the animals while we are here. We need to relieve them from doing this as soon as possible. We hope to visit you more often."

Her mamm tilted her head. "I wish we had more time to spend with you. I'm looking forward to getting to know you better."

"Ruth and I talked. We assumed you would want to return home for the reasons you mentioned. Please stay with us at my house tonight. Becca can stay with us too. I have plenty of room. If you agree, we will have more time to visit." He addressed Grace. "You are welcome to come too."

Mamm gasped. "We don't want to intrude on your wedding night."

"Ruth and I don't mind putting off going to Canton for our honeymoon for a day. We will leave after you do."

"Joseph, what do you think? I would like to accept Isaac's invitation."

"Of course we'll do it. You are a gut mann, Isaac."

Becca wished Matt wouldn't stand close to her. She wasn't being honest with herself. She liked his arm touching hers. Should she say something to him? Before she could say anything, he held out his hand to her parents.

"I'm happy you both could be here today."

Her daed put his hand on Matt's shoulder. "It's a pleasure to meet you again, son."

Matt shook Mr. Yost's hand. "I'm glad you could make it to Ruth's wedding." He gestured toward Becca and Ruth. "Your visit has made this an even more special day for your daughters."

Becca bit her bottom lip. He approached her parents with ease. She wished she could do the same with his mamm.

Mamm folded her hands. "We have missed our dochders. We didn't want to miss Ruth's wedding, and I wanted to meet Isaac. He seems like a nice mann. There is no mistaking he loves Ruth. His eyes sparkle when he talks about her. When he invited us to join them this evening, I was shocked. His thoughtfulness shows what a kind and caring mann he is. I can see why your schweschder fell in love with him." She pulled Benjamin close to her side. "Now I will have time to play a game or two with this one."

The child bobbed his head up and down, then grabbed Grace's hand and pulled her away.

Matt had done it again by saying all the right things. No matter how hard she tried, her mind wouldn't let her erase the memories she had made with him.

Matt put his hand on her elbow. "May I accompany you to the celebration?"

Her elbow ignited with fire at his touch.

As they entered the room where they would enjoy the wedding meal, she waved at Kate and the ladies from the church. They poured steaming carrots, green beans, and corn into large china bowls. The mouthwatering aroma of roasted turkey on a beautiful platter alongside a dish of sliced potatoes garnished with apples filled the room. A butter cake with icing sat on a nearby table decorated with elegant pink fabric. Thick white candles added to the décor.

Matt led her to her parents, Grace, and Benjamin, where they stood in line and filled their plates with food. She chose a table, and they followed and sat. Matt sat next to her. Her heart raced and her hands trembled. Unable to touch her food, she sipped her water.

What a relief. Benjamin had not stopped sharing his fishing stories. Her parents and Grace seemed to enjoy him. She wasn't in the mood for conversation and welcomed the child's chatter.

Matt leaned into her. "I need a few minutes with you before you leave."

Before she could respond, Ruth insisted the unwed ladies line up to pick up her bouquet. Becca dropped her arms to her sides. She hoped Grace would pick it up. The flowers lay on the floor. The ladies stared at her. She retrieved the flowers from the floor and waved them at Ruth.

The bride mouthed *thank you* to the other ladies, then she winked at her sister.

Becca studied Benjamin, who had climbed on her daed's lap and was chatting away about school.

Mamm and Grace pulled Becca aside. "Isaac told us about the robbery, and he said you saved Matt's mamm's life and the lives of an entire family. I was horrified to learn you experienced such an ordeal."

"I didn't write to either of you about it because I didn't want to worry you. The bad experience is behind me now. Benjamin takes my mind off my troubles."

Mamm glanced at the child. "He is a cute and sweet boy." She tilted her head and covered Becca's hand with hers. "I sense something is wrong between you and Matt."

"As you know, Matt and I are only friends now. His mamm still doesn't approve of me."

Mamm squinted and cocked her head. "Nothing has changed?"

Grace leaned in closer to her. "What is wrong with this woman?"

"In her opinion, I do not fit in with her high society world. I am not the kind of woman she had in mind for a prospective daughter-in-law."

"What does his daed say?"

"His daed approves. He claims Mrs. Carrington has had a change of heart toward me, but she hasn't spoken a word to me."

Mamm kissed her cheek. "Continue to pray. God

will intervene if Matt is the right mann for you to marry."

Grace patted her arm. "I'll pray God works a miracle in your life. I believe you and Matt are meant to be together."

Becca had missed spending time with Mamm and Grace. Their words comforted her. "I appreciate your encouraging words. Your support means a lot to me."

Mamm and Grace circled her in a hug then joined Becca's daed, Matt, and Benjamin. They watched as Ruth and Isaac cut the cake.

Two hours later, the men and women helped clean and straighten the tables before leaving with the other departing guests. Matt and Isaac gathered the gifts and loaded them in both their respective buggies.

Becca stood with her parents.

Isaac came toward them. He spoke to Becca and his new in-laws. "Becca, your parents can follow Ruth and me to our house in your buggy. Benjamin wants to ride with Grace in their buggy. Matt has agreed to take you home to fetch your clothes and bring you to us. I invited him to join us. He wants to talk to your parents and Grace more before heading home."

She had wanted to separate herself from Matt. It had been difficult to breathe in his scent, listen to his voice, and have him near her most of the afternoon and evening. Her self-control was dwindling. She could do this. She could stand to remain with Matt a little while longer without crying. "All right. Matt and I will come to your house soon."

Before Ruth left, she strolled over to Becca and

whispered in her ear. "I never imagined I would marry again and have you and our parents attend the wedding. This day has been perfect." She nudged Becca with her shoulder. "Miracles do happen. I believe before the sky grows dark, a miracle will happen for you and Matt."

Becca waved to Mamm and Daed, who had joined Isaac. She waited to climb in Matt's buggy until they had left with the newly wedded couple. What did Ruth mean? It was as if she knew something Becca didn't. What could it be?

Becca waved farewell to everyone, waited until her family and Grace were out of sight, and then climbed in Matt's buggy.

Horace Carrington ran toward the buggy waving his hands. "Wait! Please wait!"

Becca's heart sank. Why was Matt's daed here? Was something wrong?

Matt reined in the horse. "Is everything all right?"

"Yes, but I need Becca to step out of the buggy for a few moments. Eloise has something she would like to say to her."

Matt turned to Becca. "Are you willing to meet with my mother? I would like to come with you."

This day had been a long one. The last thing she needed was to argue with Mrs. Carrington. What could the woman want? She blinked a few times, and then it dawned on her. Was Eloise here to say she was sorry? "I am all right meeting with her alone, but you are welcome to join me." She stepped out of the buggy and hoped for the best.

Matt's daed kept his distance. Mrs. Carrington stood a few feet away. Becca approached her.

"Mrs. Carrington, I understand you would like to speak with me."

Mrs. Carrington held out her hands. "Please, call me Eloise. What I have to say is long overdue. I am sorry for all the hateful words I have spoken to you and for the things I have done to cause trouble for you and Matt. Please give me a chance to prove to you how much I want you in our lives. Say you will marry my son. It would be an honor to have you for my daughter-in-law."

For the first time, Matt's mamm seemed sincere. The harshness in her face and words had disappeared. God had answered Becca's prayer. Her heart soared. This was the first glimpse she had gotten of the mamm Matt claimed doted on him throughout his childhood. No doubt Eloise would get on her nerves now and then, but under these circumstances, that was something she could handle. "I accept your apology. It means so much to me."

Mrs. Carrington gently squeezed her hands. "I am sorry to have chosen this particular time to apologize, but I did not want to wait any longer."

"I'm glad you didn't. Miracles happened today, but this is the best one of all. I will burst if anything else surprises me."

She startled when Matt knelt on one knee in front of her. "Matt, what are you doing?"

He opened a small box and a diamond ring glistened. "Becca, will you marry me?"

She pulled him to his feet. "Yes! Matt, yes!"

Mrs. Carrington turned to Matt. "I am sorry to have caused you such grief, son. Please forgive me. I love you. I will treat Becca with the respect she deserves. I want you to bring Benjamin with you when you visit. We would like to get to know him better too."

Matt kissed his mamm's cheek as he held Becca's hand. "I am proud of you, Mother. Soon you will realize what a vibrant, sweet, smart, and beautiful person Becca is inside and out."

Mrs. Carrington moved next to Becca and touched her hair. "We have a wedding to plan. Do you mind if I help?"

She never thought she would see the day when Eloise Carrington would ask to help her do anything. This was a nice change. "I would love us to work together on the wedding." She could not wait to tell Ruth. Her sister had been right. She had received her miracle today.

Becca and Matt bid his parents farewell, and then he kissed her full on the lips. "I love you and cannot wait to spend the rest of my life with you."

Becca twisted the ring on her finger. "This is the best day of my life."

Matt kissed her full on the lips, then helped her in the buggy. She chattered about what kind of wedding she would like all the way home.

They stepped inside and both gasped.

Becca touched the beautiful wedding gown hanging on a hook in the parlor. She covered her mouth with her hands. What an elegant gown. The prettiest one she had ever laid eyes on. Lace, buttons, and pearls decorated the dress in all the right places.

Matt stood beside her. "Ruth must have designed and made this gown for you. It is amazing." He removed a note pinned to the gown. "This note is addressed to you." He passed the paper to her.

Her hands trembled as she stared at the words. She recognized Ruth's handwriting.

> *Becca,*
>   *Eloise came to the shop yesterday and told me she planned to apologize to you after the wedding. She asked me to keep this a secret from you. It was hard to do!*
>   *When you and Matt first began courting, I made this bridal gown for you. I tucked it away in my closet and prayed you would reconcile. This morning I asked Mrs. Cooper to go to our house before the wedding and hang the dress in the parlor and pin this note to it. We will plan your wedding when I return. I am anxious to get started. God has been good to us. I could not be happier for you and Matt.*
>
>   *Love,*
>   *Ruth*

She wiped away tears staining her cheeks. She fell to her knees and Matt wrapped his arms around her. She prayed aloud. "Dear Heavenly Father, thank you for Matt, Ruth, Isaac, Benjamin, my parents, and Grace. Thank you for the Carringtons' change of heart. I love you. Amen."

Pennsylvania Dutch/German
Glossary

boppli   baby

daed   dad

dochder   daughter

Englischer   non-Amish male or female

fraa   wife

gut   good

haus   house

kapp   covering for women's hair

kinner   children

kumme   come

mamm   mom, mother

mann   man

schweschder   sister

Please turn the page for an exciting sneak peek of
Molly Jebber's next
Keepsake Pocket Quilt romance,

GRACE'S FORGIVENESS,

coming in February 2016!

Berlin, Ohio, 1900

Grace Blauch pushed the door open to Grace and Sarah's Goods Shop on Monday morning, and shut it against the June breeze behind her. Who was the attractive Amish mann laughing with Sarah? *No beard. He's unwed.* He towered over her friend and partner's petite short frame. She dropped her birthing supply bag on the board floor, removed her light shawl, and hung it on the knotty pinewood coat tree. "I'm sorry I'm late. I had trouble milking our cow."

Sarah Helmuth waved her over. "Don't apologize. I'm glad you're here. Meet Mark King." She hooked her arm through Grace's and grinned. "This is my friend, Grace Blauch."

Mouth in a wide grin and hat in hand, he bowed slightly. "It's a pleasure to meet you. Please call me Mark."

Her cheeks flushed and her heart raced. Most

strangers turned away from her face the first time she met them, but Mark held her eyes. He didn't stare at the red apple-sized birthmark on her right cheek. What a welcome change. "Please call me Grace."

He had a small jagged line under his right eye. The scar added character to his handsome face. What was the story behind it? She liked his thick, dark, wavy hair, straight white teeth, structured jaw-line, and broad shoulders. He held his tall black hat by his side with not a speck of dust on it. Dressed in a crisp white shirt, black pants, and suspenders, he had a neat appearance. "If you'll pass me your hat, I'll hang it up for you." She hung his hat on the knotty pinewood hook next to her shawl.

Sarah pushed a stray curly blond hair in her black kapp. "Mark moved to Berlin from Lancaster, Pennsylvania, on Wednesday." She separated from Grace and leaned against the counter. "The Stolzfuses sold him their place next to us. He visited Levi and me before supper last night and introduced himself. He's showed us Mr. Stolzfus's, now his, workshop. What beautiful furniture, toys, and other items he's handcrafted." She bounced on her toes. "Mark showed Levi oak shelves he had for sale, and Levi wasted no time in buying them. Mark's offered to hang them, and I accepted. No telling when Levi would ever have built them for us. No doubt he means well, but puts things off."

Mark would be working in the shop. What wonderful news. "What a relief. We have no room to hang new quilts on these worn planked walls."

"I need to plant hay in the fields and vegetables for my garden. Do you mind if I hang them tomorrow?"

"Grace opens early most days, and I come in a little later. She doesn't have a husband to cook breakfast for yet. Today, we switched to give her a break. You can schedule a time with her to start work." Sarah winked at Grace.

Grace's cheeks heated. Sarah's attempt to play matchmaker was far too obvious. She glanced at him. His face had reddened, but his grin remained. His reaction couldn't have been any better. Mark was a fine gentleman.

He cleared his throat. "Miss Blauch. What time would you like me to be here tomorrow?"

"Is eight all right?"

"Ja, eight is fine with me." He put on his hat. "Have a gut day." He paused, held her eyes for a moment, and then left.

Grace's heart pounded against her chest. His smile, sparkle in his eye, and strong but kind voice lingered in her mind. She couldn't wait to learn more about him, if Sarah hadn't scared him away with her obvious matchmaking. Grace lowered her chin and crossed her arms. "You embarrassed me when you said I was unwed."

Sarah gently tapped Grace's nose. "I didn't exist after you walked in the room. The mann is smitten with you." She giggled. "I'll not apologize. His face brightened when I told him. You're glad I blurted it out. Admit it."

Grace's face softened and she smiled. "He looked

at my eyes while talking to me, instead of staring at my cheek like most people I meet. It was refreshing."

"Since he'll be working in the shop, you'll have a chance to learn more about him."

"What have you found out about him?"

"Two years ago, a stagecoach hit his parents' buggy and they didn't survive." She leaned against the pinewood table. "I asked him if he had siblings, and he said not anymore. You came in before I could find out what he meant."

Grace moved to the small wood-burning stove in the corner, opened the door, and found logs inside. She lit a match and coaxed the fire with a poker to take hold. "Maybe his bruder or schweschder died, and the subject is too painful to discuss. You said he visited you and Levi. What was Levi's impression of Mark?"

"Levi likes him. They talked about carpentry, farming, and fishing for over an hour. Levi promised to help Mark plant and has asked six other men to assist them as well. Mark will need all the help he can get if he plans to open a store in town and plant crops."

The door opened and interrupted her conversation with Sarah. Two Englischers entered. The tall, elegant woman wore a printed, fitted, red and blue dress to her ankles. A button-down white sweater draped over her shoulders. The short, round woman with full cheeks had on a too-tight yellow dress. She scurried to catch up with her long-legged friend.

Grace faced them. "Wilkom. How may I help you today?"

The two women narrowed their eyes, frowned, and stole glances at her right cheek. "We came in to browse."

She held a hand to her face. Would she ever remain unaffected by strangers' stares? "Take your time. I'm happy to help you with whatever you need."

The taller woman raised her eyebrows and leaned close to her friend. "Did you notice the poor girl's face?"

"Yes, the discoloration is hard to miss. What a pity."

The Englischers should talk quieter. Her birthmark hadn't damaged her ability to hear. Grace hurried to the back room but left the door open to view the patrons.

Sarah followed her. "Don't let our customers' comments upset you."

Her friend meant well, but Sarah had flawless skin. She had no idea what it was like to have strangers wince and stare at her. "I am working on it, but it's difficult."

Sarah put her hands on Grace's shoulders. "God gave you beautiful brown hair, deep brown eyes, a petite nose, and a tall, thin frame. Concentrate on those features."

She shouldn't complain. God had blessed her with a healthy body. She straightened her shoulders and smoothed her white apron. "You're right." She threw back her shoulders and took a deep breath. "I'll assist the women, while you check supplies."

The tall woman fingered the pinwheel green and

white quilt hanging on the wall. She patted the pocket on the quilt. "What's this for?"

"You write a meaningful letter to the person you are giving the quilt to and tuck it inside the pocket. We call them keepsake pocket quilts."

The short woman with curly brown hair held a white eyelet quilt. "I want this one for my daughter. Who came up with this wonderful idea?"

"My friend, Becca Carrington and her schweschder, Ruth Kelly. Ruth's late husband bought her a mending shop in Massillon, and she sells them there. She gave us her blessing to sell them in Berlin."

The taller woman extended her hand. "I love the idea. I must tell my friends to shop here when they travel."

Sliding back the curtain, Grace removed the dinted gray metal box hidden behind the pinewood table used for checking out customers. She opened the box containing coins separated into square sections. How exciting to sell two more quilts. She never tired of recording a sale. She picked up her pencil and wrote the prices and type of quilts the two women were buying in the store journal.

Both women read the pinned price note on their purchases and opened their reticules. Each woman passed two dollars in coins to Grace.

"Danki." She dropped the coins in their proper spots, closed the box, and hid it behind the curtain under the counter. She and Sarah would have extra money to pay Mark for building the shelves without taking it out of the money they'd planned to use for buying new fabric. "I hope you will have a chance to visit us again. Have a safe trip."

Grace joined Sarah in the supply room in the back of the store. "With the two quilts off the walls, we have the perfect spot for Mark to build shelves." She pulled a sheet and cotton blanket from the top of an old oak chest and put them on a cot. "The shelves will allow us to display more of our products, and we won't have to store as many of them back here. I need this space to work if a pregnant woman needs a midwife in a hurry."

"I could never be a midwife. I can't stand the sight of blood. I'm glad you're able to find time to help me with the shop and deliver boppli. I wouldn't want to manage this shop alone, and I love our quilts." Sarah frowned and crossed her arms. "Something you said earlier bothered me."

Grace paused and raised her eyebrows. "What did I say to upset you?"

"Don't tell our customers Becca and Ruth gave us the idea to sell the quilts. If Bishop Weaver finds out, we'll be chastised. We must shun them for joining the church then leaving our Amish community."

Grace opened her mouth to speak, but shut it. Becca was her dear friend. She missed her. Shunning Becca hurt her worse than customers making rude comments about her face. Sarah hadn't had a friend leave to become an Englischer. It was easier for her to adhere to Amish law where Becca was concerned.

"I'll honor your wishes about Becca and Ruth."

"Like I said, we don't need to discuss it further." She nudged her arm. "I'm more interested in talking about Mark. Are you excited he'll be working here?"

She clasped her hands. Of course she was, but she didn't want to dwell on him. New in town, it wouldn't be long before other women would find him handsome too. "I am, but I don't want to get my hopes up." Grace stepped out of the back room and shook the kettle on the wood stove. Water slushed inside, and she set it on top to heat it. The door opened and Mark entered. She blushed and her eyes widened.

He strode over to her and removed his hat. "Did I leave my paper with the shelf measurements here?"

She glanced behind the desk and found a paper on the floor. She passed the note to him. He was handsome. "Is this what you are looking for?"

"Ja, now I don't have to measure the walls again."

Sarah grabbed a small, plain reticule. "Mark, I apologize for not offering you anything to drink earlier this morning. I was too excited to talk about the shelves. Please stay and enjoy a cup of hot coffee with Grace. I'm going to the General Store, and I'll be back in a few minutes."

"No need to apologize."

She waved and left.

Grace waited for the door to shut. "Would you like coffee?"

"Ja, danki."

This mann affected her like no other. She couldn't explain it. Grace poured him a cup of coffee and passed it to him.

The mug slipped through his hands. *Bang. Splat.* He shook his head and frowned. "My fingers are cold and stiff. I'm sorry about the mess." Mark bent to pick up the shards and cut his hand.

She waved a dismissive hand. "Accidents happen. Are you all right?" She grabbed a clean towel and threw it to him. "Wrap your hand. I'll be right back." She ran to the sink in the back, wet a towel, grabbed two dry ones, and picked up her medical supply bag by the front door. Next to him, she stooped, threw open her bag, dug out what she needed, and tended to his hand. *Large strong calloused hands.* He must be a hard worker. "You don't need stitches and the bleeding has stopped. The bandage can come off in a day or so."

"Are you a nurse and a shop owner?"

"I'm a midwife and a shop owner."

Grace lifted the soiled cloths, lifted an empty flour sack from under the shelf, and dropped them out of sight behind the counter. "I'll pour you another cup of coffee."

"Sounds good." He grabbed a broom and dustpan propped against the wall behind the counter, swept up the broken pieces, and threw them in the trash bin. He returned the broom and dustpan where he found them.

Grace passed Mark a cup of coffee with steam rising off the top and glanced at the floor where the glass had been. "You didn't have to clean up the mess, but I appreciate it."

"It was the least I could do." He leaned against the counter. "Did Sarah tell you I bought the shop next door? We'll be neighbors. I'm anxious to open my store after I finish my planting."

What wonderful news. "No, she didn't." She slid her hands into her white apron pockets. "Did you have a store in Lancaster?"

"No, I built log cabins and barns. I handmade tables, chairs, trains, and horses at night out of pine, oak, and maple wood. I wanted to have a lot to sell before I bought and opened a shop."

"Why did you choose to move to Berlin?"

"My haus caught on fire and burnt to the ground. Mr. Stolzfus lived next to me in Lancaster and offered to sell me his farm here in Berlin."

Grace gasped. "What caused the fire?"

"Someone was in the barn during the night, left a lantern lit, and it fell over."

Mark had endured a lot of pain in his life losing his parents and his haus. It must be hard to move to a new place where he wouldn't know anyone. She couldn't imagine doing the same. "I'm sorry. It must've been disheartening for you to lose everything."

"My handcrafted items were in the workshop, and they weren't harmed. I was fortunate. I can replace furniture, clothes, and household items."

She shook her head. "I'm surprised you bought his haus sight unseen."

He laughed. "We had become fast friends. I trusted him." He shrugged his shoulders. "I needed somewhere to live. The Stolzfuses planned to move back to Berlin someday, but they liked Lancaster better. The price was right. If anything was wrong with the haus, I could repair it." He walked over to a Jacob's ladder–patterned quilt. "This caught my eye while we were talking. Did you sew this quilt?"

"I did. The Jacob's ladder pattern is my favorite one to stitch."

He put his mug on the counter. "This would be

perfect to drape over the back of my settee." He shoved his hand in his pocket and pulled out coins. "I'll buy it."

She lifted his purchase off three wooden pegs, folded the material, and unpinned the small white paper. "The price is two dollars." She showed him the pocket. "You could write a letter, tuck it inside, and give the quilt to someone special for a keepsake."

He pressed the money in her hand. "Maybe I will someday."

His rough-skinned fingers grazed hers, and she warmed. The mann had left his friends, church, and everything familiar behind. How intriguing. She doubted she'd have the strength to do the same. "Won't you miss your friends?"

"Ja, but I'll write to them." He lifted his purchase, and then glanced at the clock. "I should go. I bought livestock, a rooster and hens, from an Englischer I met at the General Store after I left your shop this morning. His name's Jed Post. He told the store-owner he was moving and asked if he knew anyone who would be interested in buying them. I introduced myself, and the mann sold them to me for a gut price. He's bringing them to me around ten."

"The mann's timing and yours couldn't have been better. Have a gut day. I'll meet you here tomorrow morning."

He grinned and closed the door behind him.

Grace smiled as the door shut. Tomorrow couldn't come soon enough.